Heddy Simmons

Relative-ly Dead
A Family Tree Mystery

Heddy Publishing

The Library of Congress catalogue information is as follows:

Relative-ly Dead: A Family Tree Mystery.
Copyright © 2024 by Heddy Simmons.
All rights reserved.

ISBN

Paperback
979-8-9923441-6-5

ebook
979-8-9923441-1-0

Book design
William Riggs Fulton

Acknowledgements

Thank you to Bill Fulton, who created the beautiful watercolor for the book cover. Thank you to Dave Peterson, who did a wonderful job wiring my writing shed with electricity so I could write in comfort. Thank you to those who patiently read Relative-ly dead as beta readers, and thank you to Lauren Raybould of Freshly Brewed for being my copy editor. Thank you to Veronica Presley for graphics and layout advice and help.

Chapter 1

"So long as my harvests are plentiful, I sometimes forget how others may be in need." The Towne Family Almanac, 1647, Anne Barstowe, daughter of Alena Towne.

Denny stood peering in on the other side of the rain-spattered, glass door. He slumped as though he had lead weights sewn in the front-facing hem of his heavy, wool coat. His beard and stringy, wet hair dripped rain over his unbuttoned lapels, and his blue eyes stared blearily in at me. He attempted a watery smile.

I sighed, slid the deadbolt, and tugged the door open for our unhoused neighbor.

"Did you get any sleep last night?" I asked Denny as he hung his water-logged coat on a peg.

I didn't expect an answer. Denny needed coffee. He shuffled toward the small table near the gas-powered fireplace. I poured him a cup and brought him a hot cheese muffin and a large sack of day-old bread and pre-made sandwiches. My boss and I knew he took anything we gave him to share with homeless friends at Tent City.

As Denny recovered from the night and the weather, I finished prepping for our Dirty Dozen Bakery customers. With the door unlocked, they pushed in before I could display the OPEN sign. For the next 85 minutes, I worked nonstop, mired in a bewildering fog of orders for specialty coffee, tea, hot chocolate, and pastry.

By 8:30, most of the breakfast crowd were skedaddled. I finished wiping down the main counter as a tall man in a dark blue, creased-to-perfection, TM Lewin suit thrust open the door with the air of someone who thought he owned Dirty Dozen Bakery. Lester Stoats was the new city manager of Brocklebrook, and from his perspective the coastal village was his. Looking over his shoulder at Denny, Stoats shook his head in disapproval before condescending to glance in my direction. He ordered a five-ingredient, large coffee to-go, and a cheese and sweet pepper muffin.

As Stoats paid for his breakfast, he spoke in a strident, carrying voice. "You know, Betts, you might want to warn your dead-beat friend over there that the city council is seriously considering closing Tent City."

I paused in my counter scrubbing. "That would be a shame. The camp has been an important part of our community for seven years now. I can't imagine why you'd want to shut it down."

"It's a financial burden," Stoats said with scorn disguised as business polish. "Taxpayers should not have to support lazy, dirty campers who don't contribute to the economy or general welfare of our town."

"I didn't realize taxpayers had to support anyone living in Tent City." I strove to keep my voice even. Being cordial to this man took effort, chiefly because when I was a middle school teacher, I dealt with self-important school administrators just like him. "I didn't think Tent City cost much of anything. It's a simple place to camp with a bathroom and showers, but that's no more than at our other city parks."

Stoats turned away from me and aimed his stare at Denny. "The freeloaders who live there are a liability. Potential lawsuits are the biggest cost to the city." He turned toward the door and marched out of the bakery, his Harry's of London shoes clicking out a brisk staccato on the wooden floorboards.

"Whoa," a warm and recovered Denny said to Stoats' back. "Just, whoa."

Picking up a pot of coffee, I strode to Denny's table, pulled up a chair, and set the pot between us.

"He's a farging icehole." I smiled.

Denny laughed long and hard.

"Our crew has enough legal knowledge between us to take down the federal government let alone Brocklebrook City Council," he said with more confidence than reason, but I almost believed him. According to Denny, many people who resided in tents had high levels of education and work experience. I didn't know why they'd ended up living in tents. Some claimed being unhoused was a choice. Others lost jobs and families, ending up with next to nothing. Everyone's story differed. Many unhoused residents were older, living on fixed and insubstantial incomes.

"He's probably feeling more spiteful than usual today," I said, referring to Stoats. "Nothing to worry about yet."

Denny lifted the bag of day-old bakery goods and sandwiches and thanked me.

"See you tomorrow, Betts. I better transport these to the tents. Most everyone will be waking up right about now." He got up and forced his arms through the sleeves of his water-heavy coat, turned and followed Stoats out the door, leaving me alone for the first time since 5:45 a.m. Maggie, Dirty Dozen's owner, would take over the shop and the sales counter in another hour.

While constructing pie crusts, I tuned into the news on our local radio station. The lead report concerned a midnight fire at one of the storage businesses. I wondered if my Warren had been there. He was a retired, big-city fire chief, but served as a trainer and educator with our small-town, volunteer fire department.

The announcer's voice echoed with tinny static off the cupboard doors. "Fire fighters discovered the man's body in a fire-damaged storage unit. The victim's last known address was Tent City, Brocklebrook. A fire department spokesperson said the man appears to have died from smoke inhalation. Police are withholding the man's identity until they notify family and friends. The cause of the blaze is yet to be determined."

My rolling pin pressed hard into the dough as I thought of Denny and everyone else at Tent City. Homelessness was an ever-expanding problem in Washington State - the whole country for that matter. I guessed the poor man caught in the fire tried to sleep in the best place he could find on a rainy night.

The back door opened then, and Dale, our bakery delivery driver, stepped in with stainless steel holding racks balanced on his right shoulder. Earlier, I'd stacked boxes of baked goods near the loading door, ready for transport to several coffee houses and restaurants in the area.

"A blessed good morning to you." Dale presented as a short, fleshy man with an expanding middle. He was a holy brother at the local Happy Potluck Church, as we called it. Its actual name was Brocklebrook First Children of God.

My best friend, Philly Rand, walked out of any room that Dale entered. Something about the man made her feel as though a complete stranger just handed her used underwear in a thrift shop, she said.

Dale called me Sweets, which I didn't care for, but I called him Pinky to even the score.

"Hey, Sweets," he hollered, "got a hot cuppa for me? It's gonna be a cold day."

I put together a large coffee-to-go, complete with three sugar packets, and I stuffed four iced donuts in a white paper bag and left them in the cab of the bakery truck. Pinky never worried much about fat, sugar, or exercise. He was a body full of contradictions, trying to be a slap-on-the-back 'good ole boy', but more often stiff and particular about rules and procedures. The man took pleasure in pointing out imperfections in other people's accomplishments.

"Just heard on the radio about a fire at one of the storage unit businesses last night," I said. "Some poor fellow died."

"Yup. Heard that too. Makes one less homeless guy to worry about," Pinky said.

That seemed heartless, even for Pinky, and I said so.

"Look, Sweets." Pinky hoisted stacked bakery boxes on his shoulder. "We do what we can at the church for these has-beens, but they keep multiplying. No matter how many shoes and sweaters and little bottles of shampoo we give out, they still roam the streets. Nothin' changes."

I wanted to ask Pinky if people without homes in the world shouldn't just lie down and expire for all our sakes, but I decided sarcasm would ruin my own day, not his, particularly if he agreed the suggestion had merit. A deep breath helped me stay calm, but my exhalation was a sigh, and I was gladder than usual to hear the delivery truck back onto the main street and take off.

"Did you know that 150 million people in the world are unhoused?" I asked the double wide, reach-in refrigerator. "You should be aware that 20 percent of the world's population lacks adequate housing," I informed the stainless-steel commercial bakery oven.

By the time Maggie arrived to take over, I was revising and rehearsing speeches about unhoused souls and cold neoliberalism and its effects on humanity, all with Pinky and Lester Stoats in mind. Only the appliances and a customer I didn't see right away would ever get the benefit of my passion-infused orations, but I felt better.

My boss, Maggie, was apron queen and bakery entrepreneur extraordinaire. She trusted me with the morning crowd and early morning baking, even encouraging me to experiment. Dirty Dozen Bakery was 37 years old, though Maggie inherited the thriving business from a great aunt and uncle only a decade ago.

In contrast to its name, there was nothing unclean about the bakery except what the customers brought in. When Maggie was the proprietor, her staff quickly spotted and dealt with bits and pieces of grime and dirt deposited from the bottoms of people's shoes. She often said, "The real dirt is in all those steamy stories and the gossip people share over cups of coffee. One bite of our sweet treats and their tongues start to wag."

A full-figured Hispanic woman with snapping black eyes, bright red lipstick, and an out-sized mass of permed black hair, Maggie always said 'yes' to an indelicate story or spate of scandalmongering.

"Get yourself ready to go home. I'll take over in a minute." She began hanging aprons on the rack near the register. "I just finished new bibs, pinafores, and a smock," Maggie explained, pushing a couple of folded creations my way for inspection. "Found these brilliant fabrics at a basement sale up north."

I shook open a sassy, rainbow-patterned, salon apron, complete with three layers of ruffles above the hemline. "You've got to have the biggest apron collection in the state," I said, admiring the pinny.

"No honey," Maggie said. "La mayoria de el mundo … the biggest in the world."

Some women create lucrative designer collections of maternity clothes. Maggie had a line of aprons she sold in the store and online. An award-winning baker, Maggie embraced me a year ago as a newbie bread maker, taught me all I know about pastry dough, and encouraged me to start my genealogy business.

Countless heart to heart talks in my boss's kitchen, all of which helped ease my retirement woes, meant Maggie had come to be a mentor and a friend. That's why I felt especially remorseful about the disturbances I caused for Dirty Dozen in the coming weeks.

Chapter 2

"An unresolved tragedy foreshadows a chain of heartbreaks to come." The Towne Family Almanac, 1727, Hannah Gould Towne. Wife of Jacob Towne Jr. and guest contributor to the almanac.

After updating my boss on the morning's events, I pulled on my chunky, worn cardigan, grateful to head home to my white-washed fisherman's cottage and to the brunch Warren would cook.

There he stood in my tiny kitchen, thick-striped suspenders holding up square-pants Carhartts over a chestnut brown work shirt. I couldn't help but smile at the unintentional wiggle going on in the seat of those pants as Warren's whole frame took part in scrambling eggs. He scooped a generous spatula full and set the eggs beside vegetarian sausage on oven-warmed dishes, depositing the plates on my kitchen table.

"Hey," he greeted me with a warm, white-bearded smile. "And before you say anything, I knew you would ask about last night's fire, so I took notes. I even took pictures."

"Well, aren't you the investigative reporter." I reached my arms as far as I could around his solid waist and hugged him. Warren looked inordinately pleased.

With my access to daily bakery gossip and Warren's work with the volunteer fire department, we enjoyed puzzling through what we called 'Brocklebrook's little mysteries'. Like crows to roadkill, we couldn't resist stories about what was happening, legally and illegally, in our little ocean-side town. Poking into other people's business was a thousand times more satisfying than working through a jigsaw puzzle, but in a world where gossip fuels the flames of social media, we mostly kept our speculations and our 'solved' cases to ourselves.

This morning, though, our whodunit guess work was more serious than usual: a fire and a man's life.

Tired and sober, Warren sat in front of me and dug into his pepper and egg scramble. His brown eyes were bloodshot from smoke and stress, and his brow tightened as he reviewed what happened during the night.

"Doug found the body." Warren's speech was slow and careful, his tone grim. "We weren't looking for people because it was a storage unit. But, you know, Doug's only nineteen. He took it pretty hard."

I grimaced. "That's not a surprise I'd wish on anyone. Poor kid."

"No one is supposed to sleep in those units," Warren continued, "but this miserable little guy must have had a key and made himself at home. The chief thinks a cigarette started the fire. A few Red Buck stubs lay flattened outside on the driveway. Anyway, the scene is too full of smoke right now to see a whole lot." Warren stopped to shake a few drops of pepper sauce on his sausage. He resumed talking only when his plate was clean.

I slid the last English muffin and the marmalade his way.

"Been to hundreds of fires over the years and this one strikes me as odder than most." Warren waved off the muffin. "Four or five boxes of clothing and papers were smoldering, so it's mainly smoke damage. That's what the guy must have died from, smoke inhalation. We got there before the fire burned out of control. Someone called it in. Saw smoke seeping out from under the unit's door."

"Do you know the man?" My interest was keen, but I was also feeling uneasy.

"No. His name was Liam Huong."

I shook my head, never having heard the name before, but I would ask Denny about Liam the next morning.

"Now, why would a fire be confined to the contents of a few boxes?" Warren drummed the fingers of his right hand on the table. "It's almost as though this Liam fellow flicked cigarette ashes into each box one at a time, which doesn't make a whole lot of sense."

"When will the fire investigators finish up? Maybe they can answer your questions."

"I'll be there when they come," Warren said. "They know my years of fire experience and asked me to help out." He yawned. "In the meantime, I'm off home to take a nap."

"Hey Mr. Fire Chief. You should have called to say you couldn't do brunch today. You almost fell asleep in your toast."

"Wouldn't miss our morning ritual." Warren winked. "Besides, I figured you'd be pacing the floors with questions if I didn't come soon."

We both laughed because he was right. Cupping Warren's face in my hands, I kissed him and let him leave so he could sleep at his own bigger house and in his more generous bed. My afternoon would be full of study and investigation, as the DNA results had come through for some of my clients and a few of my friends.

Yes. I was a part-time baker who liked to solve riddles about my Brocklebrook neighbors' lives with my fire chief boyfriend, but I also liked to solve a different kind of puzzle, the kind that involved digging up perplexing mysteries about past lives.

A year ago, I started my own business as a certified forensic genealogist, or DNA investigator as I liked to call myself. Helping people fill gaps in their family trees didn't pay all the bills, but that's what the bakery job and my teaching pension were for.

Warren hired me early on, when I first started the business, both to help me out and because he had a genuine wish to find a long-lost loved one, his son. We had Warren's DNA results, and there was someone in the database who was almost a 50 percent genetic match and who shared Warren's Y-DNA. Much to Warren's regret, the individual preferred to remain anonymous on the genealogy site. He failed to reply to our messages, and that was either because he hadn't been checking the service for a long time, or he didn't want to respond. I felt a twinge of sympathy for Warren every time we monitored DNA links to see if there was an answer.

"Someday he'll want to reach out," I told Warren the last time we checked.

"Someday might be too late. I'll be in my seventies before the year is out." Warren turned away to hide his heartache. I crossed my fingers that a reunion was possible.

Finding ancestral ties could be exhilarating for me and for the people making connections. Revealing family associations could also be complicated and fraught with old wounds and knotty stories. I understood the teeter-totter of emotions my work let loose.

Still, on the morning of Liam's death, how could I have known that my family history inquiries would unearth a secret powerful enough to threaten the safety of those dearest to me and force my involvement?

Chapter 3

"I see now that when my herbs and medicines are sold, their value is defined by numbers of coins and their true value counts for less. When I give gifts of herbs and medicines from my heart, their honest worth is recognized and strengthened." The Towne Family Almanac, 1534, Cecily Gardyner, niece of Rose Sherwood.

I often lose myself in the branches of family trees, and Warren and my good pal Philly help me climb out of them on a weekly basis. Kinship charts, old photographs, public records, diaries, memories, and the analysis and comparison of DNA molecules pull me into knotty, convoluted worlds. Without my two best friends, I forget to eat and sleep when I find myself captured by a stack of clues and a string of leads to family connections.

On this afternoon, I was eager to focus my energies on a difficult and confusing family history, one with intimate links to an inscrutable saint of a woman with an extraordinary purpose. Joon O'Neal, a Tent City leader and organizer, had a past as a pharmacist, a wife, and a homeowner. Now, unhoused, all Joon had left were social security benefits, hospital bills and a small pension that would never keep up with inflation. She also had secrets, some of them heavy loads to carry, and one of them an artifact with extraordinary value.

I pressed the start button, and my computer screen blinked on. In accord with my anthropomorphic tendencies, my trusty laptop became Deputy Delilah, helping me find links to family riddles.

"Let's see if we can root out some lineage names," I said to Delilah. "Then you can search the entire online world for family ties."

Yikes. I needed a furry friend. I might get away with chattering to a cat but talking to a computer could qualify me as being a few pecans short of a fruitcake.

Sources for heritage links and family data weren't always discovered through computer searches. Family artifacts could provide precious clues. I'd packed one such artifact with care in my side desk drawer. It was Joon's most precious secret.

"I've been carrying this monstrosity around with me for twenty odd years," Joon had said when she handed it over for safe keeping. "Parts of it might be more than 500 years old, you better believe it."

I ran my hand over the tome in its ancient leather cover. As large as a full-sized Oxford English Dictionary, most of its worn pages were a combination of hand-made and water-milled paper.

"Mom gave this to me years ago, before she died, you know. She said mothers passed it to daughters, or aunties passed it to nieces. For many British and then American centuries, we Towne family women acted as protectors to the manuscript."

Joon called this musty-grassy-vanilla-smelling compendium an almanac recipe book or The Towne Family Almanac. The day we placed it in my desk drawer, Joon opened some of the back pages and turned the book around for me to look. "See. Here's a handwritten index of the almanac's caretakers. The women each added their own recipes, stories, and thoughts about life until they passed the book on to the next generation."

To my mind, the most valuable parts of the family almanac were the seed packets that went with the recipes and stories. These seeds sprouted unusual and specific heirloom plants, with qualities that enhanced recipes for foods, liquors, tinctures, and medicines. As the book's most recent caretaker, it was Joon's responsibility to keep planting from each packet to grow fresh seed. Replacing the old seed with new ensured that the heirloom seeds stayed young enough to germinate. The practice prevented each historically tended genus from going extinct.

"Joon expects me to do two things," I told Deputy Delilah. "She wants me to grow her a new batch of seeds, which I did. Some of them are harvested and some are almost ready out there in the garden and the greenhouse." I patted Delilah on the side of her screen. "You couldn't help me with the seeding part, but you can assist me with my second job."

Joon was set on finding a woman in her kinship line to take on the responsibilities of the book. Having no children of her own and few connections to her mother's extended family, Joon, seventy-two, wanted a trustworthy home for this family legacy. She intended to pay me for my labors with some of the seeds, and I could think of no remuneration more valuable. As a budding herbalist and serious gardener, I gloried in the project and felt honored by Joon's trust in me.

Before this summer, my gardens bulged with the same, unremarkable varieties of cucumbers, tomatoes, green beans, and squashes common to most backyard horticulturists. With the addition of Joon's family heirlooms, my garden and greenhouse exploded with color and lush flora. I was a garden diva in my melodious topophilia of raised beds, vine-covered mounds, tuber-rich trenches, and rows of heavily fruited nightshades. Jewel-colored pots and hanging planters delighted my senses whenever I had time to sit on my garden bench and simply enjoy them.

At the rough center of my garden stood a pillar of river stone, my chimney water fountain. It was a gift from Warren the first time he asked me to marry him. I turned down the marriage offer but not the gift, and he disappeared for a few weeks to lick his wounds. When he returned, he built the chimney and installed the water cascade, and I loved him all the more for it. He's grown used to my refusal to accept an engagement ring, but he doesn't like it.

From Warren's fountain I could peruse the whole backyard, and because of Joon's seeds, my garden rows and greenhouse pots burst with everything from heirloom selections of nettles to amaranth, a beautiful wine-colored Aztec grain taller than me.

One day, over cups of tea, I made the mistake of suggesting Joon publish her family almanac.

"You could make some money from selling a line of the tinctures and medicines from these recipes." My insistence that the almanac held lucrative value sparked our first serious argument.

"Miss Betts, these recipes and seeds are passed down to help family and friends and not to sell for money." Joon's ragged voice scolded me.

"But that was way back when people didn't have a lot of money," I said, slow to understand. "Maybe you could market enough to live in a house again."

"Those are the rules of the almanac." Joon folded her arms across her chest, emphasizing the importance of her words by pronouncing each syllable with slow deliberation through clenched teeth. "And I don't need a house. I'm happy where I'm at."

When Joon's DNA results came in, we spent several days looking over the lists of genetic relatives on the website. Second cousins were her closest matches. We composed a letter for kin on the website. In plain words, Joon wrote that she had family history information and wanted to find who best to share it with. She also let her cousins know she had an heirloom to pass down but left out the fact that it was an almanac.

"I want to find a young woman who cares about family, history, plants, cooking, and healing. I'm searching for a close relative, if at all possible," Joon wrote.

Today I had a few email answers for Joon. In one of them, a Lenora Stanton, said that she served as her family's primary historian and that Joon should send her the heirloom since Lenora had so many more connections and might better determine who should receive it.

"You know, dear," Lenora wrote at the end of her letter, "there are far fewer young women in the world who are interested in gardening, cooking, and healing -

or in family history. You might want to reconsider your expectations. Maybe if you told me what the heirloom is, I could better help you."

Around lunch time I heard the expected knock at my door and welcomed Joon to my kitchen for a bite and to go over what we had discovered so far. I'd grown fond of this large woman with her sunburned cheeks and webs of hairline wrinkles concentrated around her firm mouth and fierce eyes. Today Joon fashioned her gray ponytail with a thick rubber band that once held together a bunch of broccolis.

"Hey, ya," she greeted me at the door.

I ushered her to the table for tuna sandwiches and hot tomato soup, wondering for the hundredth time why she chose me to help in her quest. Joon trusted very few people, and yet she signed a contract making me executor of her family treasure should she pass away unexpectedly. Over the last several weeks, she told me much of her life story, and I admired her passion and tenacity. I was committed and willing to protect her family's precious seeds and recipes.

As she said to my lawyer while we were drawing up the contract, "These recipes and seeds are for sharing, not selling. They have more power when they're given out of honest generosity."

While I settled the sandwiches on the table, Joon pulled off her fingerless mittens and wool coat before sitting down and wrapping her hands around a mug of tea made from herbs her own seeds produced in my greenhouse. "Police are all over Tent City today," she announced in a voice more raspy than usual, which suggested chronic bronchitis. "Our city manager is on a rampage because of the storage unit fire.”

“What’s he jumped up about?” I asked, surprised.

“We’re a menace.” Joon looked up and gave me an ironic, crooked grin. “Something about trespassing and damaged property.” She did a fair job of imitating Stoats’ liquid drawl when she quoted him as saying, “Things like that fire are bound to happen with so many people hanging around too irresponsible to have jobs or homes.” Joon made light of Stoats’ accusations, but her booted left foot tapped out a constant beat on the floor, a signal she was worried.

Just as I managed to set down bowls of soup without spilling them, someone else tapped at the kitchen door. I grinned when I saw Philly’s thirty-five-year-old face peering in like a peeping Tom through the space between the upper and lower door curtains.

“You’re just in time for soup,” I greeted her as she slipped out of three-inch heels, which she said were crap for her feet but radical for her outfit. She loved clothes, and today she wore a stylish, meadow-green Bellissimo dress with a V-neck, silky, three-quarter length sleeves, and three, soft pleats at the waist. Philly joined us at the table.

“Jeebus!” she sang out. “Stoats is on a rampage.”

Philly is one of two city recorders at Brocklebrook city hall. She’s good at her job and selective about who hears about the underbelly of city business. I’ve known her long enough to recognize that since the towns people elected the new city council, who then hired Stoats, the city’s underbelly acquired several dark blemishes.

Joon’s eyes narrowed. “That man is too big for his fancy pants and too small-minded to fill those thousand-dollar, polished shoes. I guarantee he's never missed a meal in his life, and I'm sure the biggest trauma he's ever endured is moving to this small town where he might have to get his socks at Wal-Mart or J.C. Penny rather than Oslo's or Lisa Kline Men." Philly and I looked at her in surprise. "You think we poor folks don't joke about the habits of the manic elite?" Joon asked. "We know where they shop."

"Hey, don't I know." Philly endorsed Joon's pronouncement with a hearty guffaw. "He's got two suits hanging in his office closet that are worth the entire budget of our fire station." She ran slender, brown fingers through her thick patch of dark hair, curly and soft like the texture of Love in the Mist, a sweet blue flower with delicate, ferny foliage. "When he heard the prelims about the fire this morning, he literally made a running leap and slid those polished kicks over our newly waxed floors and into the office. He was flying high. It's giving him ammunition for his case against Tent City, and he's going to use everything he can to dirty the people who live there. This whole thing blows."

Looking especially tired, Joon shook her head, ventured to say something, and started to cough. When her cough subsided, she said, "They're making a big deal because some of us at Tent City shared that storage unit. Liam didn't have permission to use the space, and he didn't have access to the key, so we don't know why he was there or how he got in."

"Who was Liam?" I asked. "I don't remember seeing him at the bakery."

Joon shrugged her sweater-clad shoulders. "We don't really know. He was new to the camp; we caught him stealing, so Denny and I asked him to leave. He wanted to fight us; said we had no right to tell him what to do because it's a public camping place. After that, most everyone paid him no never mind; just acted as though he wasn't there. People usually leave on their own once everyone in the camp starts avoiding them."

"Do you think he stole the key to the storage unit?" I plunked an elbow on the table, settled my chin in the palm of my hand, and squinted in puzzlement.

"Must've," Joon said, "Except it's not missing."

"Ooooh," said Philly, startled. "That's why the police are talking about an arrest."

"Yeah. And that's why they pumped questions at Denny and me all morning." Joon examined her weathered hands as though they were a book she was reading. I could see she was thinking hard about something. She finally squared her wide shoulders as though making up her mind. "That's why I need to tell you something right now. Before …"

"Before what?" I softened my voice.

"Well, before they come and arrest me." Joon emphasized her pronouncement with an impatient shake of her head and a swing of her gray ponytail. "They're talking about Liam's death being peculiar, and I know us Tent City people are going to be the first ones they blame."

"Surely not." My voice petered out. I realized that the location of Liam's death looked suspicious for those who rented the unit.

We were all silent for a long moment. This was a turn of events none of us saw coming. Philly couldn't sit still for long; she never could. She jumped up to pace on those long, slim legs in front of the kitchen window. Giving in to impulse, she threw her arms around Joon's shoulders and hugged her, but Joon seemed to shrink further into herself. She didn't take well to physical contact.

"I've got to tell you to hold onto that book I gave you." Joon looked over at me with pleading eyes. "Don't let anyone else take it. There's someone after it, but he can't have it. He's not the one. And if I get arrested, you know what to do. You finish what we started."

Joon was so earnest that I felt afraid for her. "You're going to finish the job yourself," I said. She waved a hand as though to swat off a no-see-um, one of those tiny, blood-sucking bugs that live in our Northwest, ocean-side forest.

"I just want your word," she said in an impatient, clipped rasp. "I want to know that our contract protects the book."

I nodded. "It does. I had my lawyer look over it again. But can you tell me more about this person who wants the almanac and shouldn't have it?"

"No. No more'" Joon waved a weathered hand with finality. "That's all I'm going to say."

Philly and I looked at each other, and I could see my friend was as puzzled as I was. We sat down to finish lunch, and when our spoons scraped the last of the soup from our bowls, Philly got up to return to work. "I'll let you know if I hear anything." She pushed her long feet back into those sharp-toed pumps and steadied herself toward the door. Her shoes looked dangerous to me, like weapons.

Joon and I spent the next few hours talking about the

new correspondences from cousins and the recent DNA matches that came up on the genealogy site. Done with the paperwork, we strolled into the greenhouse where I showed her how the pots of seed plants were coming along, and we stepped through garden rows to look at the tall, burgundy amaranth and deep green nettles that were living representatives of her family's horticultural, medicinal, and culinary past.

Tears pooled in Joon's eyes as she touched the velvety amaranth seed heads, whose tendrils drooped like tassels on a knitted winter hat. Nearly ready to harvest, I would dry the tiny black seeds and then store them in a seed envelope, secured to the proper page in the recipe book.

"These came from Central America to the colonies after The Towne Family Almanac was moved to Salem from England all those years ago." Joon stood next to one of the six-foot-tall stalks so I could take her picture.

As we turned to go back in the house, two police officers, weighing heavy with holsters, pistols, and night sticks, pushed through the gate into my back yard garden. They offered only perfunctory nods at my quizzical greeting, moving closer until Joon was between them.

"Are you Joon O'Neal?" The taller officer looked down at my friend. She nodded, shoving her rough, square hands deeper into the outsized front pockets of her coat. "Ms. O'Neal. You're not under arrest, yet, but we need to take you to the station for questioning. We've arrested Dennis Woodman, and we need you to clarify some details about your whereabouts last night."

"Arrested Denny for what?" My stomach turned queasy in alarm.

"Murder," the second police officer said. "The murder of Liam Huong."

24

Chapter 4

"I buried an old and great love today amongst the dandelions on the hill behind the church, but my heart swelled with renewed love for the friends who stayed to comfort me." Towne Family Almanac, 1833, Cora James Penny, niece of Mattie Singleton Hireman.

I woke at 3:30 a.m., grateful for morning rituals. Mine involved switching on bakery lights, heating ovens, and assembling mountains of butter, sugar, and flour.

Warren stayed with me through the night, and I was grateful. Images from the fire photos Warren laid out on the kitchen counter after dinner still flashed one at a time through my head as though from an old slide projector. The coroner concluded Liam died in the storage unit a few hours before the fire started. Cause of death was still undetermined, though vomit and seizures were involved. Investigators noted someone searched the storage room before the fire started, overturning packing boxes and tossing their contents.

Philly called before we went to bed to inform me the police questioned Joon at the station.

"But they didn't arrest her. They took her back to her sleeping area in Tent City. All the cops have to go on is Joon and Denny's fight with Liam and the problem with the key that's not missing." A long sigh escaped Philly's lungs, steeped in exasperation. "But they're harassing these old folks as though they are some kind of third world terrorists."

"Apt way of putting it," I said. "I guess Tent City seems like a primitive encampment to a lot of people in town. But these are mostly older people who keep a kind of law and order in the camp. The police don't know how much harder their work would be without Joon and Denny and some of the others."

"Well to the men in blue it looks like Denny and maybe Joon took the law into their own hands in a very nasty way," said Philly. "Get this. There is one remarkably interesting piece of evidence. Investigators found a Dirty Dozen Bakery wrapper inside Liam's shirt pocket."

As I dressed that morning in my usual black leggings, ankle-high leather boots, a brown knit boot skirt, and my hand-quilted maroon vest over a long-sleeved, white cotton shirt, I thought back to Philly's words about the police and Tent City. I splashed chilly water on my round cheeks and into my sleepy eyes and dried them with a towel, noting the dark circles developing under my lower lids from tossing and turning most of the night.

No, I wasn't a fresh, young thing anymore. I was sixty-three, but I was pleased with who I'd become. When I was twenty-six, I got over not looking like Linda Ronstadt or Kim Basinger and grew content with being Betts Harvey. A journalist once did a feature story on me and my eighth-grade students. I'd always appreciated her newsprint description of me:

"Set over a dignified square jaw, friendly, approachable, brown eyes stare out with composed scrutiny from below a noble forehead."

I grinned at the memory as I pulled on a royal blue sweatshirt, ready for my walk to the bakery.

The subdued hum of streetlights and the tapping of my boots on concrete were the only steady sounds in the wee hours of the morning. Shaking my head in consternation, I kept thinking about yesterday's events. For Denny or Joon to kill someone was unimaginable. I trudged down the sidewalk toward the bakery, exhausted already, and looking forward to an afternoon nap, but that would be hours away.

Not another soul was out and about at 3:55 a.m. when I unlocked the bakery door, let myself in, and then re-secured the bolt. It wasn't until I mixed several kinds of cookie dough, set the bread dough to rise, and started defrosting the strawberry freezer jam for scones that I decided to take out the garbage. Bakery garbage goes out the side door and into a dumpster on a cement pad in an alley between our store and the Drive Yourself Wild car parts shop.

As I worked my way down the steps to the alley with two heavy plastic bags, I noticed bits of garbage strewn near the dumpsters. I groaned aloud. If there's one thing that ruins my morning schedule it's having to pick up after raccoons, dogs, or alley cats. Most of the time, the heavy dumpster lids are shut tight, and they remain impenetrable except, perhaps, to insects. Sometimes Pinky forgets to shut the lid when he cleans out the delivery truck in the late afternoon.

Bags in hand, I approached the mess. A streetlamp

several feet away helped me discern familiar shadows of equipment and garbage cans from our neighbor's shop. Just the same, it was dark, and I failed to see the obscure, motionless form of a human body on the ground until I was right on it. I tripped. Bags went flying. One burst open as it hit the side of the dumpster. I fell on hands and knees having nearly flown over the body and into something cold, wet, and sour.

The body was behind me as I worked to push and pull myself to a standing position. I recognized how stiff the body felt when I tripped over it, so I realized this person was no longer alive. I knew if I turned around, I would see this dead someone. I didn't want to. I wanted to march down the alley toward the street and never look back. My whole body ached, especially my right knee and my elbows. Tears welled in my eyes from pain and fear. The wet stuff I fell into was ripe, and I tried to clean my hands on my apron.

Standing there in the dim glow of the streetlamp, I knew that in time I would have to circle myself around. Sooner or later, I would have to call someone. Not until I heard a car pass by on the main street did I shake off my paralysis. I pulled my phone out of my pocket and then I turned.

Oh God. The face I saw caused me to convulse in a choking sob. This was simply not possible. Why would she be here in this alley? I knelt beside Joon O'Neal and touched her face. It was ice cold. I gasped out another sob and squeezed my hands together, and the hardness of the phone between my palms reminded me to make a phone call. The light of its screen drew my attention away from Joon's frozen face. I dialed 911.

A night patrol car arrived first, within five minutes of my call. Maggie, hair uncombed, came twenty minutes later to supervise and take over the baking, and Warren was there with me as I answered police questions. He brought me a change of clothes, knowing that the bakery had its own shower, but the police insisted I explain everything and submit myself to pictures before I cleaned up. They wanted me to show them where I was when the garbage flew out of my hands and to identify the trash that was already on the ground before I contaminated the scene.

I hated watching people discuss and photograph Joon as though she was just a body and not a beautiful, generous, cranky human being. There was so much they didn't know about her, such as how much of her life she'd surrendered for the sake of others. I wanted people to understand all the things that led her to living in a tent, foraging for food in an alley in the middle of the night.

"It's the same modus operandi as the Liam death," I heard a detective say to the police chief in hushed tones. "There's evidence of seizures. There's the vomit nearby. Ten to one the autopsy will show she died of respiratory failure, just like Mr. Huong."

"Well, hell. What is it, an epidemic?" Chief Clarence McCleary growled with a puzzled frown. "Food poisoning? Is it something to do with the bakery? Damn. Do we need to seize all the food at Tent City?"

"Maybe a good idea," said the tall, forthright detective. "Or is it a simple case of two murders very much alike and maybe connected?"

"Simple case," mumbled the chief. "There are very few simple murder cases." His hat was askew, and his rough lips pursed in skepticism. "But I think we need to take precautions. Get the food safety inspector into the bakery and make sure to record every scrap of food confiscated from Tent City."

Philly drove up just as they lifted Joon into the coroner's van. A big-hearted soul who doesn't believe in hiding her emotions, Philly, tears rolling down her cheeks, told everyone who would listen what a wonderful woman Joon was. Later, pacing in front of the big storefront windows, Philly waited in the bakery with Warren until I showered and changed. I stuffed my dirty clothes into a plastic bag to throw away, but not my boots. I'm careful with money, and I don't usually waste things, but I knew I couldn't wear that skirt or vest again without reliving the morning's events.

Maggie served free coffee to a full crowd. Word about the fatality in the alley spread fast, and Brocklebrook residents wanted to find out for themselves what happened. When the location of a mysterious death is a bakery, people have a ready-at-hand place to sit down and swap ever escalating theories and rumors.

"Honey," Maggie said to me when I joined Warren and Philly, "I can't erase this morning for you, but I want you to know I wish I could." She handed me a light package wrapped in bakery paper. "This is to cheer you up a little cause I know you've been looking at it."

Maggie gave me the rest of my shift off, so I hugged and thanked her. Philly and Warren had plans to take me home, wrap me in a blanket, and not let me out of their sight. Once in Philly's car, I opened Maggie's little package. It was one of her aprons, the one with the DNA molecules stretched like ladders across pockets and the hemline. I laughed and then I cried, using the apron to wipe my wet eyes.

A person can take only so much mothering, patting, and cups of hot chocolate before they've got to escape and find a hiding place. Philly and Warren by themselves could be overwhelming, but together they were like whipped cream smothering a blueberry. I couldn't breathe. To stave them off, I kept my eyes closed and pretended to rest, but I wasn't sleeping. I was thinking.

At 11:15 a.m., I opened one eye to scope the hovering caretaker stakeout. My gaze went to the DNA molecule apron, draped over my living room chair, and an idea began to percolate. *Problems are like staircases*, I thought. *There are sequential steps, a bit of stretching to climb to the next level. Each step taken enhances the view.* On the double helix-shaped spiral stepladder of a DNA strand, each nucleotide rung reveals something about the whole person. Joon had confided in me. Her stories were like rungs on a ladder; they helped me understand her intentions and her homelessness. I reasoned that her stories would also help me understand her death.

I slid, silent as a jellyfish, off the couch and tiptoed into my work room.

Did Joon die because of an accident? I didn't think so. Was it suicide? I couldn't see Joon killing herself in a muddy, old alley. I never heard her say anything that would lead me to believe she would commit suicide anywhere. She was strong. She was a survivor. Remembering the investigator's words about how similar Joon's death was to Liam's and considering the chief's orders to check out the food at Tent City and in the bakery, I was ninety-nine percent sure she'd eaten poison.

Denny was in jail when Joon died, charged with Liam's murder. He couldn't poison Joon from behind bars, and why would he want to? Joon's death reinforced my certainty the police made a mistake with Denny's arrest.

For convenience, I'd covered a wall of my workroom with dry-erase paint when I organized my office. I used it to chart genealogical connections when I wanted to see the big picture. Instead of feeling caged on the couch, I would start my search for answers to Joon's death by mapping out the basics, the who, what, when, where, why, and how questions. I would create a sort of investigation board with Joon at its center.

In minutes, I was busy writing big-lettered questions on my wall. Ten minutes into my brainstorming, Philly came in. She said not a word but picked up a pen and started adding her own questions. With her long, slim legs she stretched higher than I could, and we wove in and out of each other's reach as though Sufi whirling.

Lastly, Warren joined us. He knew a hatful of connections between Tent City, the police, and the fire department that I would never have put together in my list of inquiries. We bumped into each other, sometimes repeated each other's work, and now and again, we drew arrows between our questions and people's names as we connected Brocklebrook relationships, histories, and ties to Tent City.

When we laid down our pens and stepped back to look, Philly broke the silence. "Do we have to answer all these questions to know what happened? There must be twenty brain teasers on that wall."

"Some of these we can answer right now." Warren

grabbed a pen and started writing under the question asking about current camp residents. "We've got about twelve unhoused people camped out now, in the middle of fall. In other seasons, those numbers increase, especially if entire families move in. Sometimes the Tent City population is down to half a dozen or so. Joon, Denny, and some of the others are always there, and have been since the camp opened seven years ago."

"They are the elders," I said aloud, my throat catching on the last syllable.

"You alright?" Philly put an arm around me. I laid my head on her shoulder and gave her a squeeze before grabbing my rolling office chair to sit down.

"Joon and Denny and Stan and the other older people at Tent City, they're the elders," I explained. "They set the rules and enforce them, and it means most people in Brocklebrook don't have much to complain about when it comes to our unhoused citizens. They don't think about Tent City much because they don't have to."

"There's trouble in Tent City sometimes, no doubt about it." Warren capped his pen and shook his head. "That usually happens when drugs and alcohol are part of people's lives. When a newcomer sneaks in unhealthy substances, it effects all their fellow campers."

My phone pinged next to my elbow, an ad for a candidate running for office, but it reminded me of the pictures I took the day before with Joon and the amaranth. I showed them to Philly, and for a few moments we stared at the images, feeling as though our friend was still with us.

The photos inspired Philly to pick up blue and green markers and sketch a picture of Joon on the wall. She drew arrows and lines highlighting the more personal links between Joon and city employees who worked to maintain park bathrooms or did garbage pickup. Philly even color-coded relationships with green for 'friendly,' blue for 'strictly businesses,' and red for 'unfriendly.' The thickest red lines went from Lester Stoats to Denny, Joon, and the other older members of Tent City.

"Love it," I told Philly and began using her color code to circle questions and connect them with lines and arrows to other questions.

"You know this kind of reminds me of all of those crazy maps and newspaper articles that Russell Crowe - well, John Nash, tacked up in his garage in that film *A Beautiful Mind*," Philly said, laughing. "You don't suppose we're all mad geniuses, do you?"

"We're definitely mad, but I'm pretty sure none of us are geniuses," I answered.

"Hey," Warren said. "Speak for yourselves. I'm here to keep you two from getting into more trouble than you can handle."

"Oh ho, Mr. stay-up-till-all-hours playing League of Nations and Counterstrike and Dota II with sixteen-year-olds. You're the craziest of us all." Philly scrutinized Warren and snorted.

"Keeps me young." Warren was laughing too. "I never reveal my age."

Hearing my friends needle each other lifted my spirits. Warren could blend in with about anyone, including his macho fire-fighting buddies, sixteen-year-olds on multiplayer online computer games, computer programmers, and even with Philly, a fiery, single woman who was deep into work, Friday night dating, and the local fitness-and-figure competition.

My puzzle-solving partner might be able to mix with kids, teens, and younger adults, but he really was old enough to be a grandparent. For all we knew, he might be a grandpa. He had that missing son out there somewhere.

I squinted at the wall and our dozens of colored lines connecting questions, names, businesses, and organizations. I couldn't see how the squiggles and arrows helped expose why Joon died, but something might pop out and grab me later.

"Oh finknoodles," Philly said, checking her watch. "I've got to get back to work. Will you be okay, buddy? I'm talking to Betts, not you Warren. I know *you're* never going to be okay."

"I'll make it," I told Philly. "Go to work. I'll ring if I need something."

"If I find out anything at city hall, I'll call. I can scope out police scuttlebutt, too." She pursed her lips and half closed her eyes, pondering. "They might know more about whether Joon and Liam were poisoned or not."

When Philly was gone, Warren and I sat and talked. We tried to work out a tie between Liam and Joon that would explain why they both died so suddenly.

"I had no idea Joon got food from the dumpsters. It's sad the police didn't feed her last night before sending her home, but I guess that's not something that police stations do." I shivered, thinking about Joon's last moments, sick and afraid in that dark alley.

"Look," Warren said, getting up from the couch. "I've got errands to run, but I don't want you to be alone tonight. I'll be back in time to cook you up a fried chicken dinner."

I nodded, grateful. Together we could watch a silly comedy before bed, hoping a nonsensical distraction would help us sleep better. I kissed him as he headed out the door; then I went out back to take care of my garden and the greenhouse.

Feeling gloomy was more challenging among my vegetables and late-season flowers. In early fall, most of the plants were either done producing or at their peak. I whistled the tune from a song called *Plant A Rose For Me*, by Malvina Reynolds, while I gathered tomatoes for dinner and ground cherries, garden huckleberries, and beans for freezing.

Seeing the familiar plants from Joon's seeds brought tears to my eyes. I would share the harvest with her friends and save the seeds to grow new plants in her memory. According to Joon, several heirloom varieties were quite rare, even valuable. I wasn't always sure what she meant because *valuable* in her mind did not necessarily connect to financial wealth or money. Whatever their worth, I would honor Joon's precedence and protect the recipes from financial exploitation.

I heard my phone ringing through the open back door of my house. Because I forgot to bring the phone with me outdoors, I rushed to answer it, thinking the caller might have important news about Joon or Denny. However, my body simply couldn't move as fast as usual. I felt as though I was trying to walk through cheesecake batter, sore all over because of my fall. The phone stopped ringing by the time I got to it. No one left a message; probably one of those fund-raising college students, calling to see if I would donate to my alma mater. Just as I turned back toward the garden, the phone rang again. I picked it up, eager for news.

"Ms. Harvey?" said a low, dry voice. The connection sounded muted and scratchy. I thought I heard a working clothes dryer in the background.

"Yes, that's me," I answered.

"You have something that belongs to me."

"Who is this?" Now I was on my guard. "What do I have that's yours?"

"I'm Joon's heir. I want what is mine. I want the book she left with you." The voice tightened on the last sentence with suppressed emotion.

I thought hard about what to say. This was unexpected. "I'm happy to meet with you, but Joon was extremely specific about how she wanted to decide who received her book. It could be that you meet the criteria, but we would need to talk."

The caller answered with low, sarcastic laughter. "Joon is dead. What she wants doesn't matter anymore. That book is mine, always has been, and let me warn you. You could meet the same sad fate as Joon if you don't do the right thing."

"Are you threatening me?" I was more than confused. I was angry. "Because that doesn't work with me. I'm not giving Joon's book to someone who threatens people. Did you kill her?"

Hostile sniggering replaced the low laughter and caused heat to rise along the back of my neck to the crown of my head.

"You leave that book outside your front door tonight and I'll leave you alone." The caller sniggered again. "If I don't get the book tonight, you'll find out just how Joon was killed."

My vision blurred and the bright colors in my garden faded to shades of gray.

"No tricks," said the voice. "No police. No one watching the book. Do you understand? I'll leave you alone if I get the almanac. If not, you'll wish you never met Joon O'Neal."

The line went dead, and I still had no idea if the caller was a man or woman.

Chapter 5

"Those who love life will see beauty in the flower of a powerful plant. Those who despise life will discard the flower and transform stems, leaves, and roots into weapons." Towne Family Almanac, 1763. Mattee Singleton Hireman, daughter of Ellyner Salter.

I was afraid to leave my house, and I was afraid to stay in it. If I left, someone might invade and damage my home. If I stayed, someone might break in and damage me.

Warren wasn't answering his phone, but his battery was low when he left after lunch. I recorded several messages on his voice mail, explaining the threats and my concerns about the book. *I'm even afraid for Joon's plants,* I told Warren in a message. *If this person knows I have the book and what it is, there's no telling what they know about the plants I've been growing in the greenhouse.*

When I couldn't reach Philly's cell phone, I tried to call her through city offices. A receptionist explained Philly was in a meeting and would call back once she got my message.

Should I call the police? What would happen to Joon's family almanac/recipe book if I did? Would it become evidence? What happened to pieces of evidence when the police took hold of them? If law enforcement got involved, would they help or hurt the situation? Would I be withholding evidence if I didn't call the police? Was I really in danger? All these questions and more ricocheted through my mind like synthetic rubber superballs let fly in a handball court.

I made a decision. First, I wrote down everything I could remember of the caller's words. Then I retrieved Joon's bulky family heirloom from my desk, wrapped it in birthday paper and ribbon to disguise it, and carried it to my car, careful to lock the doors of my compact home behind me. Dr. Dillinger, my black and white cat who died of being ancient only weeks ago, came to mind. While I missed him every day, I was glad I had no animals to leave behind today.

Nervous, I checked the street for strange cars or people. Everything was quiet. My retired neighbor, Carl Safina, watered his flowers to my left, and perpetually-unemployed Anna Blommaert looked through her mail, the weathered metal lid of her mailbox hanging open.

My first stop was a printing and packaging shop. Claiming one of the copy machines, I settled in. It was going to take a few hours to copy every oversized page of Joon's book and to meticulously double check that the seed packets remained in the right slots in the correct pages. One hundred fifty minutes later, I asked the young male store attendant to bind the copied pages for me. While I waited, I packaged the original, leather-bound manuscript in a large mailing box and addressed it to me. I would send it third class to myself at the bakery.

I wasn't sure my behavior made any sense, but it

meant I could postpone thinking too hard about a plan-of-action concerning Joon's compendium. If it were in the mail, there would be no conceivable way to hand the book over to this phone bully and probable murderer.

"Here you are, ma'am." The store attendant handed over the new copy, bound with cardstock, and I passed him the boxed and addressed almanac, the one that had come across the Atlantic in a sailing ship and was hundreds of years old.

I was ready to talk with the police.

Brocklebrook police station was in the same concrete building as city offices, so after I finished my obligations with the investigators, I could find Philly, and we could go out for coffee.

Detective Edward Crumley introduced himself. He was one of the officers who oversaw Joon's crime scene investigation earlier that morning. My police department host was one of those people who couldn't help but look like a road construction supervisor, no matter how professionally his hair was styled or how nicely pressed his suit.

Keeping his rough and weather-tanned face impassive, he led me into what looked like a conference room and invited me to sit at a large, oval table, shiny between an accumulation of scratches and dents that reminded me of the crisscrossed lines on someone's open hand. I wondered if it was possible to read conference tables the way some people read palms. The chair the detective offered was ladder-backed all the way down to its cushioned seat, recently stained with coffee.

Sitting on the edge of the cushion, I waited for Crumley's questions. None came. He sat next to me and waited. Two minutes into the silence, I started talking.

"A few hours ago, someone called my phone and threatened me. They ordered me to leave a copy of a book belonging to Joon in my front yard tonight or I might end up cold and dead."

Crumley sat back and stared at my face, his eyes scrutinizing mine as though assessing my sincerity. "Tell me about this book. Why would someone want it."

"It's old, ancient really. It's an heirloom, a book that women passed down to each other through the generations since at least the 1600s. Joon and I were working to compile her family history and find a keeper for the heirloom. She gave it to me for safe keeping."

"Besides being old, what's so special about it that someone would threaten you for it?" Crumley regarded me with skepticism.

"I don't know. It's full of old recipes and seeds. Here's a copy." I pushed the duplicate almanac toward him on the table. "Joon made it very clear that this is a private book that should not be shared with anyone."

"Where's the original?" Crumley complained.

"I sent it to myself in the mail just to make sure it was out of reach for a while." In defense of my decision, I folded my arms over my chest and kept my eyes on the photocopied compendium between us. He, of course, wanted the original as evidence, but Crumley would have to wait to see it. I didn't tell him about the key for the codes that went with the recipe book. Many ingredients for the recipes were unnamed. Instead, the almanac caretakers used symbols to indicate ingredients. The symbols referred to plants connected to saved seeds. There was a key to the symbols hidden in a fold of the back cover. The copy of the heirloom book that I gave to the police did not have a back cover or a symbol key.

When I showed him the phone number of my caller, Crumley's laugh conveyed a tone of irony.

"That's a throw away phone," he said in his usual short-sentenced staccato. "It'll be near impossible to trace. Now then, we can investigate everything Joon gave you. We can examine her DNA record. We can try and find some evidence, but I'm going to warn you. Our case against Denny Woodman is getting stronger. We let him go this morning. We didn't have enough to keep him, but we're building up to a second arrest for both murders. He might very well have been your phone caller."

I could feel my face flush, stunned over Crumley's easy conjectures about Denny. "So, you're identifying both deaths as murders?" I put both hands inside my sweater pockets and balled them into fists. "And if you're calling them murders and Denny was locked up last night, how could he have killed Joon?"

"You don't have to be with your victims to poison them." Crumley's manner and his tone bordered on scornfulness. "You just have to make sure that you've planted the poison. Put it in food or drink that your target eats."

"What kind of poison?" I remembered the phone caller's threat.

"May I call you Betts?" Without waiting for an answer Crumley continued. "We found a toxic substance called cicutoxin. It was in both victims. We think someone took parts of roots or seeds of the plant *Cicuto douglasii* and added it to food that Liam and then Joon ate."

I looked hard at Crumley. "I may have a garden, and I may love plants, but I still need to know the conventional name of a plant to understand what you're talking about."

"Okay, Betts." He leaned in to put a hand on the copy of Joon's heirloom. "We're talking here about water hemlock. Toxic. Grows right here in western Washington. Animals or humans have been known to eat certain parts of this plant. If they go untreated, they can die within fifteen minutes. On the other hand, they might be in agony for up to two hours and still live through it. Water hemlock has a kind of carroty smell; it's a member of the carrot family. Carrots seem innocent enough but some of their relatives are deadly."

"Oh, those poor souls." I thought about the pain and confusion Joon and Liam must have experienced. "But I don't think Denny did it. What motive would he have? Why him?"

"Look, Betts. There's water hemlock growing along the stream bed down the bank from Tent City. It's right there. Denny and Liam were close to blows the night before Liam died. Joon was a witness. Denny could have lost control and taken the fight to the next level." Crumley leaned back, sliding the book towards him. "These are homeless people, Betts. Their lives are extreme. They're often mentally ill. Joon might even have been a witness to more than the fight. Denny needed her gone."

"Did you ever spend time with Denny, I mean, outside of the police department?" My voice was hard. "Do you have anything to go by other than 'could haves' and speculation?"

When Crumley began shaking his head in would-be sympathy, I stood to leave, wanting to get out of the room before I lost my temper.

"Look. I'll send a patrol car by your house. One or two times tonight just in case your caller is more than a prankster." Crumley's clipped sentences were starting to get on my nerves, but he continued. "You might want to stay somewhere else. Maybe have someone with you. You live alone, am I right? A spinster, aren't you?"

"I'm a widow," I said, irritated with myself for caring about his spinster jab. To my mind, the police could have acted more proactively, maybe with a stakeout, one that ended with arresting anyone who came to take items from my front porch. I didn't look forward to some so-called *prankster*, as Crumley referred to them, victimizing me.

As I left the police offices behind me, I thought about what I'd learned. I knew something about the toxicity of water hemlock. As a student of garden plants and wild herbs and vegetables, I'd studied some of the florae varieties around Brocklebrook. I knew how to identify water hemlock and poison hemlock flowers, both of which were often confused with the sweet and innocent Queen Anne's Lace. I also knew people without experience might easily mistake hemlock for wild parsnips. Cattle and other mammals have perished from eating it. Convulsions are one symptom, and animals die from cardiovascular collapse due to asphyxiation.

Remembering the caller's words, I tightened my arms to my side to quell a shiver. *If I don't get the book tonight, you'll find out just how Joon was killed.* Of course, I would rather go the way my furry Dr. Dillinger went, of being ancient, and not from a dose of cicutoxin.

Unable to shake off the patronizing tenor of Crumley's self-assured verdict about Denny, I kept my focus on the exit sign. His attitude about Denny fanned the newly fired coals of resentment I carried in my belly toward the police department. I strode up the stairs to the city offices where I would find Philly. Her meeting was just ending, and she looked as harassed as I felt. Her face relaxed a bit when she saw me. The coals in my belly cooled a bit, and I felt better, safer, in her presence.

"Got time for coffee?" I asked.

"I'm gonna make time. Let's get out of here."

My friend walked so fast up the street toward Hot Shot Coffee Shop that I needed to run to catch up with her. As a fitness and figure competitor, Philly was in great shape, but even so, this was high speed for her. I figured she had some strong emotion she needed to walk off. I couldn't keep up, but I knew she would save a seat for me in the café. Sure enough, five minutes later I found Philly in a window seat, staring at the sugar bowl as though she wanted to do it mortal damage. I moved it out of her reach and sat down across from her.

"Okay, spill," I said.

"I don't want to make your day worse, Betts," she said.

"It's already in the trash without your help."

"Okay, but you asked for it." Philly scowled. "You're not going to like it, but here goes. None other than Lester Stoats, King of Brocklebrook, called the meeting I just got out of. He outlined a plan he wants all of us to get behind, a plan to wipe Tent City off the map and out of town. The murders, he says, make this the best time to act, politically speaking, and according to him, the murders prove that the camp is a legal liability to the city."

"What has he got against Tent City?" I felt those

coals in my belly heat up again. "I mean what's his real problem?"

"I don't know for sure, but I can guess." Philly pursed her lips and strummed nervous fingers on the table between us. "He wants to make Brocklebrook into a high-end tourist attraction. He's fully focused on gentrification. He says the city council hired him to bring a more corporate-style business model to town government, and if something doesn't fit into that model, then it's not sensible. So, if you're old or sick, or your store is a little rundown, or if your job doesn't earn what he considers good money, you're not worth talking with, nor are you worth representing. Tent City simply doesn't have a place in a corporate-style city where to be anybody, everybody must contribute to an elevated bottom line."

"That's not how humanity works, nor has it ever worked that way." I stirred my coffee with vigor, even though I hadn't added anything to it. "People have a whole array of needs that don't fit into an economic formula. People also have a whole variety of ways they contribute to a community that most economists or officials never include in economic figures and measures."

"Listen to us." Philly burst out laughing. "We sound like a couple of academics, but yeah. Some of us mentioned that. You know what he said to us? 'Get behind me or pack up your belongings. I decide who works here and who doesn't. If you're not with me and the big vision, then you're not part of my team.'"

"So, the King of Brocklebrook really is an authoritarian." I was disgusted. "What does the city council have to say about all of this?"

"There are a few who want to have more discussion, but a majority of the councilors are somehow enamored of Stoats and don't seem to care that his methods are without empathy or compassion." Philly held her head in both hands as though it hurt. "They've bought into the philosophy that humans are operative robots, mostly concerned with economic progress and that if it doesn't make a profit, it doesn't belong. They're rewarding Stoats and his conceit."

"And Tent City is the antithesis of the corporate, money-making model," I said, adding to Philly's assessment. "So, it drives someone like Stoats absolutely crazy."

We sipped our coffee drinks for a while, each with our own thoughts about CEO types we'd known who wanted to impose their organizational values on every corner of the world.

"What are you going to do?" I asked Philly.

"Well … I'm not behind Stoats and his vision, as he puts it." She leaned back and looked hard at the ceiling. "So, if he stays, and the Brocklebrook City Council goes along with all of this, I'll either have to pretend I'm something I'm not and forsake my own ethics and morals, or I'll have to find another place to work."

"You can always get a job here at Hot Shot Coffee," I teased.

Philly toasted me with her empty coffee mug. "In the meantime, Denny has become the poster child for why Tent City has to go."

"Denny's out of jail, for now," I reported. "I sure hope he comes into the bakery tomorrow so we can talk. I'm worried about him. What if he's arrested again? Does he know anything about who really killed Joon and Liam and why?"

I told Philly about the phone call and my trip to the police station.

Her countenance changed from petulant Persian feline to protective gargoyle. "I want you to get away from your house this evening." She leaned over the table and lowered her voice. "I want you and Warren to go out to dinner with me, and I want you to meet a new man in my life. His name is Roger Ingold. If you eat dinner with us, you won't be sitting and waiting for something bad to happen on your front porch."

"Well." I caught my lower lip between my teeth, thinking it through. "I'll have to check with Warren, and he hasn't been answering his phone."

"I'm a big believer in spontaneity." Philly straightened, face alight with a mischievous grin. "It'll be fun. I promise we won't go where there's a loud Salsa band, as much as I love to dance. It'll just be a quiet dinner at a nice restaurant."

"I'll text him," I said. "No guarantees."

In the end, we did go to dinner with Philly and Roger, but only after I met with the police a third time. Philly and I decided to gather at the French Door Cafe at 7 o'clock, if Warren agreed. I stopped for groceries and chose only food supplies in well-wrapped containers. I was starting to over think my new need to double check for food tampering and protect my supplies from doses of water hemlock.

When I brought my groceries in through the kitchen door, I was relieved to see that the house was in the same order I'd left it. I saw no signs that anyone gained entry when I was gone, but I did lock the doors behind me, something I only ever did at night. Remembering that I hadn't finished watering my greenhouse plants, I slipped on my greenhouse rubbers and stepped out to finish the job.

The greenhouse door was wide open. Had I left it that way to get the phone? I didn't remember, but I was cautious as I approached the entry way. As soon as I could see inside, I knew something was wrong. Little piles of spilled soil fouled my ordinarily well-swept cement floor. Someone kicked a pot of Astragalus into a corner where it lay on its side, broken. What brought a groan to my throat were all the empty spaces where potted plants rested a few hours ago. Someone took every last one of Joon's seed-producing plants and none of my own. How was that possible? Who would be able to distinguish between Joon's plants and mine? My mind went to the afternoon caller. How had they known about the book in the first place? Could they have known enough about Joon's project to identify and steal the seed plants that went with the book? Such a connection boggled my mind. Then again, was it even the caller who took the plants?

Some of Joon's words from yesterday came back to me. *I've got to tell you to hold onto that book I gave you. Don't let anyone else have it. There's someone after it, but he can't have it. He's not the one. And if I get arrested, you know what to do. You finish what we started.*

Why hadn't I pressed her to tell me more? Who was this someone after the book? I stamped my foot hard in exasperation and groaned as bolts of pain shot up to my bruised knee.

While most of the seed packets in the heirloom book

were already replenished, some seed varieties were late and still unripe. Now those were gone. If they were monetarily valuable, the thief could be profiting. Plus, it looked as though I would have to go through another growing season before I could harvest more seeds and finish the job I'd begun.

Disheartened, I called the police and reported the theft. This time they sent an officer to take pictures and record a statement.

"Ms. Harvey," the officer said, his young brow crinkled in puzzlement. "This doesn't make a whole lot of sense to me. Why would someone take a bunch of plants that had gone to seed, and what does this have to do with Ms. O'Neal getting killed?"

I told him I was as mystified as he was.

Not only was I perplexed, but I also felt violated. Those angry coals in my belly started to smoke again, and I was dipping my toes into a rising pool of resentment and annoyance - the kind of anger that could become fury if I didn't check myself. I needed to sit down and review who I was angry with and what I was mad about, but for now I had designs on catching the phone caller and the bastard who took my plants. I pictured subjecting them to the same kind of fear-of-God questioning I put my eighth graders through the day they became eco-terrorists and perpetrated a canola oil spill in the biology teacher's fish aquariums.

I locked up my greenhouse for the first time in months. Looking around, I observed that my outside garden seemed fine. I saw no evidence of digging or plant mutilation. Not for the last time I thought about what it might be like to have a dog as a companion, but also as a kind of house and garden protector.

Warren finally phoned. When I explained about the malicious caller, Warren's fire fighter, man-in-charge ethos blazed. There were times I barely tolerated this demanding, macho side of Warren.

"Don't go all schoolteacher on me," Warren said. "No lectures. There's something I've got to do."

At his words, I felt myself shape shift into my don't-mess-with-me persona. I was ready to defend my independence like a hornet zeroing in on a clueless intruder. I was ready, but holding back, because once in a very great while it's a relief to have a good friend who wants to protect me and demands I follow reasonable safety measures. It means I'm not alone in a bewildering and dangerous situation.

"Betts," he said before I could explain about dinner, "I'm coming by in 15 minutes to pick you up. I'm leaving a guy in your house to watch over things tonight. He'll sleep on the couch. You're staying over at my house."

I didn't protest. Frankly, I was relieved, so I shelved my independent bravado for another time, gathered up Deputy Delilah and other essential items, picked out clothes for dinner with Philly and her new man, and got ready to leave. At the last minute, I decided to conduct a little experiment. Wrapping an old, substantial phone book in brown paper, I positioned the package above the steps of my front porch. I wanted to see if someone came by to retrieve it.

"You ready?" Warren walked through the front door without a hello or smile, grabbing my overnight bag and heading out to his truck. He returned with a young man dressed in fashion ripped jeans and a black t-shirt, tight over his muscular upper torso. "This is Joey. I've already given him my extra key, and I'm going to show him around while you climb aboard."

After I settled in the passenger seat of Warren's pickup, and Warren jumped in at the wheel, he kept his eyes focused upfront, careful not to look at me. I slapped him lightly on the knee. "Your bulldog is showing." I offered a sideways smile. He turned his head a tentative few inches in my direction, his jaw muscles set and stress lines creasing his brow. When he saw my wink, he softened a bit. I decided to tell him about the missing plants later when he was less edgy.

"I thought you were going to fight me on this," he said, "and I wasn't taking no for an answer this time."

"I'm just looking forward to going out to dinner." I leaned over, gifting him with a light kiss on his left cheek. "And I really am grateful that you got someone to spend the night, so my house won't be left empty."

Warren breathed out a sigh of relief and started the truck. His vocation included giving orders as a fire chief, so he had to work hard at compromising and toning down his take-charge impulses. I surprised him with my lack of protest.

"When I get a hold of the guy who made that phone call-," Warren muttered under his breath.

"You'll let the police take care of him or her," I whispered in his ear.

Chapter 6

"Yarrow and borage grow among the wild plants that border my garden. Both are herbs of courage. They remind me that people who help in times of need are mightier than my fears. Yarrow and borage reveal that I am most afraid of how powerful I can be." From the Towne Family Almanac, 1708. Ellyner Salter, daughter of Emma Flower.

The four of us settled at a table near the front window of the French Door Café, and Philly introduced us to Roger. About forty, he was a fit man with a toned physique and a winning smile. It was obvious to me Philly was taken with him, and that was unusual for her. She liked to go out with a succession of men, but she mostly saw them as friends or acquaintances. Roger, it seemed, had managed to tune a few of her heartstrings.

"We met at the fitness center," Philly said. "After a week of coffee breaks together, we discovered we share very little in common." My friend laughed as she put her hand over Roger's. "So, we've been going out every Friday night for more than a month now."

I gasped in mock wonder. "And now you've invited your 'parents' to meet him. This is serious."

"Well, you're old enough to be my parents, that's for

sure." Philly chewed on her stuffed mushroom and winked. "But mostly you're my good old friends."

Over our pre-dinner appetizers, complemented with white wine, Warren and I learned that Roger was new to town and looking for volunteer work. He retired early the year before with a substantial pension and lucrative stocks from a computer programming company. He'd moved to Brocklebrook for a change in scenery and to find a new focus on life.

"And Roger's like me," Philly said. "He's taking time to look for missing family. He wants to locate one lost relative in particular. I told him about your genealogy business, Betts, but he's already done DNA testing."

"That reminds me. With all that's been going on," I said to Philly, "I haven't had time to check and see if anything came up for you. Have you looked at your genealogy account?"

"Same as you. Too much happening." Philly waved a forgiving hand.

"I'd love to get your advice someday." Roger backed up his plea with an earnest nod of his head. "I have questions about how to contact people if they turn out to be related."

"I'm at your service," I told him.

"Philly tells me you're good at unravelling more than genealogy puzzles. You and Warren like to put your heads together and solve Brocklebrook mysteries."

"In other words," Warren said with an embarrassed chuckle, "we're nosy neighbors. I confess that I'd rather talk about town secrets with Betts any day than sit hunched over a crossword puzzle. Keeps our brains active without having to know the names of has-been,

Hollywood celebrities."

Roger sat up straighter in his King Louis side chair, his eyes intent on Warren's face. "Are you two figuring out how that poor guy got caught in the storage unit fire?"

"We've talked about it." Warren stopped short of giving details. "Betts, would you mind telling us again about that phone call you got after finding poor Joon this morning?"

For Roger's sake, I repeated the details about finding Joon in the alley and recited the words of my threatening phone caller. "And then, to top it all, when I got back from reporting the call to the police, I discovered my greenhouse had been robbed of all Joon's seed-bearing plants."

Warren scooted his chair back and stood, clearly upset. I had forgotten to tell him about the greenhouse burglary.

Philly looked livid. "As if you hadn't gone through enough today," she said, "and all that hard work. Gone."

Roger looked up at Warren with an odd, assessing expression.

"And you thought it was a good idea to stay put at your house tonight?" Warren stood over Betts and put a protective hand on her right shoulder.

"No. I'm grateful to be spending the night with you," I reassured him.

When Warren returned to his seat, we dropped the subject of stolen plants and murder. Roger told us he was staying at a hotel until he could find a nice rental. "Most of my things are in storage, so I feel a little homeless. I like this little village, and I think I might want to stick around." He turned toward Philly and nodded.

After entrees and shared desserts, we got up to leave, and it was then that I saw Roger's hat. A standard beanie variety, it had to be hand knitted, mostly with thick, rustic sheep wool but displaying a pattern of green and brown mandalas. I stared at it for a long minute.

Disconcerted, I studied Roger's face and scrutinized the hat again.

"You like my hat?" Roger eyed me with a quizzical frown.

"Oh," I said, coming out of my momentary trance. "Oh, yes. The colors are so distinctive, and it is beautifully hand knitted. Do you have a matching scarf?"

In my mind's eye I recalled one of Warren's photos portraying Liam's murder scene. The pattern and colors of Roger's hat exactly matched a scarf pictured amongst the burnt boxes in the storage unit.

"I used to, but I seem to have lost it somewhere. I bought the hat and scarf from a woman who was selling them on the street, over between Third and Jackson."

"I see," was all I could think to say. Joon often sold hand-knitted items on that very corner.

We parted at the front entrance of the restaurant, Warren and I trudging to his truck, and Philly and Roger walking hand in hand to a gold-tinted SUV.

I needed to clear my head and put my thoughts in order. Was it time to put together a suspect list? Roger's name would be on it, no matter how nice and polite he seemed.

An October chill took charge of the dark evening, so Warren turned the heater on high and passed me a lap blanket.

"Let's drive by my house to see if that package is still

on the porch," I said to Warren.

Warren frowned. I could tell he thought this was a bad idea, but he turned the truck in the direction of my street. When we got closer to the house, he switched off the truck lights and cut the motor. We coasted toward the white picket fence surrounding my steep-roofed cottage. On a moonless night like this one, all we could see were the shadowy silhouettes of my front yard apple trees and the outline of the cement walkway leading to the porch. Joey had the front room lights on, and they helped illuminate the rhododendrons on each side of the porch steps. We parked across the street.

"Is Joey going to be alright if someone tries to break in?" I asked.

"Oh, I think so." Warren chuckled. "He's equipped with a few weapons, knives and tear gas, and he's eager to use them all."

"Well, I hope at least part of the house is left standing after he's done," I said with some acerbity.

We sat there in the dark for a while, holding hands. I enjoyed the scent of Warren's aftershave and moved closer. He slipped an arm around my shoulders.

"Mmmm," I said, enjoying the feel of his lips on my forehead.

His warm, moist mouth moved down to the tip of my nose and then lower. Just as our kiss deepened, the windshield exploded, enveloping us in a violent, shattering paroxysm. A blast of sharp, diamond-sized pieces of safety glass showered over our faces, necks, and hands. It took a short bleep of Warren's horn for me to realize that the irritating, ear-splitting screech I heard was me screaming. As the glass storm petered out, I held my breath to gain control. Beside me in the seat rested a large igneous rock.

"Are you alright?" Warren yelled. At my head nod, he was out of the pickup in a flash, tearing off to catch our attacker. But he returned in a matter of minutes.

"Dressed in black," Warren said between clenched teeth. "Bastard ran when he saw me. Leaped into those woods over there. I had no chance of spotting him in those trees without a flashlight."

By then, I realized I was in shock, trembling and still sitting on the front seat of the truck with those bits of safety glass all around me. Faceted squares and rectangles invaded my hair and even my sandals. Warren cleared glass off the seat so I could slide out, and we worked to brush each other off under a nearby streetlight. I tried to make sure the sharp edges hadn't cut or skinned Warren. In the meantime, Joey sidestepped out of the house.

"Identify yourselves, or else," he yelled.

Neighbors rushed out to investigate. One called the police.

Forty-five minutes later, law enforcement had left, the neighbors shuffled up their walks, and Joey returned to my living room, shutting the front door behind him. As the officers explained to us, a broken windshield wasn't enough provocation to bring in reinforcements. We swept all the glass we could see in the dim light and got back in the truck. It would be a breezy trip to Warren's house. I was still shivering with nervous energy, and the cool air wouldn't change that. Just as we pulled away from the curb, I remembered the reason we'd come in the first place. As the headlights illuminated my front door, I could see the package I'd installed on the steps was long gone.

I shuddered, thinking about the marauder and how they would react when they discovered it was merely an old phone book instead of Joon's heirloom compendium. There would be hell to pay.

Rubbing the sides of my arms to generate heat, I tried to make sense of the situation. Who were the most obvious suspects? Could Roger drop off Philly in time to throw a rock through our windshield? I supposed it was possible. Might it be Denny? I couldn't see Denny throwing a rock at anyone, let alone at Warren and me. My imagination took a leap, and I pictured Lester Stoats in a black ski mask running from Warren into the woods, concerned about getting dirt on his flawless, polished shoes. The thought almost made me laugh.

Who else could be so obsessed with Joon's book? Who else even knew about it? Did the book have anything to do with the murders? The phone caller implied there was a connection, as farfetched as that seemed to me. Right then, I wished I had made two copies of the book before sending it in the mail, one for the police and one that I could look through, page by page. The book might contain hints or clues about its value and why someone might want it badly enough to kill.

By the time we turned into Warren's driveway, exhaustion took over. My shower lasted all of five minutes before I climbed into Warren's four poster bed. I couldn't tell you how long Warren's shower lasted because I was fast asleep before he slipped under the thick, hand-stitched quilt. About 3:30 a.m., I woke with a start, comforted to find my arms around the very warm and sturdy frame of a man I was growing ever fond of.

It was time to go to work, and Warren insisted on

driving me, broken windshield, and all.

With purposeful resolve to be brave, I opened the door to the bakery while Warren parked the truck. He wanted to be in the building with me during those first, lonely work hours.

Most days I loved the time to myself, listening to the radio as I baked. This morning, though, I was concerned about every distinguishable noise, inside and outside the bakery. Each little squeak and scrape teased out the more morbid digressions of my imagination. I especially wanted a friend with me when I took the garbage out. Warren grabbed one full garbage bag, and I took the other. Maggie, bless her heart, must have worked with due diligence to make sure the alley way was spotless. I could see no residue of yesterday's events as I lifted the dumpster lid and deposited my load.

Aromas of lemon loaf, whole-grain bread, rum cake, and cinnamon scones captured every corner in the bakery and helped abate the memories of finding my friend lifeless. I put together a package of day-old bakery goods and sandwiches for Tent City, wondering if the police had confiscated most of the campers' food and, if so, had the food been replaced to keep the unhoused men, women, and children from going hungry? If Denny didn't make it to Dirty Dozen, Warren could drop the care package off at Tent City once Maggie came to take over.

Denny did make it. His thin form, silhouetted outside the front door, reminded me more than ever of a wild, bedraggled Tomcat. Warren ushered our friend into the café, thumped him on the back, and brought him over to where I was ready to serve coffee.

"We've been so worried about you." I searched

Denny's face to assess his wellbeing.

He took some time removing his coat and getting into his chair. His hair looked unwashed. Dark circles accentuated the watery tiredness of his blue eyes.

"I'm in hell. I can't stop thinking about what happened to Joon," were his first words. He looked on the verge of crying, which was enough to start tears falling down my own cheeks. Even Warren, usually stoical about these kinds of things, was misty eyed.

When our waterworks settled, and we could all breathe normally again, I told Denny that I had half an hour before opening the doors. Warren and I wanted to hear everything so that we would know how best to help.

So, Denny told us about Liam and how fellow campers caught him stealing. He'd also smuggled meth into camp and was trying to sell it. "You know there are Jake and Penny who work hard to be drug free and are really struggling. They've been attending Al-anon twice a week. Joon and I decided that Liam could not stay. We told him to take his filthy wares and get out of town. I'm afraid I was rough with him after he insisted Tent City was a public place, and we had no right to stop him. I kicked his skinny butt out into the road and told him that if he ever came back, I would call the police. I should have called the police right then and there."

"Did he come back?" I asked.

"I never saw him again." Denny poured himself a second mug from the coffee pot. "How he got in our storage room and how he even knew we had one is a mystery. Apparently, Liam or someone else searched the room and dumped most of our belongings. I can't imagine what they were looking for. Mostly, we don't have anything worth more than a few dollars. But I did have a box with money; I was saving it for something important. I don't even know if the box is still there."

I sighed. "Denny, did you call me yesterday?"

"No, Betts. I'm sorry. I should have. I knew you must be really upset after finding Joon, but I was so busy trying to help Stan calm everyone at Tent City that I didn't get to it. It's chaos down there right now. You were on my mind though." Worry lines dominated his forehead and concern tightened the muscles around his eyes.

"I knew you were dealing with the police, and I didn't expect you to call," I reassured him. "It's just that someone did, and they didn't leave their name. I wanted to make sure it wasn't you."

Warren cleared his throat. We waited for him to speak. "Denny, there might be a connection between Joon's murder and a family heirloom book she had." I passed Denny another cinnamon bun, and Warren continued. "We can't for the life of us figure out what it would be, but did she talk about the book to you? Do you know why anyone might want it badly enough to steal it or do violence for it?"

"Do you think Liam was looking for the book in the storage unit?" Denny asked.

"I hadn't thought of that," Warren looked at the ceiling, considering. "But why would he?"

"I don't know." Denny shook his head and studied the table. "Joon talked about the book sometimes. I was the one who recommended she take it to you, Betts. I knew she could trust you with it. She told me mothers passed it to daughters or aunts passed it to nieces from generations back, perhaps as far back as the 15th century, or longer. She knew the cover was from the first original book and that somewhere along the line someone recopied the pages by hand because many of the older dated parts and some of the newer parts were all written in the same script."

"Yes. She told me all of that, too." I nodded for Denny to continue.

"Us unhoused people don't have many physical things to worry about. We don't usually carry around heirlooms or other valuable stuff. This book was an exception, and Joon felt a strong need to protect it. It was a huge responsibility for her. I know she wanted very much to pass it on down to the next generation. She didn't want to be the one out of all those cohorts of women to fail at finding an heir. That book was the main reason we decided to pool some of our social security money to rent a storage unit." Denny looked up from his coffee mug. "Joon wanted a safe place to keep it."

"Is it worth money?" Warren asked.

"I suppose it's worth some money," Denny said, "because it's old. Joon kept saying the recipes and the heirloom seeds were valuable, but I don't think she meant that someone could collect a fortune from them. I suppose if there were recipes that could cure cancer or worse diseases, they would be worth millions, but I don't know if there's anything like that in Joon's almanac."

We repeated to Denny the book might connect the murders, at least from the police's point of view.

"Will they be able to say you were motivated to steal the book?" I asked.

"They'll be able to say whatever they want." Denny shrugged his shoulders in bitter resignation. "If they can arrest me for Liam's murder on rumors of a fight, then they can say I killed Joon for a stupid book." Tears welled in his eyes again and he brushed them aside with a dirty shirt sleeve.

"But I tell you, if I was out for money, if I wanted to be rich, I would be." Denny curled his hands into fists. "I know how to make money. I had several cool millions once, and I learned that when people have gross amounts of money, they usually get it by being ugly. I'm not talking about people who make enough money to live in simple comfort. I'm talking about those guys who have way too much, the ultra-rich. It's rarely done without hurting a lot of people. That's why I stopped playing the game, you know." Denny looked fierce. "It's why I stay unhoused. I'm trying to help people who have nothing. I'm trying to make up for what I did to families so I could have more than my share."

"What do you mean?" I sat back, unsettled. In the past, Denny hinted that he was well educated and that he used to have a high-status job, but he kept the details close to his chest.

"I'm going to tell you my story because I don't want you to think twice about me wanting to steal Joon's book or killing someone for a pile of boodle." Denny's jaw was set, his chapped lips pressed together in a stern line.

My impulse was to tell Denny he was under no obligation to divulge anything, but I kept quiet because I was curious; Warren would call it nosy. I wanted to hear Denny's story. Here was this thin, muscular man with skin so grooved and weathered by living outdoors his face could have been a contour map. I tried to imagine a tie around Denny's neck, setting off the collar of a crisp, blue shirt under a business-quality suit jacket, but I couldn't do it. The contrast to Denny's secondhand work shirts and worn jeans was as incongruous as picturing Lester Stoats in oil-stained mechanics overalls under the chassis of a pocked and faded Plymouth Fury.

"When I was in my early 40s, I was a CEO for a large, energy systems company." Denny started his narrative in slow, deliberate phrases, like a TV news host. "We were good at convincing smaller, less democratic countries to let us do energy projects for them, like building dams. Putting money in the pockets of government officials and politicians for their support was a lot cheaper and quicker than going through international legal procedures set up to protect human rights. We did it in Panama. We got the Panamanian officials to let us start building hydroelectric dams in their mountains. We paid key leaders under the table for their cooperation."

A sardonic half smile deepened the grooves on the left side of Denny's sun-weathered face. He picked up his beige, ceramic coffee cup and jerked it in a rotational pattern until the coffee inside swashed and seethed like a tiny, wind-tossed sea.

"We took the bulk of the profits made by these dams for ourselves. The thing is, there were Indigenous people living up in these mountains who had been there for centuries. They fed themselves with small-scale farming, hunting, and fishing. I was one of the CEO's who ordered them removed. I considered them to be nothing more than problems in the way of progress. We stole their lands for little more than pennies, forced them out of the mountains and into the slums of big cities, where they became indigent."

Denny let out a sad, bitter snort and slumped his shoulders further into himself. "I thought nothing of it in those days, believing that these people were backwards and that we needed to herd them into what I called the 'real' world. No more of this living off the land sort of thing. Time for them to grow up and find their place in industrial modernity. We built the first dam and then the second dam, and we filled our bank accounts at the expense of these people. They literally received nothing for the lands and rivers we destroyed."

Denny pulled a thick square of old, frayed leather layers from his pocket, a wallet. Out of it he removed two creased, partially faded pictures. One showed a beautiful, forested valley. The other showed the same valley, bulldozed, scarred, and barren, filling with water. "Before and after," he said, pushing the photos across the table in our direction.

Regret for the loss of forest and the loss of people's homes filled me as I focused my eyes on the wrinkled and cracked snapshots. I couldn't help but wonder why some people still seemed to think they knew how the rest should live, that subsisting on the land had little value for those who only saw space as profit-making property. Stoats and his beliefs about Tent City came to mind.

"It wasn't until I was visiting the mountains to look over the area for the third dam that I realized what a bastard I'd become." Denny took up his story again. "There was an earthquake, and we couldn't get off the mountain. A rainstorm drenched the whole region, and I had no shelter or food. I was hypothermic. One of those Indigenous families took me in, fed me, helped me get dry and treated me as though I was a brother. For three days I stayed with these good souls. I knew this same family would end up in the slums of Panama City one day because of me and the company I worked for. When I got back home, I found that I couldn't look in the mirror anymore. The closer we got to finalizing the deal with Panamanian officials for the third dam, the more I thought about that family. All this time we were doing less than the law required to compensate these people. We did everything possible to increase our profits, and we got away with it. You can't give people who have made a living from the land for hundreds of years a pittance for what the land is worth to them and expect them to prosper."

Denny inspected me for signs of shock and judgment, and then he looked at Warren. I understood that he both anticipated and dreaded criticism. I'll never know what Denny saw in our faces, but he looked away, his eyes half lidded and bitterness thinning his lips.

"They say I had a nervous breakdown because I sold and gave away everything I had, ended my relationship with my girlfriend, and started traveling around the United States with just a backpack." Denny slid the photos back in his wallet. "If it was a nervous breakdown, then more people at the top of these big corporations need to break down. Many of them steal resources and create situations of great poverty for people whose voices are silenced. Since quitting my job, I've refused to return to that world. I want to mend some of the wrongs that I did. Sometimes I think of myself as Marley's ghost, working to shorten my chain of shame. So, killing someone over a book that may or may not have some valuable seeds or recipes is laughable." Denny ended by removing a third ragged piece of paper from another wallet compartment. "I keep a picture of the mountain family to remind me. They call themselves Ngöbe Indians."

Denny handed us the worn picture of a large group of smiling people gathered at the foot of a simple wooden home built on stilts high above the ground. "I did my best to make sure they had a place to move after the third dam was built, with acreage to grow their crops, but their friends and the other villagers didn't have anyone like me to help them out."

Taking a last gulp of his coffee and grabbing the package of sandwiches and pastries, Denny got up. "I'm off to feed a few people. Thank you for helping me do it." With one swift movement, his coat was around his shoulders, and he was out the door. I took in a lung-full of air and let it out through a long, strained sigh.

"Yeah," said Warren. "I don't think he killed Liam or Joon."

I didn't have time to respond, as the morning rush of customers were outside and knocking on the door to get in. I did, however, agree with Warren. Denny was no killer.

By the time 8:30 a.m. rolled around, Pinky was already in the back picking up his packages of baked goods. I greeted him with his usual bag of donuts and coffee to-go.

"Hey Sweets," he said. "Heard you had a rough morning yesterday. Man, I had no idea the bums were stealing our garbage at night. I think I should unload the truck just on the mornings before the garbage collectors come for the trash."

"First off, Pinky, I wouldn't call it stealing if it's in

the garbage, and second, I wouldn't refer to Joon as a bum." His callousness and lack of tact unnerved me. "If people are hungry, they will probably take our day-old baked goods no matter what time of day you unload them into the garbage."

"Yeah, yeah," he said in the singsong voice of a teenager working hard to irritate a parent.

"Do you usually have a lot of extra?" I asked. "Should I be baking less for the truck run?"

Pinky considered this. "Some days people just don't buy everything. It's hard to predict. But if there's extra that doesn't sell, I mostly take some home for my kids, and if it's church dinner night, I take some to the church. Otherwise, it goes in the trash. Most days it's just maybe a few dozen rolls, half a dozen donuts, and a few loaves of bread. I just don't like the idea of people taking stuff. I work for what I eat. These lazy guttersnipes need to get a job and stop stealing off the backs of us honest, hard-working citizens."

I refrained from aiming a middle finger at his back as he took a load of baked goods outside and returned for more. Someone might see me.

"What was it like?" he asked on his return. "I mean what did the old lady look like out there in the alley?"

"Her name was Joon, not old lady," I told Pinky, "and she looked dead."

"Well, yeah, but did she look like she was in a lot of pain? Was her mouth twisted and foaming? Were her eyes open like in a horror movie? Do they know what kind of poison she ate? Do they know who did it?"

"Joon was my friend." I clenched my hands into fists inside my apron pockets. "So, your questions are highly inappropriate."

"Okay, okay." Pinky put up his hands as if in surrender. "It's just that the kids on my route are asking. But, hey, I can make it up. They don't care. They just want to hear a good story."

Pinky finished loading the bakery truck but then he was back, leaning on the door frame, watching me cut butter into the pastry.

"Heard maybe this friend of yours, Joon, had a valuable book. Is that true?" He took a noisy sip of his coffee.

I looked hard at him. "Rumors abound. She has a recipe book that women pass down through the generations of her family, if that's the one you mean. I gave the copy I had to the police. Why do you ask?"

"Well, yesterday I saw Mrs. Hester, who lives across town." Pinky spoke in that annoying, portentous voice he uses when he has something important to say. "Her husband is a police officer; he came home talking about this book and how it's probably the reason for Joon's murder. Mrs. Hester says she is a third cousin of Joon's. She says she's heard stories about the book from her family since she was a little girl. She thinks the book belongs to her now, cause she's the only relative around. There's a lot of yak yakking out there right now, but Mrs. Hester told me to tell you she'll be around for a visit to talk about it."

"Alright, Pinky. Thanks for the information. Now, I don't want to be the reason for late Dirty Dozen baked good deliveries." I worked to hide my surprise at Pinky's account of Mrs. Hester and her claims.

Maggie arrived in another hour, and I modeled the

apron she gave me, thanking her for making sure the alley was so clean. Maggie nodded. "Betts, I'd hire a guard to be with you every morning, if I could. It's reason enough to consider opening later in the morning when there are more people around."

"I'm going to be fine, Maggie. I haven't heard of anyone in the whole history of Dirty Dozen Bakery finding bodies in the alley before. It's a one-time deal. I love early mornings, and in a few days I'll be okay again." I gave my boss a hug, hung up my apron, and grabbed my backpack.

My bakery hours over and done, Warren and I stepped out to the pickup, missing front window and all. With Joey as my bodyguard, I intended to return home to work while Warren kept an appointment with the window repair shop.

I opened the passenger seat door, and I screamed.

Chapter 7

"It was no coincidence that I learned my calling as soon as my mother's sister brought it to me between a leather cover. It was the family book of seeds and receipts. I began to realize that the power that germinates seeds and opens flowers also caused my own birth, and it is the same power that gives us our life vocations." From The Towne Family Almanac, 1599. Alena Towne, niece of Alis Dinley.

It was just a little scream, but it was my second in so many days.

I quickly forgave myself for losing control. On the seat of the truck was a jar containing three large brown spiders with long reddish legs like bent, synthetic wig hairs. A typed note taped to the jar identified the spiders as brown recluses. *I have more of these*, the note said. *You gave the book to the police. Get it back. Leave the book outside on your front porch in three days or I will let my spiders loose in your house and greenhouse.*

Beads of sweat formed on my forehead, and my pulse raced. I would never be able to sleep again. This was cruel and it was vile. The coals in my belly fired up again, more out of fury than fear. How did this troglodyte even know the book was with the police? Warren was furious too. His hardened jaw jutted forward like a battering ram; his eyes focused intently ahead in a 'warpath' stare. He took an old napkin from the dashboard and used it to lift the jar with its note into an empty grocery bag.

"I'm taking this to the police," he growled. "And Joey needs to hear about it."

"Do you think this fungus-headed potholder already let spiders loose in your truck and in my house?"

Warren knew all too well that I sometimes threw together words when I was angry, but he raised an eyebrow anyway. "If he did, I'll exterminate him," said Warren. "But no. If we found one of them, there wouldn't be much use to give him the book like he wants, because the threat would no longer mean anything."

"What if it's a woman who's doing this?" I told Warren about Mrs. Hester and the conversation I had with Pinky.

"It's always possible, but the person I chased into the woods last night had the build of a man."

I sat in Warren's truck not understanding. What was so special about this recipe book and its seeds that had people bedeviled? Was there something Joon forgot to tell me? Part of me wanted to give it to this creepy lout so I could stop feeling afraid, but the other part remembered Joon's mission and her trust in me.

"We need a bun fight tonight," I said to Warren. We were in the habit of calling our meetings to hash-out-hot-leads bun fights, or BFs for short. I loved the metaphor because we always ended up in heated disputes as we sorted through clues. We were much like buns that rose higher because the air was warm; our ideas expanded in the heat of the moment, augmenting the "yeast of debate."

Like risen dough, cooked in the oven at 375 degrees and then cooled on racks, our brainstorming sessions went through a similar process. We sorted through clues and mixed them with facts, which cooked in our brains and cooled after debate. Often, the result was fresh insight. I hoped our brains would heat up with ideas that evening, but mostly I looked forward to making up after the argument.

"I feel as though I'm being bullied and just letting it happen. It's time I get proactive. I'm going to find this person and bring them down." I stamped my foot to emphasize my frustration and then rubbed my sore knee.

We both chuckled as Warren looked sideways at me. "Not without me, you're not. How about right after dinner we set things up for a bun fight. Do you want Philly there?"

"I want Philly to come, but I'm worried about Roger." I explained about the hat and the scarf.

Warren nodded. "That's something to consider. We can ask Philly about it."

"I think Philly really likes Roger." I rubbed my forehead, which felt knotted from stress. "And for that matter so do I. How will she react if we put Roger on our suspects list?"

"Remember rule one in detection. Everyone is a suspect." Warren turned his head my way and delivered a wink. "We can put all of our names on the list and then Philly won't feel her new friend is being singled out."

Joey was busy with a computer game in the front room when I finally got home. He managed to look up from his X box controller long enough to greet me with an easy smile, which enhanced the charm of his bright-eyed, Hispanic features.

"Hey hi," he said, his young voice friendly. As much time as this young man spent sitting on a couch playing video games, I wondered how he managed to keep himself as fit and healthy as he was.

"I'll be in my office," I told Joey.

I wanted to check Joon's DNA information to see if there was a Mrs. Hester among her relatives. I also had a list of relations that Joon and I had decided to try and contact. Drafting email letters to people on the list would take up most of the afternoon.

I also wanted to see if Philly's DNA data had been uploaded. She was so excited to be looking for her biological parents after all these years. Philly, whose adopted parents were white, knew she was part Black, and wanted to find real-life connections to her birth family.

Starting with research about Joon's relatives, I discovered that a Mrs. Marta Hester did show up on the DNA site as Joon's third cousin. She also showed up on my front porch.

Peering around the door frame to my office, Joey cleared his throat. "Uh. There's someone in your living room who says she's got to talk to you. I let her in; hope that's okay. She says her name is Mrs. Hester."

I pulled myself away from my computer screen and went out to meet my surprise visitor. Mrs. Hester was a short, plump woman, whose rounded cheeks could, and did, shore up substantial amounts of makeup. She'd had her bleached blond hair cut in a flawless bob, and she shellacked it with enough hair spray to decoupage a child's handmade place mat. Everything she wore was some shade of peach. Her expensive-looking fall blouse served as the backdrop for outsized, silk-screened, peach dahlias, and she'd draped it over peach slacks which brushed the tops of kitten-heeled pumps. She shook my hand in a business-like manner and proceeded to explain herself.

"Ms. Harvey," she began, "I am Joon O'Neal's cousin, Marta Hester. Joon and I met a few times over the years, and I was deeply sorry to see her become homeless. To get to the point, I know that Joon had in her possession an incredibly old and precious recipe book. My great aunt talked about it when I was a girl." Marta cocked her head to the side in a coquettish motion, as though to portray herself as an innocent Shirley Temple. "I approached Joon once about getting the book from her to protect it. She was living in a tent after all, and it is difficult to take care of things when you don't have a place to sleep every night."

I wondered when Mrs. Hester would need to take a breath, but she kept on. "Joon said she was looking for the right person to pass it down to. I offered to be that person, but she said she wanted someone closer to her own family line. I let it be. But now she is gone, and I understand you have the book, and you are not related at all. Don't you think it would be best to give it to *me* now? It really doesn't belong to you, as I am sure you would agree." Mrs. Hester finished her speech with a wide pastel, lip-sticked smile, trying, without success, to appear friendly and accommodating. "It might become a burden to you," she added, "finding someone else to give it to. I can help ease your responsibility."

"Mrs. Hester, it's good to meet you," I began. "I'm wondering how you know that I have this family heirloom. Did Joon tell you?"

"Well, no." Mrs. Hester waved her hand with a dismissive flick of her plump fingers. "My husband works as a lieutenant for the police force. He told me last night that Joon's murder might be linked to a strange, old book. He said you brought a copy of said book into the police station as evidence. I asked him about it and came to realize that it is the very book that Joon and I discussed only months ago."

"Maybe you can help me understand something, Marta." I used her first name to minimize the formality. "But first, can I offer you some tea or coffee. Do you want to sit down?"

After settling us with a pot of blackberry tea at the kitchen table, I shared with her my picture of Joon standing next to the amaranth. Mrs. Hester's eyes barely scanned my phone screen before she waved it away.

"Can you tell me, Marta, why so many people are interested in this book of Joon's? Someone threatened me yesterday with an anonymous phone call, and today I received a hostile note demanding that I hand over the almanac to an unidentified person. Now, here's you claiming it. I do understand parts of it are incredibly old and that some of the recipes for medicines are extraordinarily helpful, but I'm starting to think Joon might have been killed over this compendium. Do you know why?"

Marta Hester sat biting her lower lip in deep thought and did not answer right away. At last, she said, "I hope you don't suspect me of murdering Joon."

I wondered where her question had come from. Aspersions of her involvement seemed out-of-the-blue, but I assured her that was the last thing on my mind. It was a lie, but I hoped to keep the conversation friendly. "I just want to know why people have been inundating me with threats and requests concerning this book. What is so special about it?"

Mrs. Hester clasped her hands in front of her. Her face lit up as she began talking about the Towne Family Almanac. "As a girl, I grew up imagining that I would have the book someday. I often made up stories about what I could do with it when it was mine." Marta assumed a wistful half smile and a dreamy-eyed expression. "I've never seen it, or even the copy of it you gave to the police. I heard about it from my great aunts and my grandmother. It has become a kind of family icon, and there are so many stories and legends around it."

I looked at Marta in amazement. "What do you mean legends?"

"Well, for example, I heard there is a recipe in it that cured my great grandfather of tuberculosis. I heard there is a recipe in the book that gives people several hours of brilliant insight. When I was a girl, I dreamed about a recipe called 'You Can Do Anything'. My Great Aunt Sally said that drinking the mixture of herbs - made from plants that grew from the seeds in the book - helped you believe you could do anything. Someone who drank the potion was suddenly one hundred percent sure that they would succeed at what they wanted to do. Because they knew for sure that they would succeed, they always did. My great uncle took the potion and was suddenly sure that he would find gold in his back yard. He started digging, and sure enough, he found a sack of gold nuggets secretly buried there a century ago by an old miner. So, you see, people want the book because of all the wonderful stories.

They want it for the fantastic recipes."

"Do you think these stories are really true?" I refilled our teacups and studied my guest. "Don't you think storytellers might be exaggerating a bit? Might the legends just be family fairy tales?"

Marta shook her head. "It doesn't matter if they're exaggerated or not. We grew up hearing them and loving them. At least some of them must be true." She hugged herself with excitement. "My great aunt believed whoever had the book needed to be interested in herbs and cultivation. I'm a gardener. I have a beautiful greenhouse, and many of my flowers win awards at the fair and the garden club. I would be the perfect caretaker for the book."

"I'm not disputing that," I said. "It's just that Joon had a list of qualities that her grandmother, aunts, and mother passed on through the years. There are specific guidelines about who should have it. Joon told me those standards are as old as the book. According to Joon's instructions, third cousins are just too far removed. She wanted to find a closer relation."

"Well, that's a problem," Marta said. "My great aunt and my mother talked about how much our part of the family resented Joon's part of the family just because of that expectation. Many of us feel we are more qualified to handle the recipes and the plants than some of the women who were given the book. Look at Joon. She did little with the heirloom except keep it and make sure to replenish the seeds every few years. Think of the good she could have done for the family and others had she taken more interest in the recipes and what they could do for people."

"I think she did use some of the recipes to help

people feel better," I said. "I know she made medicines to relieve people in Tent City who suffered from the flu and headaches and such. She was careful, though, to encourage people to see a doctor if things got bad."

Marta sniffed and frowned. "If she really used the book for her own good, I don't believe she would have been homeless. If the stories are right, there are recipes to help her get what she needed to live in comfort."

"As to that, I do not know." I sat up straight, weary of Marta's accusations. "But I understand a little bit more about why the book might be important to so many people. You have been extremely helpful. I appreciate it."

"So," said the lady in peach, tapping her apricot-polished fingernails on the table in accelerating rhythm, "are you willing to hand the book and the seeds over to me, or do I need to find a lawyer to make it happen in court?"

Marta's sudden and unexpected threat startled me. I worked to calm myself before answering. "I think, Marta, that to ease your own mind, you might want to find a lawyer. I warn you, though, that Joon and I also visited a lawyer, and we drew up a contract giving me certain rights of decision making should something happen to her. I believe it will be difficult for you to challenge the contract, even in court."

Marta Hester's face reddened under her pastel makeup. "What did you do, drug Joon - threaten her? What kind of power did you have over her that she would create such a contract? You're not even family, and if I must prove that you coerced Joon to sign the agreement, believe me, I will." With that, Marta grabbed her shiny, mother-of-pearl purse, and stomped to the front door.

"You will be hearing from a lawyer soon," she called out as she left.

Joey, who moved his computer gaming operation to my office while Mrs. Hester and I talked, reappeared in the kitchen. "That was craptacular. That lady reminds me of a crocodile, if you don't mind me saying." He offered me a crooked grin. "I won't be letting her in the house again."

"*Craptacular*. I like it." I grinned back at my amateur bodyguard. "It fits."

Joey went outside to make sure no one was prowling around and then moved his computer back into the living room. I returned to my office and my genealogy work. Marta Hester would be another name on my suspects list, even though she seemed to prefer getting her way by using threats and lawyers rather than violence. Still, she might have poisoned Joon. She knew about plants and might even know about the powerful, poisonous characteristics of water hemlock. She probably didn't expect resistance to her claim for the book after Joon was gone. Still, her relationship with Joon didn't explain a connection with Liam and his murder, and I believed the murders were linked.

My experience with Mrs. Hester motivated me to draft emails and letters to a large list of Joon's relatives. I hoped Joon's third cousins could give me information about closer relatives, ones who might qualify to receive the recipe heirloom book. I crossed Mrs. Hester off my contact list. After today, I wanted as little connection with her as possible.

I also wondered what Marta Hester knew about spiders. I had a tough time picturing the plump, peach-bedecked woman as a spider terrorist, but what did I know?

Once finished with my email letter writing, I decided to glance through Warren's DNA data. Sometimes I wondered if it was Warren's loss of his son and wife so early in life, and the fact that he never remarried, that made him in such a hurry to marry now. Our disagreement about marriage was the one issue we couldn't seem to get past. The first time I said no to his marriage proposal I thought our relationship was over. He left town and for at least a fortnight refused to answer phone calls or emails. My heart ached for him and for me. When he returned, I welcomed him back with open arms, but I rejected his engagement ring. We might be a couple right up to the end of our lives; I just wasn't willing to be a married couple, at least not yet. I loved my independence and my ability to simply have days when I was alone to do exactly as I pleased.

"I'm just an old badger," I'd tell Warren.

I peered at Warren's DNA connections and finding nothing new on Warren's account, I decided to take a break.

"Want a piece of ice cream cake?" I called out to Joey. Happy to share a mid-afternoon snack, we took our treats to the picnic table out back. Joey told me he was a community college student, currently taking on-line classes and majoring in computer programming and business.

"Thanks for the job," he said. "I can always use some extra cash."

I laughed. "Warren's your boss. He hired you. But I hope you don't get too bored here. Hanging out with someone who's old enough to be your grandmother can't be your first choice."

"There's a lot more snap here than at my parents' house." He eyed me over a large fork, piled high with stiff chocolate pudding and whipped cream. "Broken windshields, people dressed in black stealing phone books off the porch, burglaries, strange sounds coming from under the house, and old lady rumbles. You got a way about you Ms. Harvey."

"Usually it's nice and quiet here," I said, "and that's the way I like it. But what do you mean strange sounds coming from under the house?"

"Oh. Didn't I tell you? This morning, about 2:15, there were scratching sounds under the floor, close to the front door. I thumped on the floorboards and the sounds stopped, but then they were back." Joey squared his shoulders. "I put a flashlight up to the screens on the foundation of your house but didn't see anything. Plus, I went all around the house and didn't find any way a dude could get in there. Decided it was just a twitchy mouse or a rat."

I'd lived in the house for a few years and never heard night sounds coming from the crawl spaces, but my bedroom was upstairs. "Probably it's a rodent of some kind. I'll have to set a live trap and see what comes out. Thanks for letting me know."

It was time to get back to my genealogy work. I wanted to check and see if Philly's DNA records had surfaced, and then I had ground cherry jam and pie filling to make.

When clients send in their saliva as a DNA sample, the company usually takes a month before results come back.

Philly sent hers in about five weeks ago.

"I love my mom and dad," she said about her adoptive parents. "I never want to replace them with anyone else. But I'm just curious." Philly was optimistic even though I warned her that genetic data or not, unless her biological parents had their own DNA analyzed, and included their contact information on the genealogy website, Philly was just beginning her search.

I filed records to keep track of what I'd done for Joon's genealogy project and settled down to look at Philly's case. We set up her account together, and Philly gave me access to her password so I could help her analyze what surfaced. Optimistic, I accessed her files for the fifteenth time in a week. Paydirt. Her information was downloaded, finally. Clicking on the link to her DNA relatives' folder, I waited, breath held, hoping that connections to a parent popped up.

Information for genetic relatives filled the screen, but there was no match with a parent. The closest match was with someone who shared twenty five percent of their DNA with Philly. The site listed this relative as an aunt. When I saw the aunt's identification, JO1, I simply sat there dumbfounded. If Philly were looking at her new data, she would see the aunt identified too, but she would not understand the enormity of the discovery or the coincidental significance of the connection.

"Deputy Delilah, I think we've turned up something epic. It's JO1. Don't you get it?" Not even a flicker. Delilah didn't seem to understand the magnitude of what was on her screen. But I did. I knew JO1 well. I clicked on the link from Philly's site to JO1 to double check. I didn't see how, but maybe there was more than one JO1.

Feeling lightheaded, I skimmed over the introduction JO1 and I wrote together, the one asking for information leading to first or second cousins, nieces, and nephews. I sat frozen for a good ten minutes, looking out the window toward my grape vines, not really seeing them.

This was the moment JO1, otherwise known as Joon O'Neal, had waited for - the discovery of a close relative. She would have been over the moon to know Philly was her niece. With the backs of my hands, I wiped wetness off my cheeks and realized I was crying. Were my tears due to gladness for Philly or grief for Joon? Maybe both.

Swiping another swell of tears from my eyes, I pulled out paper files of interview transcripts I'd done with Joon about her family. There was also a sealed manila envelope containing a short autobiography Joon wrote herself. "Keep this one private unless something happens to me," she'd said, and I'd honored her wishes.

Joon had only one sister and no brothers, so Joon's deceased sister had to be Philly's mother. Joon might never have agreed with me, but in my mind, Joon's sister was the cause of Joon's homelessness.

I could picture Joon sitting across the kitchen table telling me some of her story. She had a lengthy career as a pharmacist, and her husband was a house builder. They had no children, but Joon once tried to adopt her sister's little son. I checked my notes to verify Joon's sister's name: April.

According to Joon, April got pregnant out of wedlock when she was sixteen. Their father's response was to expel her from the house and disown her. April, with an inadequate level of education and little chance of procuring a job, began a life of survival on the streets.

Star bursts of wrinkles at the edge of Joon's eyes deepened as she described pleading with her father to allow April and the little boy back home. "He was a hard, man," Joon said. He claimed a strong affinity with strict, Christian rules and forbade Joon from seeing April. Joon made a habit of disobeying her father, bringing her sister whatever help she could, trying to get her re-enrolled in high school. April was soon an addict as well as unhoused. More than once, social services took her son from her, and more than once, Joon and her new husband took the boy in as foster parents.

"We begged April to let us take permanent custody of the boy, but April refused," Joon told me one spring morning. "We would have let her see him anytime she wanted. But when we asked to adopt her little boy, April left. She just disappeared with her son. Completely gone. I didn't see her again for many years." Joon always believed April left to keep Aunt Joon and Uncle Giles from taking her child. I looked through my notes for the name of April's son and was astonished to find Joon left that information blank. I did not know his name.

In all my records, I could find no reference to a girl being born to April. Joon had said nothing about a second baby. It was likely that April never told Joon about a lost, infant daughter. I could only surmise that Philly was born and put up for adoption sometime after April disappeared.

"April came back into my life just as I was retiring," Joon revealed. "My husband, Giles, died of a sudden heart attack only a few years before. And when April came back to me, she was dying of cancer. She could barely take care of herself in the bathroom let alone get in and out of bed."

As Joon told it, April had no health insurance, and

what the state provided in indigent care was inadequate, so Joon tried to cover doctor bills herself to get April the best help she could.

"My sister was as tough and as bitter as a thorn-guarded quince," Joon told me as we set up her DNA search. "All those years and she still hadn't made peace with anyone, herself most of all."

By law, Joon was not legally responsible for her sister's healthcare. Still, she signed the essential papers and spent every hour she could with April, keeping her at home when possible. In the end, after April died, the hospital, ambulance, and doctor bills led to a sell-off of Joon's home to make payments.

When all was said and done, Joon owned nothing but her social security and a small pension, not enough to live comfortably from month to month. She might have qualified for low-income housing and other assistance programs. I didn't know. I believed it was Joon's stubbornness and a broken heart that led her to living out the rest of her life in a tent.

As I sat back, going over Joon's story in my mind, I wondered about April's son. Had he survived? If so, Philly had a half-brother she might be able to locate.

Little did I know that the wisest course was to let sleeping brothers lie.

Chapter 8

"Learning about the power of plants has been all about false starts and new beginnings. But then, that describes life in general, doesn't it?" From The Towne Family Almanac, 1920, Fannie Lee, daughter of Hannah Hyndman.

Like that ancient and archetypal messenger, the one with bad tidings, I had to tell Philly about her aunt as soon as possible. If I'd had my way, I'd help her celebrate news of her biological family and leave the shocking news till later. But as Father Flynn from the movie *Doubt* said, "There is a wind behind us that we cannot command."

I called Philly as soon as I recovered enough from my bittersweet discoveries to locate my phone. "Philly? Yes, it's me, Betts. Have you been looking at your DNA account? No? Well, you might want to. I've got something to tell you about the results, but I want to do it in person. Yes, I'll be there soon. Get yourself a pint and be prepared for a bit of shocking news."

We agreed to meet at Shifty's Shanghai Tavern for something topped with foam. Before our meeting, I photocopied the notes I took during Joon's interviews so I could pass them on to Philly. As I placed the stack of papers on the passenger seat of my car, I pondered their significance. They were Joon's last words, so to speak, and I was passing them on to someone who would appreciate their value.

The tavern's dim light reflected softly on golden brown, paneled walls and sturdy, thick oak tables, each surrounded by rock-hard chairs and benches. Philly waited in a corner booth, looking at her iPhone, boots rapping out a quick, two-footed percussion roll on the rough-hewn, wood floor. Locks of curly black hair brushed her high cheek bones and delicate nose.

"I'm looking at my DNA results," she called out when she saw me. "Look at all these cousins. Over eight hundred fourth cousins and eleven third cousins and an aunt. No mother or father, though."

I gave Philly a quick hug before sitting down myself. "Those numbers will change as more and more people get their DNA tested," I said. "It's possible that one day your dad will show up or a brother. Your mother won't, though. That's some of the sad news. She died in about 2006."

"Betts, how do you know that?" Philly scanned her phone. "I can't see anywhere on here where it says stuff like that."

"Brace yourself, Philly." I wanted to measure out my news. "I'll tell you all about it after I get my apple cider." A cheerful server plopped my foamy, golden half pint on the table only seconds later, and Philly looked at me with a raised left eyebrow and an expectant, "So?"

Sighing, I sipped the fragrant, ice-cold, apple bubbly. "Like I said, Philly. Brace yourself. I know when your mom died because I knew your aunt - the aunt that comes up here on your DNA match." I put Joon's typed and copied interviews on the table and the sealed manila envelope with the autobiography that Joon wrote, and I pushed them over to Philly. "These are copies of interviews I did with your aunt, and in the sealed envelope is a description of her life that she wrote. I've never opened it. She asked me not to unless she was gone. I think you should be the one to open that envelope now we know this woman is your aunt."

Philly's enthusiasm seemed to scatter in her confusion. Her smile faltered and she looked at me sideways. "Are you sure this person you interviewed is my aunt? Can I meet her? Does she live close by?"

"Philly, I'm sure she was your aunt because I recognize her DNA-codename on your genealogy results. From your account, I clicked on your aunt's identification number and looked up her biographical information. I recognize it because your aunt and I wrote it together. Plus, you've shown up on her DNA account as her niece. I'm one hundred percent sure the woman who wrote the autobiography inside this envelope was your aunt."

"What do you mean *was* my aunt?" Philly looked down at the notes I gave her and the heading, *Interviews with Joon O'Neal*. Philly's head shot up and her eyes widened. "Do you mean that *she* was my aunt?" I nodded. "You're telling me that Joon O'Neal was my aunt?" she asked again. My answer was a thin-lipped, sympathetic smile.

"Oh God," said Philly, her eyes brimming with tears. "Why didn't she tell me? I feel like I have to start grieving for her all over again."

"Philly, I don't think she knew you were her niece. I don't think she knew she had a niece." I told Philly what I learned about Joon's sister April. When I finished the story, I motioned toward the interview notes. "It's all there, everything I know. If Joon had realized you were her niece, I believe she would have been overjoyed."

"But what if she was afraid to let me know because she was embarrassed about how she lived?" Philly wiped her wet cheeks with a sleeve, her eyes imploring me to answer.

"That's not how Joon worked," I reassured her. "She wouldn't have asked for sympathy or handouts, but she would have wanted to acknowledge you as her niece. There's just no record or mention that Joon even knew her sister had a daughter."

Philly cried some more and then dried her eyes. I reached over to hand her more Kleenex and watched the expression on her face change from sad to fierce in the blink of an eye.

She said, in a hard voice, "If some selfish monster hadn't murdered Joon, she would know today that I am her niece. Someone took her away from me, and I want to find out who. Betts, I want to help you and Warren find Joon's murderer."

I slid out of the booth on my side of the table and onto her bench so I could hug her. "I'd be grateful for your help," I told her. "Tonight, Warren and I want to invite you to one of our famous 'bun fight' meetings. Bring your brains and your quick wit to Warren's at 7 o'clock. We could use them both."

"Bun fight meetings?" Philly used more Kleenex to wipe smeared eyeliner from around her moist eyes.

"*Bun fight* is slang from the old British Commonwealth meaning petty argument. It's just something Warren and I started calling our nosy neighbor investigation talks." I shared a wry smile with my determined friend. "Our debates became 'bun fights' because if we argue over clues, and take our disagreements too seriously, our feelings get hurt. It takes time and energy to set things straight between us. You know how Warren sulks sometimes when he thinks I'm rejecting him. By calling our arguments 'bun fights,' it's easier to laugh about ourselves and keep arguing at the same time."

"Bun fights," Philly mused. "Sure. I'd love to join you in a 'bun fight.'"

"It's settled then. Bring those dazzling powers of critical thinking with you."

"Thanks for these." Philly picked up the papers and hugged them to her chest. "They are already very precious to me."

"I hope they help you find your brother," I said, "and maybe even your father."

"I have a brother?" Philly looked across at me, her mouth a surprised, rounded 'O'. "I wonder why my father didn't help my mother when she got pregnant with me." Her eyes narrowed. "Why did my mother have to put me up for adoption?" Philly's emotions revved up to third gear and for good reason.

"As to that, I couldn't say. Even Joon didn't know about you. There could be so many reasons or circumstances we don't understand."

It was 5 p.m., time to go and finish dinner for Warren, Joey, and me. The roast was in the slow cooker, but I stopped at the grocery store to get fresh items for salad, and only enough for dinner so there would be nothing left over. Earlier, I emptied the refrigerator and cupboards of anything that I'd already opened and hadn't sealed in its original packaging, just in case the phone caller made it into the house and got liberal with water hemlock root, seeds, juice, or any part of that beautiful but deadly plant. I made sure to buy nothing to do with carrots so that we would be wary of carroty smells or flavors in our food. The phone call threat actuated a hard hit to my pocketbook.

My homemade mixes of cooking herbs and herbal medicines seemed irreplaceable to me, so I arranged them snuggly in my safe, hidden behind the steps of the stairway leading up to my bedroom.

We would eat dinner and then leave Joey to guard my house. As soon as the three of us, Warren, Philly, and I, gathered at Warren's, our bun fight could commence.

Joey finished off the last of the roast beef and potatoes before I served the chocolate cream pie.

"You sure you don't need someone permanent here?" He licked chocolate from his upper lip.

"If anyone is ever permanent here, it's going to be me." Warren pointed a butter knife at Joey to emphasize his firm proclamation.

I laughed. "You stay with me long enough and you just might run screaming into the night. I'm not always easy to live with."

"Who is?" Joey shrugged. "But dessert helps."

We were quick and efficient cleaning up, and I teased Joey about finishing the pie as soon as possible before someone got a chance to poison it. He assured me he could empty the pie dish in fifteen minutes.

I came to our bun fight armed with notebooks, colored pencils, and several pictures I printed featuring my dry-erase wall and its mapped-out genealogy of Joon's local relationships. I wanted everything possible at hand that might help us figure out why two Tent City residents lost their lives and how to connect the killings. Did the murders have anything to do with my potted plants burglary, the broken windshield, and the spider and phone call threats?

Yes, it's true. I could have been more patient and relied on the police investigation, but no matter how far along the police were, I wanted things to move faster. It was the threat of a spider infestation that motivated me more than the fear of poison. Besides, Detective Crumley seemed obsessed with Denny as his murderer, and I wasn't buying that conclusion.

Philly already parked her car to the side of Warren's long driveway when we arrived, each of us bringing our own vehicles. As we approached the big red front door, set back within the brown and green painted wrap-around porch, Philly got out of her car. To our surprise, so did Roger. Warren and I exchanged questioning looks. We wanted to be free to express whatever came to mind, and we didn't know Roger well enough to trust him. Plus, he was on my suspects list. If he joined us, I might have to confront him.

"Look, I hope it's alright that Roger came," Philly said to both of us when Roger went back to get his favorite coffee cup out of the car. "I really like him and he's so easy to talk with. I told him about Joon, and he immediately volunteered to help us out with our private investigation. He said he had experience with criminal research when he was in the Army."

"We trust you, Philly, but we don't know him."

Warren's tone was less than enthusiastic. "All we can do is see what happens."

"I'm willing to include him, at least this time," I said, "as long as you don't mind me asking him a few touchy questions. You should know he's on my suspects list."

Philly huffed in surprise and narrowed her eyes. "Knowing you, the whole town is on your list." I stuck out my tongue at her and chuckled.

Warren's house was bigger than mine, with a large wooden patio off the dining room and a fireplace made of river boulders in the living room. In contrast to the soft, cream wool carpet in my home, Warren's floors were either hardwood or indoor/outdoor gray and gold carpet. My furniture tended to be antique hardwoods, overstuffed couches, and cut-glass decor, like the windows in my China cabinet centerpiece. He preferred leather easy chairs, more leather easy chairs, and sharp-steel standing lamps. A row of prominent shelves, close to where the walls met the vaulted ceiling, displayed his antique telephone insulator and geode collections.

Roger, Philly, Warren, and I pulled up chairs around Warren's pride-and-joy replica of a large, 17th century drawing table. We turned on every light as we could find so we could stay alert and better see the notes and pictures which made up our scanty evidence pile.

Once each of us had a steaming mug of hot cider at hand, I suggested we create a suspect's list and review the nitty gritty details about each of the accused.

"And the first person I want to discuss is you, Roger." I straightened my back and scrutinized Roger's face to read his reaction.

Focused on the pictures of the storage unit fire, Roger looked up with a quick upward jerk of his square-jawed chin. "Me? What about me?"

"It's your hat," I explained, passing him a selection of photos showing Liam's murder scene. I pointed out the scarf that matched Roger's hat laying across one of the scorched boxes. "Your hat matches this scarf, and since they are both handmade from an old sweater, these have to be one of a kind."

We passed the pictures around the table, along with a magnifying glass so everyone could see the evidence.

"You haven't been in town long. We don't know much about you or your history." I raised my eyebrows and pressed my lips into a straight, stern line. "You could be posing as someone you're not, and you got into town not long before all of this started happening. Put all those things together with the scarf at the scene, and it looks a little suspicious."

Philly grabbed more photos from the table and started going through them. She found another snapshot with the scarf and picked up the magnifying glass. Roger leaned over her shoulder to look too.

"Fair enough," he said. "That does look a lot like my missing scarf."

"How did it get there?" Philly resembled a trusting puppy as she studied his face. She really did seem smitten with this guy, and based on the way he looked at her, the affection was mutual.

"I have a storage unit two rows back from the one that caught on fire. A week ago, I moved most of my belongings into it, just until I can find a permanent place to stay. I am ninety nine percent sure that I wore the scarf and my hat on moving day because it was cool and rainy, and I just bought them the day before. I'm sure I took off the scarf, and I must have left it outside my unit."

"There you go," Philly said. "Someone else could have picked up the scarf, especially if Roger forgot about it and it was there overnight."

We all stayed quiet for a good, long minute. Warren and I looked hard at Roger, Warren flicking the photo that displayed the scarf as though it was a playing card.

"That's plausible," Warren finally said. "There is no way to prove it one way or another, not right now anyway. In your favor, you don't fit the typical arsonist profile."

"Let's see," Roger said. "I'm not young, I don't have a criminal record as far as you know, and I'm not white."

"And Philly wouldn't be with you if you had below average intelligence or had more than the normal trouble with relationships." Warren chuckled. "How do you know so much about arsonist profiles?"

"I had experience assisting a criminal investigator when I was in the Army. We get all types there. Stuff happens." Roger tossed the pictures on the table, and they slid in my direction. "But I will say that if the fire in these pictures was set to cover another crime, we're not looking for someone who fits the typical fire-setter profile."

"Uh huh. Someone who uses fire to destroy a crime scene is not necessarily a dude with a sorrowful set of psychological problems. He's more likely to be a criminal psychopath." Warren inspected Roger with calculated scrutiny.

"As for who I am and why I'm here, I can give you my information and you can run a background check." Roger let loose a weary sigh. He looked past our faces as though summoning memories of something or someone we couldn't see. "I've also got references. I can give you their phone numbers and addresses." Roger's countenance was serious, even earnest.

"Look son," Warren said to Roger, "I'm ready to give you the benefit of the doubt. You seem like an honest man to me, and I think we could use your help with this. What do you say, Betts. Should we put him on our fellow investigators roster?"

"For the time being." I crossed Roger off the suspect's list with reluctance. "If a new clue pops up, you're back on the list. Leave your references' contact information with me before you leave."

"I'm honored." Roger offered me a comical bow.

We sat facing each other, like dogs who finished circling and sniffing each other and were now ready to join forces and hunt down the track of some wild animal. Philly and I readied ourselves for writing - pens in hand - the blank pages of notebooks in front of us.

"Suspect number one," said Philly, "Lester Stoats."

"Suspect number two," I said, "Marta Hester."

"Suspect number three," Warren said, "Denny Woodman."

"Suspect number four," Roger said, "that homeless guy Stan, who's been helping Joon and Denny for so many years."

We all laughed in unison and then sobered.

"You're right." I felt a need to sum up our hilarity. "None of these people seem like the real deal. But let's list the pros and cons for each one anyway. It's a way to start. Let's begin with Marta Hester. By the way, Mrs. Hester is Joon's third cousin. That makes her related to you too, Philly."

"I don't know much about her." Philly stuck the eraser end of a pencil in her mouth. "Except she did come to city hall a few years ago to file a formal complaint against a neighbor because his barbecue smoke kept drifting onto her property and into her screened-off back porch."

"Pinky told me she's publicly claiming Joon's recipe book should be hers." I snorted to express my skepticism. "Pinky got the idea from her that I've as good as stolen it, and she came by my house today to collect the book. She's threatened to hire a lawyer and take me to court."

"If the same person who killed Liam also killed Joon, we're looking at an arsonist and poisoner," Warren interjected. "Does Mrs. Hester seem like a murderer, or is she simply a pain in the ass who uses lawyers and bureaucrats to get what she wants?"

"She's a nightmare in girly makeup," Philly said, wrinkling her nose.

"We worked on a case where a general's son was poisoning his parents." Roger sat up straight, his tone professional. "We got training on the psychological profiles of poisoners. I don't know enough about this Mrs. Hester to make any kind of a judgment. Consider this, though. Poisoners often have a strong need for control. The crazy thing is that they can pretend that they're doting and caring. A lot of them are in the medical professions, and they act as though they are tender, self-sacrificing attendants to their victims. When General Stebbins and his wife started getting sick, their son came off as the one most concerned about their wellbeing. He tended to them day and night. All the time he was adding poison to their 'curative' apple juice every morning."

"Clever, sneaky, emotionally immature, methodical, and self-centered. These are typical traits of poisoners," Warren added, reading off a sheet of paper in front of him. "I've been doing a little research too. I think the scariest thing about poisoners is that they always premeditate their murders. To poison someone, you've got to plan ahead."

"And they like to stay and watch the poison do its work, if they can," Roger said.

Roger's description horrified me. "Do you think there was someone in the alley watching Joon die that night?" I looked down at my list of facts and hunches about some of our suspects. I'd run out of notepaper and used some old stationery to jot down notes. It seemed appropriate the likeness of faded purple pansies framed Mrs. Hester's information.

"It's hard for me to picture Marta Hester as a doting, tender caretaker," I mused. "Then again, I can imagine her acting sickly sweet when she wants something. I just don't know her well enough to be sure."

"Based on your descriptions, if she's the one who threw a rock through your windshield, I'm surprised she didn't paint it pink." Philly smirked. "Plus, Marta would need a good strong arm and impeccable aim to make a direct hit."

"It was a man I chased into the woods," Warren said, "but she could have an accomplice."

"Her husband's a police officer. He might have taught her how to get into a locked storage unit, like the one Liam died in." Philly's speech quickened with enthusiasm as she laid out possibilities. "Maybe Mrs. Hester thought Joon stored The Towne Family Almanac there and she went to filch it. What if she found Liam sleeping in the unit and decided to get rid of him so he wouldn't tell on her?"

"What about the spiders?" I sketched a tiny spider in the margins of my notes as I talked. "Is Mrs. Hester likely to have brown recluses on hand? They don't survive well in our climate. Someone must be breeding them in a controlled environment. She mentioned she's got a greenhouse. I guess that might work as a spider incubator."

"It's just hard for me to picture those pudgy little hands with their peach-painted fingernails getting anywhere close to spiders," Philly said. "But I can conjure up an image of her brewing a pot of poison."

"What about Lester Stoats?" Warren cut in, "I can't imagine the man brewing much of anything, including his own coffee. I also can't see him caring for a dog or a cat, let alone taking care of spiders."

I stared at Lester Stoats' entry on my suspects list, pressing down my pencil to darken each letter of his name as I tried to picture Stoats setting fire to the storage unit.

"Still, he's not the type to settle issues upfront with a physical fight. He'd do it like a poisoner, secret and subtle," Roger put in. "He'd do it without getting his hands or his shirt dirty."

I laughed in agreement. "But really, with water hemlock, there doesn't have to be much brewing. You just need some fresh seeds or grated root, and you've got a lethal substance. You would want to wear rubber gloves when you gather the stuff and when you use it, so there's no dirtying your hands. You might get mud on your shoes, though. Water hemlock is partial to wet areas."

"I don't have trouble believing Stoats could murder someone. He's scum." Philly emphasized her words with what I called her fierce mountain lion rumble.

"He's the milk scum that collects on top of an otherwise good cup of hot chocolate," I said. "He has no sympathy for every day, hard-working people, let alone people living in tents. I honestly think humans repulse him if they aren't rich and powerful."

"From what I've heard, he's overly ambitious. A reliable source told me he's planning to be a senator someday." Roger looked sideways at Philly. She answered him with a conspiratorial smile, and he continued. "Stoats must prove himself by demonstrating he can turn this town around and make it into a tourist showcase, a destination to bring in the big money. I just don't know how killing two unhoused people factors into his plan."

"Contrarian," Philly said to Roger, pretending to lean away from him.

"Okay. Okay." Roger waved his open hands in front of his chest in supplication. "What if… What if he was so intent on getting rid of Tent City that he killed Liam to frame Denny and the others at the camp? That way he'd make the campers look more like derelicts so he could get his way. He killed Joon because she knew or saw something, or he poisoned her to make Tent City look doubly dysfunctional."

"But who stole my plants?" I wailed. "And would milk-scum Stoats want Joon's recipe book?"

"I suppose Denny Woodman knows the value of Joon's book," Warren said. "If he killed Liam, it wouldn't have been about the book, though, because he knew that

Betts had the almanac. The recipe book might not link the murders. Crumley thinks Denny killed Liam out of rage and Joon to cover his tracks, but I don't see it."

"I don't believe Denny had anything to do with it" My voice came out tight and angry. "If he was the one demanding the book and breaking into my greenhouse, where would he keep stolen plants? I talk with Denny every morning when I'm in the bakery. I know him. I've never heard a vindictive word from him about the other campers, and I know they look up to him. Plus, Joon trusted Denny. He doesn't strike me as someone who lulls his victims into adoring him while he prepares their poison."

"I may be a contrarian, too, but knowing someone well is not enough to exonerate him, I'm sorry to say." Warren blew out a long breath. "Just the same, especially after listening to Denny's story, I'm inclined to agree with you, Betts."

"Well, blast it, what about this Stan Smith who lives at the camp?" Roger moved forward to park his forearms on the table, curling his hands around his cup. "Why are police settling on Denny when the-Stan-man had every opportunity and maybe the same motives?"

"Could Stan have been the one who called you and demanded the book, Betts?" Philly asked. "Could he have taken the plants? What do we know about him? He had one of the keys to the storage unit."

"I don't know Stan as well as I know Denny," I admitted, "but for him to threaten us with spiders, throw rocks at Warren's windshield and kill his friends? Doesn't feel right."

"Besides. Just like with Denny, where would Stan

keep your stolen plants?" Roger stuck out his jaw and rubbed his chin stubble.

We all sighed, one after the other. I remembered a quote in Cameron Conaway's poetry book *Bonemeal*. "Somewhere in the shape sighs take."

"I don't really think any one of these people did it." Philly bit her lower lip in discouragement.

"Well, we certainly don't have any evidence that confirms the guilt of any one of these people," Warren agreed. "Can you think of anyone else who belongs on our list?"

We were all silent, wracking our brains.

"I think we need more information." Roger's tone was careful and studious. "We might want to do some interviewing, you know, or ask people questions about our suspects. Philly told me everything she can about what's been going on, but I don't know much about these four people, not the way you all do."

I leaned back and let my pencil clatter to the floor. "We're going to need to table our bun fight and put on our sleuthing hats."

"I was hoping for a few more bun bombs," Roger said. "This was fun, but not enough bun-bardments."

"Very funny." Philly poked Roger in the arm.

"I think we need more yeast in the ammo." Warren grinned back at him.

Philly brightened. "Yes. More information. We need to spend time with each one of these people. Something is bound to slip out if we talk with them long enough. Let's each focus on a suspect tomorrow and then report back for another bun fight, same time, same place."

"That's really all we can do," said Warren.

Philly agreed to spend extra time talking with and observing Lester Stoats. I said I would visit Mrs. Hester.

"Do I have your permission to tell her about your relationship with Joon?" I offered Philly an uncertain, crooked smile. "It might be a good excuse for showing up to visit."

"Oh, yes. Go ahead." Philly nodded her permission. "I'm not sure how she'll take the news. I'm not sure how I feel about being related to her either."

Warren agreed to spend time with Denny the next day, and Roger said he would get to know Stan at Tent City by volunteering to help with a project.

Our meeting lasted less than an hour, but it was a start. We were optimistic that in 23 hours, we would have something more substantial to share.

"Be careful," I warned everyone. "The murderer deals in poison, so don't eat anything unless it's well packaged."

"Yeah," said Roger. "Leave everyone else's buns alone."

Philly giggled, and I laughed, but I also let them know I was serious.

That night I stayed cozy and warm in Warren's four poster. I would drive my own car to the bakery in the morning.

As always, I got up at 3:30 a.m., showered, dressed, and tucked my hair into a royal blue knitted cap. I pulled on my black leggings, a denim skirt, and a big button-down shirt with a blue-green flower print. While tugging on my black leather, side-zip boots, I stiffened my resolve to treat this like any other ordinary day.

My faded green Audi sat locked all night, but I

double checked through the windows to make sure there were no jars invading my front seat - especially jars containing *Arachnida* specimens with eight legs. I suspected that the marauder would leave me alone that day and the next, but if there was no package on the front porch by the third night, I could expect more surprises the next day. *Honestly,* I thought to myself, *someone is bullying me, a ... a ... fungal-blighted, burned-bottomed pot licker no less.*

Once inside the bakery, I turned on the radio, partly to hear the early news programs and partly to block out those structural noises that old buildings make, the ones that don't mean anything but that tend to be worrying if you're listening too hard for them.

Today there was an extra order for twenty buttery pound cakes. I loved the idea of pound cake, one pound of butter, a pound of sugar, a pound of flour and a pound of milk, and of course I loved the sweet, buttery results topped with strawberries and whipped cream. My morning routine moved along without a hitch, and I felt my confidence return. Mornings at the bakery had always been a Zen time for me, and I wanted them to stay that way.

I let Warren in a few minutes before Denny entered, and by the time I had the bag of goodies ready for Tent City, Warren was set to help Denny sort the burnt boxes and establish order to the damaged storage unit. Finished with their investigation, the police gave Denny permission to clean the unit while a fire department volunteer like Warren was present.

"They tell me my re-arrest is coming soon," Denny said. I gave him a quick hug to show my support.

Thinking about how to approach Mrs. Hester later, I worked the rest of my shift. Dropping by Mrs. Hester's house seemed the best approach. If I called ahead, Marta might simply say she was too busy or that she would be elsewhere. While I worked, I sprinkled questions here and there among the customers and listened in on conversations to see if there were new insights or bits of information about the murders. When Pinky arrived, I asked him if he had heard any rumors.

"I've heard everything from the killings were drug deals gone wrong, to the whole thing being about a love triangle." Pinky snorted with laughter at the idea of homeless people being in love.

"What do you think happened?" I wanted to extract anything I could from this man who spent hours talking with customers.

"Is this the fifth degree?" he asked with sudden defensiveness. "Why would I have any idea what happened?"

"You're around a lot of people every day." Pinky was prone to switch between hot and cold in a matter of seconds. Cool or fiery, the best approach was to infuse my tone with soothing notes. "I just thought you might have heard something."

"Well, I'm tired of talking about it, Sweets. I already spent too much time and energy rehashing the lives of two people who dragged down society. I can tell you, I'm tired of serving these people soup every Thursday at church. I got better things to do with my time." He stomped out with the last of the bakery delivery orders balanced on his shoulder.

I stood looking at the back door, deep in thought.

What did Pinky have against our unhoused neighbors? He could get surly about things, but I usually understood the reasons. This time I supposed it was just a kind of prejudice, and I knew he wasn't the only one who seethed with this level of judgment against Tent City residents.

As Maggie took over the customer counter and the baking, I folded my DNA-strand apron and waved goodbye. It was time to visit Marta Hester before lunch. I made sure my clothing was free of flour dust or stray dollops of batter, then I re-packaged my hair into my roomy cap, took a deep calming breath, and drove to Mrs. Hester's north town address.

Marta was in her greenhouse when I rang her front porch doorbell, but she had a doorbell extension installed there. Just as I was leaving the porch, thinking she wasn't home, she walked around the corner of her house, pruning shears in hand. Her mascara-accentuated eyes looked me up and down as though I was a hatching of weevils in her cake flour. I was neither invited nor welcome.

"Ms. Harvey," she said in her prim manner. "What can I do for you? Did you reconsider our little talk yesterday?"

"Hello Marta." I kept my demeanor informal. "No, no. My mind hasn't changed, but I do have some interesting news I think you might want to hear."

"Hummph," Marta said, "The only news I want to hear is that you decided to pass along Joon O'Neal's book to me. Come along back. I'm working in the green house today."

I followed behind on her manicured lawn, each piece of grass the same, exact height. The stone path bordered flawless, trimmed bushes and led to a shiny, upmarket greenhouse. Inside, the floors were spotless, even gleaming, and none of her exotic plants dared to expose even a blemish on their bright, glossy foliage. Marta, it appeared, was unconcerned about being organic. My eyes scanned her rows of benches, seeking evidence of my missing pots and plants. They were not there.

"I'm glad you came by if only to see that I am a qualified gardener." With noticeable pride, Marta motioned toward the potting benches, heavy with flowering begonias and trilliums. I agreed her plants were beautiful.

"Now what is it that you want to tell me?" she said.

I took a few minutes to look at her giant chocolate lilies. "You already know that I am a genealogist. I help people organize family history. Anyway, new information came in on Joon's DNA match-up site yesterday afternoon. She has a niece. I'm sure she didn't even know about her niece. But the strange thing is, you and I know her. She lives here in town."

"This is nonsense." Fiery patches heated Marta's cheeks and clashed with her peachy blush. "Did you just make this up because of what I said yesterday?"

"Not at all." I took a deep breath to still my inner wolverine. "I was as surprised as anyone, and her niece is completely stunned herself. I've already told her because she was working with me to find her own DNA matches. She's looking for her biological mother and father, and her DNA results came in just yesterday. She never expected to find out that Joon was her aunt. I think it's a bit of a miracle."

"Well, who is this supposed niece?" Marta demanded, untying her spring-bud, green gardening apron, with its peach-piping trim. "And for your information, I will be checking on this in detail. You aren't going to be able to pull the wool over my eyes. I will want to see the proof."

"I'm getting a little too warm in here." Wiping perspiration from my forehead, I walked out of the greenhouse and began strolling along the side of Marta's property, looking at her glorious, fall flowers. Marta followed, sharp sheers back in hand.

"Who is this niece of Joon's?" Marta repeated.

"It's Philomena Rand," I said. "We call her Philly. Do you know her?"

Marta shook her head. "I'm sorry, but that's just too much of a coincidence, you being good friends with Philly. This must be something you cooked up together so you could get away with keeping the recipe book."

I decided to be as diplomatic as possible. "Marta, I thought you would like to know there is a member of your extended family here in town. It's something you might want to celebrate. As you know, the Towne Family Almanac was never likely to come into your possession, and this doesn't change that. Would you like to have lunch with Philly and I to celebrate her new discoveries? She's adopted, you know, and only just finding out about her biological family. You could be of enormous help."

"As far as I know, she doesn't garden," was all Marta got out.

"You could show her." I motioned with my arm, stretching my fingers toward the lush flower beds and beautiful trees Marta cared for. My arm stopped short in its sweep of the lawns. There, along Marta's little pond, I could see wisps of white, lacy flowers. They blossomed at the tops of long stems extending from plants I had been thinking about a lot in the last few days. Allowing any wild plant to live in her controlled landscape seemed out of character, but Marta Hester had water hemlock growing on her property.

Chapter 9

"When the new sickness overtook the village I made my medicines, but they did little good. I had to start at the beginning and try again. I taught myself new combinations and new remedies. It was a lesson about wrong turns and backtracking. I found new powers in lavender and hemp and the molds on bread. I practiced never giving up, just as my grandmothers taught me. The people started getting better." From *The Towne Family Almanac*, 1620. Alena Towne, niece of Alis Dinley.

For a long minute I just stood and looked at Marta's pond and those healthy, thick-stemmed water hemlock plants. Marta noticed my interest.

"What do you see over there?" Marta stood on tiptoes to see better. "I've been having issues with raccoons and goldfish. Is that what you see?"

In my mind, I snatched at traces of inspiration, trying to craft an answer she would accept. Finally, I fabricated a request to get a closer view of her pond. "Can I see how you constructed your pond? I'm thinking of putting one in myself."

"In your teensy, bitsy, half-acre backyard?" Marta's tone was incredulous. "It wouldn't work."

"Nevertheless, I'm sure you won't mind if I take

pictures." I pulled out my cell phone and walked closer to the pond, snapping several quick photos of the water hemlock. My photography expedition interrupted our conversation about Philly, displeasing Marta.

"Have you got what you want?" she demanded. I nodded and she turned back toward the front of the house. "I have a lot to do today, Betts, and I don't have time for chit chat. You and Philly are up to something, and it's not going to stop me from getting that lawyer."

I turned toward Marta, conscious of her self-entitled chin raise. "Look, I know you feel disappointed," I said. "But think about it. You and Philly might make a wonderful team. You could tell her so much about the family she's longing to know. If the book passes to her, you could help Philly learn more about gardening, and I expect she'll share recipes with you. Should you change your mind about getting together, call one of us. We'll have lunch someday."

I left her standing like a salt pillar in the middle of her impeccable, frog-green lawn. I had a bit more information than I did an hour ago, but it was inconclusive. When I looked back, Marta stayed rooted to the same spot, long, sharp-cutting shears hanging down from one gloved hand. Her eyes, black clouds of fury, stared at me. I shivered.

Marta's coldness stirred up questions about the inner workings of our local police investigation. Were police looking at suspects other than Denny? I decided to drop by Brocklebrook city offices and see for myself. Because Mrs. Hester's husband worked for the police department, I would wait to tell chief investigator Crumley about the water hemlock growing near Marta's pond and her threats to hire a lawyer.

"I can give you a minute." Crumley looked at me as though I was a sooty outdoor grill that needed scrubbing before the cookout could begin.

"Have you found anything? Can I stop worrying about spiders under my pillow or poison in my coffee creamer anytime soon?" I clamped my teeth together in anticipation of Crumley's clipped litany.

"We're on our way to make an arrest now," he said, narrowing his lips until they were a thin dash below his wide, sunburned nose. "We found a wooden box in the storage unit. Your Denny Woodman claims there was seven thousand dollars in it. We found no money in the box. We did find several ounces of grated root and seeds. They came from a water hemlock plant. We just got the fingerprint evidence back. The only fingerprints on that box belong to Denny Woodman. He's our do-er. Now we have the evidence to prove it."

The intensity of the sinking and swooping feeling in my stomach had me groping for a chair. No matter what the evidence showed and no matter how bad it looked for Denny, I still refused to believe he was the murderer. I knew him better than the police did, and his arrest was not going to alleviate my fears of brown recluse spiders trespassing in my shoes or of having to confront a poisoner all by myself. With a prisoner behind bars, the police were much less likely to consider my suspicions about Mrs. Hester or anyone else on our suspects list. A judge or even a jury might convict Denny of the murders.

"Got to go," Crumley said. "Got an arrest to make."

The remainder of my day passed in a blur of household chores, laundry, and genealogy research. My efforts to help Denny and figure out the identity of the *real* bad guy were as pitiable as trying to find that one stray dandelion seed in a mound of marigold seeds. Crumley's irksome words, "He's our do-er," pounded in my head to the rhythm of my washing machine. My cat was gone, but not his feline-soothing music CD. Into my CD player it went, and I sat in my oversized, wingback chair, letting the strains of harp and piano calm me until it was time to leave for our meeting at Warren's.

By 7 p.m., the four of us gathered around Warren's antique drawing table, ready for bun fighting, each of us having spent time with one of our suspects that day.

"Yeah. Arsonists usually start fires within about two miles from their own homes, on average," Roger was saying to Warren.

"Hmmm. I suppose we could draw a map and figure out how close our suspects live to the storage unit." Warren stripped a piece of paper off his legal pad. "I'd need Google Maps to calculate, but Tent City is only blocks away from the unit. Betts, your Mrs. Hester lives at least five miles away from it. Of course, Lester Stoats' office is within two miles, but he lives up in the hills in one of those million-dollar houses." Warren raised his head from the map. "Where in Sam hill does that man get all his money? No one gets rich from a city manager salary, not in Brocklebrook."

"It still comes down to motive," Roger said, ignoring Warren's question. "If the motive for fire was to cover up the crime of poisoning someone, or burglary, the distance from the criminal's home might not be a factor. But if it's a guy with control issues and he fits a typical arsonist profile, then his home is going to be close to the storage unit."

"Anger," Warren said. "Setting fires is about burning rage."

With eager relish Roger answered. "Right. Blood-boiling, out-of-control anger. The guy starts fires because he's tired of his neighbor's dog barking or some-such. He's impulsive and goes ballistic. When he gets angry, he thinks of scorching things."

What is with these two? I wondered. *They seem to feed off each other's morbid interest in the criminal element. Time to throw a bun into the works.* "That could be Stoats. It could even be Mrs. Hester," I said. "But I've never seen Denny or Stan lose control like that, and they live closest to the scene of the crime."

"Wicked cool," Philly said, in awe. "This is an honest to God brain-twister."

"Let's hope we've found enough new information to un-twist a few neurons." I sighed. "What have you got Warren? Did you talk with Denny today?"

Warren raised an eyebrow in my direction. He often gets edgy if he thinks I'm ordering him around, but this time he must have decided to take my cue as an invitation rather than a command.

"We were sorting through the stacks of boxes on the floor; a lot of it is Joon's," he said. "The smoke didn't get into the plastic containers with tight lids. We wiped those down. Then we took stock of the damage. A few boxes of knitting patterns were completely spoiled by fire. A box of Stan's family pictures was ruined. Joon had some keepsakes too, and Denny wondered if you wanted them, Philly. He could hardly keep that big grin off his face once I told him you are Joon's niece."

Philly managed a sad half smile. "Yeah. I'll take them."

"Anyway," Warren continued, "Denny thinks that if we can find out how Liam and the killer got into the storage unit, we can figure out who set the fire. He remembers about six months back Joon misplaced her keys. It turned out they were lying on the sidewalk where she usually had her little craft market. Some man, Denny didn't remember who, recognized the teddy bear flashlight key chain and brought them to her. So, Denny thinks someone either took the keys from her and copied them and then brought them back to the sidewalk, or someone found them on the sidewalk, copied them and then returned them to the Joon."

Roger shook his head. "I don't know. That all seems like unusual behavior to me. If someone found her keys, why copy them at all? Why not just keep them and not go to extra trouble?"

Warren nodded in agreement. "I ran that by Denny. He said that if the keys disappeared permanently, he and Joon would have replaced the lock. But because the keys turned up, there was no need to change anything."

"Six months is a long time." I pursed my lips together in doubt. "If someone went through all the trouble to copy Joon's keys, why wait so long to break in? What would they be looking for?"

"Maybe someone has been getting into the storage unit throughout those six months, only no one knew they were doing it," Roger suggested.

"There's the money," Philly said. "You said that they arrested Denny because they found a wooden box with water hemlock seeds in it and that the box belonged to him. And Denny said he kept his savings in that box. If someone knew that Denny kept cash there, maybe they waited until he saved up more of it. They took the money and replaced it with poison. If they used rubber gloves, only Denny's fingerprints would be on the box. That points to someone like Stan."

"If we're being thorough, it could have been Joon." Warren was playing the devil's advocate. "What if she was after the money, killed Liam, and then, feeling a huge sense of guilt, killed herself?"

Both Philly and I groaned at Warren's suggestion. "That's absurd." Philly's voice rose to a near shout. I reached over and squeezed her shoulder.

"Okay, okay." Warren relented. "I don't know who else knew about the money. Denny said he was saving to construct a few of those tiny homes on trailers we've all been reading about. He collected enough to build one house, but he wanted enough for two houses before he got going."

"Of course, the police don't believe Denny." Philly pulled at her hand-painted silk scarf in exasperation. "They don't think someone like Denny could save money. I heard them talking, and they assume he's making up reasons for someone to break into the storage unit."

Warren got up, stiff-legged, and lumbered to the kitchen. He came back with a stainless-steel carafe and four mugs and poured coffee all around. He shook his head and sat down again.

"I could have kicked something when they came to take Denny away this afternoon." Warren lifted his mug and toasted us. "Denny gave me his keys and asked me to lock up and keep an eye on the unit until he gets back. I sure hope he does get back. Watching Crumley and the others put him in the patrol car burned me. I'm more determined than ever to find the real killer."

"And you're sure he's not the real murderer?" Roger leaned back and lifted his left foot to rest on his right knee. Three sets of eyes directed glares like lit napalm in his direction. He lifted both hands in surrender. "Sorry guys. You know him. I don't."

"Roger, we almost forgive you. It's good for us that we've got someone in the group who can ask those kinds of questions." I winked at him but held back from smiling. "Why don't you tell us about your day with Stan? I don't know him as well as I know Denny. What did you find out?"

Roger's face relaxed. "I spent the day with Stan clearing out a few abandoned camps at Tent City. I like the guy. He's a hard worker. He used to be a forester for the federal government, but the agency let Stan go after he turned sixty-two, and the man doesn't have a family. He was a bachelor all his life. Stan told me he did a spate of backpacking after retirement and a few years ago, found himself in Tent City. He feels at home there."

As Roger talked, I couldn't keep my eyes off his hands and his coffee mug. His thumb stroked the upper part of the clay handle while his first finger searched for something inside the handle curve. From Philly's descriptions, I knew Roger was an avid target shooter. As he held his mug, the handle seemed to become a trigger guard, and his first finger appeared to feel for a missing trigger.

"Stan's like Joon that way," I said. "I'd try to get her to apply for reduced-rent housing. She'd look at me like I was a nagging seagull and say, 'Wrong kind of rent. Service is the rent we pay for being on Earth.' Joon, Denny, and Stan have served as camp mentors and volunteer managers for as long as Brocklebrook established Tent City."

"Stan showed me around the camp," Roger continued. "I was expecting a slum but it's pretty well organized."

"Yeah. Saint Stan," Philly said, with a hint of sarcasm, as though talking about all this virtuous goodness was somehow indecent. "But did you get the impression Stan was hiding something? Did he seem defensive at all?"

"So, Stan is confused about what is happening." Roger bypassed Philly's questions. "He was gone last week and spent most of this week visiting his godson in Oregon. When he got back, Denny was in jail and Joon was dead. He's got a good alibi, and the police checked it out. I think we can cross him off our list."

"Well then, you need to find a new suspect to add to our file." I was only partly kidding. "In this game, when you clear someone of being a miscreant, you've got to finger someone else to accuse."

"Who's it gonna be?" Philly chided Roger. "Should we put your name back on the list?"

Roger stiffened but forced a crooked smile. His right-hand fingers fiddled with his coffee mug handle again. A nervous tick? Was he more wounded by our initial suspicions of him than I'd realized?

I decided to change the subject and spotlight Mrs. Hester, who moved closer to the top of our suspects list, except some of the villainous antics of our murderer were out of character for her. Sure, she had motive, of sorts, and she had clear access to the murder weapon, but I couldn't see her peach-festooned nethermost anywhere near poisonous spiders or back-alley dumpsters. She might have gotten the key to the storage unit to look for Joon's heirloom recipe book. But killing Liam? The heirloom itself did not seem to warrant that kind of extreme behavior.

I showed everyone the pictures of Mrs. Hester's pond and the hemlock plants and then it was Philly's turn. Philly outdid herself. Counter to her strong convictions about gender parity and office behavior, she'd impersonated a 1950's secretary and volunteered to bring Lester Stoats his coffee, sort his mail, and bring him his lunch.

"I pretended to be interested in his visions for gentrifying Brocklebrook," she said, sugaring her voice. "Ooooh Lester," Philly mimicked herself. "Educate me, Lester. Tell me everything I should know about small town economics."

Philly took in a deliberate lung-ful of air. As she exhaled, she narrowed her eyes in my direction. "He's a complete turd, you know." And then those fierce eyes filled with tears, taking us all by surprise. Without hesitation Roger reached over, grabbed her closest hand, and sandwiched it between his two larger ones.

A good sign, I thought.

I wanted Philly to hook up with a considerate man who knew how to care about her. But that hat caught my attention, the one Joon knitted, folded neatly on the table in front of Roger, and I recalled the matching scarf collected in the evidence box at the police station.

"This is really bothering me." Philly got out the words as she wiped her cheeks with the sleeve of her free arm. "I hate to tell you this story, but it really shows what kind of person Stoats is." Philly looked at the notes in front of her, picked up the notebook, and hugged it to her chest.

"He left for a few minutes while I sorted his mail. He got a phone call, and his voice mail kicked in, but the speaker was on. I heard something that makes me want to gouge out Stoats' eyes every time I think of it."

Roger's left brow rose ever so slightly.

"Someone was sobbing," Philly said. "It was an older woman, and she sounded heart broken. She just asked Stoats, 'Why?' in this quavering, defeated voice. And then she was keening. I wanted to answer the phone. I wanted to ask her if she needed help, but it wasn't my phone call."

Philly had our full attention. Warren, Roger, and I sat motionless, leaning toward Philly, waiting.

"Then this poor old woman said, 'Nephew. I may be in the hospital, but my kitty, my Penny, was my best friend.' And then she started crying again, but I heard her whisper, 'Lester, you had no right to have my Penny euthanized just because you didn't want to take care of her while I was gone. My neighbor would have cared for her.' Stoats' aunt was wheezing by then, and someone took her phone from her."

My throat tightened over a painful lump. I realized then that Stoats was more than arrogant. He was also cruel. I leaned toward Warren, who had a soft place for kittens. He'd adopted several dogs and cats as life companions and understood what it meant to love animal friends.

"Damn nation. What a jerk," Roger said under his breath.

Philly wiped her eyes one last time and finished her investigation report by saying she also heard Stoats' side of a few phone conversations.

"And I learned," said Philly, "that King Leopold Hotels Inc. have their sights on Tent City land to build a conference center. They plan to construct the buildings right beside our beautiful creek with a top story view of the ocean. It's a prime location because it's just off the first freeway exit into town. Lester Stoats, our illustrious city manager, is willing to sell us all down the river. He already showed King Leopold Hotels Inc. the place and proposed it as a location."

"This is the first I've heard anything about a hotel conference center. Is that something that Brocklebrook business owners and residents want?" Warren looked at Philly for an answer.

"It's hush, hush right now," Philly said. "Stoats asked me to sit on the information because even the council members are keeping it secret. The plans include shops and an entertainment center that would compete aggressively with our local businesses. I suppose Stoats thinks that if he proposes it as a complete, profitable, and strategic package, the council would be foolish to say 'no.'"

"What does Stoats get out of it?" Roger asked.

"Well, that's interesting," Philly pulled her hand away from his so she could double it into a fist. "He's got political aspirations. He wants to be governor or senator someday and so he's using our town to show how he can accomplish an economic makeover. I kept my mouth shut, but it was hard. I'm not against economic progress; however, it should involve local people. It should be their vision, and current residents should be able to gain something from the changes rather than be shunted aside so venture capitalists can expand their bank accounts."

"Exactly," I said. "Economic progress for Brocklebrook ought to be about our community and the people who are here right now."

"Whether Stoats had anything to do with the murders, I can't say." Philly shrugged her shoulders, looking defeated. "But he's using them to his advantage to scare people. He's telling everyone that it's dangerous to help unhoused people or give them a place to stay. He has no intention of finding a new place for Tent City, should the deal go through with King Leopold Hotels."

"Stoats is no Nelson Mandela, but using the killings to his advantage doesn't mean he murdered anyone," Roger chimed in.

Philly glared. "I didn't say he murdered Joon and Liam, but anyone who kills his aunt's cat like that is capable of even more pitiless acts."

"Are your eye-gouging reflexes in check?" Roger asked, leaning away from her.

Stoats was still on our list, then, and so was Mrs. Hester. This detective work was harder than I'd imagined. "Tomorrow I'm supposed to leave the heirloom recipe book on my porch or face the consequences," I reminded the others, "and I don't think we're any closer to brainstorming our way to a logical solution."

"So, let's be illogical," Roger said, grinning and looking toward Philly as though seeking affirmation and pardon.

"What do you mean?" Philly brightened.

"Let's set a trap for our blackmailing lowlife," he said. "Let's see if we can catch him - or her - tomorrow night."

"Sounds dangerous." I was ready to put an immediate kibosh on the suggestion. "I don't want to be responsible for friends getting hurt."

"And we don't want to be responsible for doing nothing while you get hurt." Warren stood. He circled the table, clomping out a dogged rhythm with his large boots on the honey-stained, wood floor. "The police think they've got the person responsible for all these crimes, Betts. They're not going to spend effort to protect you or your house right now."

"There are four of us against one," Philly said, taking Roger and Warren's side.

"Five, including Joey," Warren pointed out.

I sighed. With my reluctant help, the other three set about drawing a diagram of my house and yard, accounting for every bush, tree, and outbuilding. They hovered over their patchwork map, planning a human snare that seemed crazy and plausible at the same time, but it left me apprehensive.

"What if this guy has a gun?" I leaned over the table looking hard at each of the three conspirators. "Then what?"

"You won't put your package on the porch until it's night. That's part of the strategy," Roger said. "The house will be dark, and we've got plans for hooding the streetlights. He won't be able to see, and he won't know what he's shooting at or where to aim. Of course, if he gets to shooting wildly, accidents can happen, but I really doubt a gun will show up.”

The twitching of Roger’s fingers on his cup handle drew my eyes and piqued my curiosity.

“I know you’ll be hiding, but he’s bound to have a flashlight that he can use to see you.” I was determined to dress down the plan.

“If he’s got a flashlight, all the better for us. We’ll be able to nab him in no time.” Roger’s eyes twinkled in anticipation.

“While Betts is at the bakery tomorrow morning, let’s meet at the Salvation Army store on Second and Pine and see what we can dig up for our stealth wardrobe.” Warren interrupted and took charge with one simple statement. “Then let’s set up before early afternoon so we draw as little attention as possible to what we’re doing. We’ll make it look as though we’re mowing the lawn, trimming hedges, weeding, and installing a sprinkler system.”

I blew him a kiss. “I think it would look more realistic if you really did mow the lawn. It needs it.”

I decided to go stare at my office wall and then sleep in my own bed that night. I wanted to write a letter to this blisterpodpopper of a human being who was compelling me to leave a package on my porch the next night. He wouldn’t be getting the recipe almanac, as he expected, but he would receive a piece of my mind.

Chapter 10

"When the victim becomes the suspect, dangerous accusations lead to treachery. A concoction of sweet forest herbs can ease the pain." From The Towne Family Almanac, 1673, Joanna Blessing Towne, wife of William Towne. Guest contributor to the almanac.

It's a good thing I did go home.

When I opened the door to my house, my plans took a hard left turn. Joey was missing. He'd left his sleeping bag bunched in a sorry mound on my living room floor, which was littered with wall pictures, toppled plants, and two overturned wing-backed chairs.

Someone broke into my home, searched every closet and every cupboard, upended lamps, and propelled my things into haphazard piles. The intruder cleared every drawer. Even my bathroom medicine cabinet was bare. Plastic medicine containers floated like flotsam in the toilet. I closed my eyes to try and calm my sense of foreboding before entering my office. Sure enough, my computer, my Deputy Delilah, lay on the floor, a dent in her computer case. My client files were strewn like wind-blown newspapers over toppled bookcases, torn books, and my file cabinet, which leaned sideways against the back wall.

I put my hands up to the sides of my head as though trying to protect my brain from exploding. Only then did I raise my eyes to the dry eraser wall, and what I saw caused my knees to buckle. I grabbed onto the side of my tipped desk to steady myself.

Thick red and black lines merged in menacing zigzags over the work that Philly, Warren, and I had done. The prowler's hand crossed out Joon's name. In bold, red letters near Philly's drawing of Joon, the intruder wrote, *YOU ARE NEXT*. Thick black letters below the death threat spelled out another message. *On the porch. Tomorrow night.*

I dialed 911, talked with the dispatcher, and then called Warren. All I could do next was wait in utter silence. Where was Joey? He was supposed to be on guard. There was no sign of him.

The police found Joey knocked out with a tranquilizer and shoved behind my grape vines. They summoned an ambulance. At the hospital, the doctors wanted to keep him overnight, though they said his injuries were minor. Until hospital staff could notify his parents, we stayed with Joey and kept him company.

Investigator Crumley took a statement from me in the hospital waiting room. After describing what I knew, I faced him squarely and gave him my well-practiced, teacher-glaring-over-the-tops-of-her-eyeglasses stare. I crossed my arms in a don't-lie-to-me gesture. "As you can see, I'm still not safe." I tapped my right foot with increasing speed. "Don't you think you arrested the wrong person?"

"Not necessarily." He looked down his wide nose at

me with a glare that nearly matched my own. "We think there are two things going on here. Someone killed these down-and-outs. Likely it was Denny. Someone else wants this book of Joon's. They are using the situation, making it look like the crimes connect."

"What about those threats on my office wall?"

"Yeah. This burglar is using the deaths to scare you. That doesn't mean he's the murderer." Crumley looked at his watch and then toward the hospital exit. I knew the watch game well. My husband used to do that right up to the day he died, that is, look at his watch when he wanted to avoid talking.

"I'd like you to catch this guy before he can do anymore damage," I said, impatient. "My friends are ready to spring a trap for him tomorrow night when he's supposed to come and pick up Joon's book from my porch. Don't you think it should be you springing the trap instead?"

"Look, all we can do is send a patrol car. We can drive by," Crumley said. "We don't have authority to be ambushing people on someone's front porch. Things aren't that bad. You said it yourself. No one took anything from your house this evening."

"An intruder tranquilized and injured a young man tonight; someone invaded my house and damaged my belongings. Isn't that enough for the police to be concerned?" At this point I'd clenched my fists. My temper was building. Those hot coals in my stomach were smoking again. "If you know that this perpetrator is expected at my house tomorrow night, the least you can do is catch him and arrest him."

"Lady, what if we catch someone stealing a package

from your porch? Then that's all we can charge him with. That's not even worth a night in lockup," Crumley said.

I hate when someone calls me *lady,* almost as much as I hate people looking at their watches while I talk to them.

"It proves he's the one who called and threatened me, put the spiders in Warren's truck, broke into my house, and left an incredibly menacing note on my wall," I said.

Crumley was unmoved. "Maybe, maybe not. The real perpetrator might not come. He might hire someone to get the package for him. The real perpetrator could have hired someone to ransack your house. No. You want us to catch him in the act of doing something really damaging; then we can keep him locked up for a while."

"Why not question the porch burglar until you get answers?" I knew my tone was reproachful, but I didn't care.

"Look, Ms. Harvey, we'll run by your house. If we see someone there, we'll stop and ask questions. The only thing we can charge them with is taking something from your porch. Why not give this guy what he wants and get it done with? It's just a book." Crumley tipped his hat, turned, and walked off.

I pictured Crumley's name at the top of our suspects list. I also had an urge to follow and kick him in the seat of his police regulation, tan pants.

Joey would be okay, according to his doctors. His darkening bruises came from being dragged down steps, and his grogginess would clear as the drug worked its way out of his system. Joey's disorientation left him with only a vague recollection of what happened. In a slurred string of words, replete with mushy consonants, he told us he'd heard sounds outside and stepped out on the porch to check things out. Someone grabbed his arm; he felt a sharp stab on his right thigh and ended up under the grape vines.

Joey's dad, a short, squarish pug of a man, who drove truck for a prefabricated housing company, was more concerned that Joey failed to keep his guard up and let someone get the best of him. Joey's petite bomber-jacketed, poodle-haired mom marched up to the hospital bed and seemed to yap like a Pomeranian. "Joey, you turkey. What was the use of all those boxing and self-defense lessons if you're just gonna let someone wipe the steps with your ass?"

After his parents finished their scolding and left, Joey fell back into a sleepy stupor. I couldn't help but feel responsible for leaving him on his own in my cottage when the devil was out there. I thought about Warren, Philly, and Roger's plans for the next day. I wanted no more injured friends. When Warren rejoined me in the waiting room, I insisted he call off their trap tomorrow.

"It's already in the works. Can't stop now," he insisted.

My house was a wreck, but I couldn't do much about it until after work the next day. Not since the vexatious days of parent teacher conferences had I felt so frustrated. A possible murderer ambushed and assaulted my security guard. My friends were busy planning a dust up that could go terribly wrong, and I wanted to turn my garden hose on our police department and soak every uniformed one of them for failing to protect and defend.

That night I tossed and turned next to Warren, who

took me in again. I felt like a homeless waif. Most nights I don't remember my dreams, and I wish I could forget the one I had that night. It made no real sense but left me feeling anxious, and it provoked a stark awareness of how helpless this situation was making me feel. I don't do helpless at all well.

In the dream I was in a beautiful field surrounded by acres of Queen Anne's Lace. Crumley stood over me, yelling, "We need more for Joon's funeral. Pick more." I had two giant bunches of Queen Anne's Lace, but I could see stray water hemlock flowers sticking out here and there. It was so hard to tell one lacy flower from the other. The bundles were each as tall as I was and as wide as my garden gate. Joey's mother and father were in the field lamenting. "We gave her boxing lessons. Why can't she carry her load?"

Crumley and Joey's parents packed the flower bundles onto my back, so I was almost crawling toward the door where Crumley stood. He pointed an index finger at the exit as though to instruct an errant child, in this case, me. In my dream I put up a valiant struggle to get myself and the flowers through the opening. After what seemed like forever, I stood on the other side, but there was no applause, only the doors closing behind me with finality. I let the bundles fall, finding myself alone in a dark alley. There, a few feet from where I unloaded the flowers, was Joon's lifeless body. My heart, already pounding hard from carrying my load, sped into fourth gear. When Joon's dead eyes flew open and focused on me, I wanted to run. Instead, I fell backward onto the bundles of tiny whitish green flowers clustered on reddish purple stems, not Queen Anne's Lace at all, but Water Hemlock.

"The book," Joon growled. Her eyes, outlined with dark circles, widened to meerkat proportions. "Don't let him have it. Keep him away from the book." When Joon struggled to sit up, there were tears streaming from those enlarged eyes. "Use the book," she said in a commanding tone. "Use the book to save the book."

Next thing I knew, Warren was coaxing me out of sleep with gentle nudges. "Betts. Wake up. You're dreaming. Come out of it."

We held each other tight after that, Warren drifting back to sleep and me working to shake the image of Joon's haunting, meerkat eyes. The dream haunted me until I got up to watch something inane on Netflix, something that would take my mind to another place. So, what if it was Andy Griffith and the sweet simplicity of Mayberry that helped me get back to sleep?

I have no recollection of what I baked the next morning in that warm, lemon-yellow bakery kitchen. I walked in a stupor, and Warren, his head on a café table, snored like a whale, his hand still wrapped around a half-full cup of coffee. He was a stubborn grizzly bear at times, but he was loyal and knew how to take care of his friends; I was glad to be one of them.

The morning crowd's specialty coffee customers might have ended up with some unusual flavor combinations, but nobody complained until Lester Stoats was the buyer. He usually had four cubes of sugar in his drink, but I lost count at three and may have added one extra. Stoats could tell on his first sip.

"When we get a real coffee shop in town," he said, "you won't be so casual with your orders. Now make me another one, and this time get it right."

"Mr. Stoats," I said, "you have never had cause to complain before today, so don't act as though this happens all the time. I suppose you've never made a mistake brewing your own coffee?"

"Well, I don't get paid to make my own coffee." He smirked, looking down his sharp nose at my tired face. I looked up at his snarky face and met his eyes squarely.

"You might want to count your money again," I told him. "You're a dime short."

His expression turned sour, but he dug into his pocket for the missing coin.

Warren had gone by then to meet Philly and Roger at the secondhand store and choose their trap-setting ensembles. I could tell that Pinky was out back because his favorite radio morning talk show blared from the delivery truck. "And we gotta give praise to our favorite philosopher, good ole Rush Limbaugh," said the announcer. "Remember what he said when those whiners complained that low-income children would go hungry come summer? You know because they wouldn't be in school eating federally funded food? Ha ha. Our good friend Limbaugh said it best. 'Isn't it reasonable to let some of those kids go hungry so they can looooze suuuum weight?'" The announcer laughed long and hard at his own joke before continuing. "And here's a recording of Rush, now, telling kids where to find food when school's out."

I winced as Limbaugh's pompous bellyaching bounced off the kitchen walls.

"Kids, there are . . . things in what's called the kitchen of your house called cupboards. . . most likely you're going to find Ding-Dongs, Twinkies, . . . potato chips. . .. If that doesn't work, try. . . McDonald's. . . and if they don't have Chicken McNuggets, dial 911 and ask for Obama. Then there's always the neighborhood dumpster."

Limbaugh's voice faded away and the local talk show host was back. "And our ever-wise Limbaugh told those oh so poooor hungry kids that's where they could 'dive and survive until school kicks back up in August.' The dumpster. Ha ha. Got to hand it to him."

I could never understand why Pinky started his mornings with the dehumanizing drivel of hate pundits. My brain hurt every time I tried to find the logic in it.

"There's a package delivery for you outside by the mailbox," Pinky said when he came in. "Been there since yesterday cause I don't think anyone remembered to check the mail."

I crinkled my forehead wondering what it could be and then remembered. It was the parcel I sent to myself with Joon's original book in it. I stepped out to retrieve the package, amazed that no one stole it during the night. What should I do with the book now, I wondered? Crumley's words came back to me. *Maybe you should just give this guy what he wants and get it done with. It's just a book after all.* And then I recalled Joon's meerkat eyes and her voice in my dream. *"Don't let him have it. Keep him away from the book."*

Tucking the package under my arm, I gathered Pinky's morning coffee and donuts and placed them on his front seat, grimacing at the spiteful commentary shouting from his radio.

"Well, what's in it?" Pinky asked, gesturing toward the package. "Aren't you gonna open it?"

"No. Not right now. It's just supplies," I said. "I've got some new recipes I'm working on."

"Have ya now." Pinky looked amused. "And what kind of recipes do you have in mind? You haven't stolen them, have ya, from some cookbook?"

"When someone publishes a cookbook and you use the recipes, it's not stealing."

"Depends," Pinky mumbled. "Mrs. Hester's been goin' on about that recipe book you got that doesn't belong to you." Then he stepped up into his truck, slammed his door shut, and backed out without bothering to close the bakery loading doors. I sighed. Sometimes Pinky was privy to way too much gossip and spent too much time spreading it around.

"Have a good day," I said to his taillights as they turned the corner onto Seventh.

Returning to the kitchen I eyed the package. Where to hide it? The safest place I could muster was up in the bakery shelves among the specialty pans that we only used for unusual occasions. The shelf I chose was at the top of a ceiling-tall cupboard and required the use of a step ladder to open. I slipped my package between several other cardboard boxes that held various kinds of pans, party supplies, and cutting tools.

Half an hour later, before Maggie arrived to claim her shop, I managed to get everything in tip top shape, despite my slow pace and my need for several more hours of sleep.

While I'd finished my bakery shift, I considered that my day had just begun. First on the list was checking in on Joey, and then I wanted to get my house back in order. After that, I was afraid to speculate. I

pictured an ending to the day that included myself and
three friends tucking in our tails with embarrassment and
licking our wounds after a takedown gone terribly
wrong.

Chapter 11

"Lure your enemies into a trap of blackberry brambles, home of fairies, and the result will always be calamitous and unpredictable, but the one who is trapped has no choice but to take notice." From The Towne Family Almanac, 1502, Rachel Ward, daughter of Rose Green.

I don't like to use the word paranoid. Let's just say I was stewed. I so wanted to check the status of my safe behind the slat of one of the steps going up to my bedroom, but I couldn't do it. I was afraid that whoever trashed my house left a bug, or some kind of spyware device. Was that even possible? Were these covert listening devices expensive? Were they available to just anyone to buy, or were they just the stuff of spy movies? Could people really stick little metal buttons behind your framed cross stitch samplers and listen in?

As one by one I picked up my belongings from the floor and returned them to drawers, cupboards, table tops and shelves, I couldn't help but feel around every corner and on every flat surface for things that didn't belong there. I used a flashlight because I also wanted to avoid angering any eight-legged, brown trespassers. In my imagination these long-legged recluses might even be guarding the espionage gadgets. In my defense, I needed sleep.

By 1:30 p.m., nearly everything was back in order. Belongings damaged beyond repair, such as my grandmother's Brown Betty teapot and an antique map of Australia, I put in a trash box next to the front door. I had yet to switch on Deputy Delilah to see if she still worked. The contents of my clients' files were in a box for re-sorting and re-filing. I wiped clean the entire dry erase wall so it gleamed white, rubbing especially hard to obliterate the offending red X.

Outside, Philly, Roger and Warren mowed the grass and installed bits and pieces of their trap. As long as no one looked too closely, they appeared to be trimming hedges and weeding, but there were incongruous rolls of thick wire and a conspicuous pile of metal posts, the kind that support electric fencing. For a few minutes, I watched them hide electrical cords under wood chips and other lawn materials. The two men were actually singing together - Jerry Lee Lewis's *Great Balls of Fire*. Philly read out directions and, on occasion, scanned the street to detect onlookers. She told me there was a big red 'X' marked on the beautiful blue door of my glass-pained greenhouse to match the one left on my dry-erase wall. I hurried to investigate. The offending graffiti boiled my blood, but thankfully, inside the greenhouse things were just as I left them. As I returned to my back porch, Warren and Roger belted out the lyrics from Lynyrd Skynyrd's *Poison Whiskey*. It was all about rotgut whisky killing a poor man dead. Roger and Warren yowled out the words, not quite in unison.

Philly rolled her eyes. "These two can't talk about anything except poisoners and arsonists when they get together." She pursed her lips and pulled on a pair of earphones.

Doctors released Joey from the hospital at about three in the afternoon. He insisted on coming over to "help," so we propped up his concussed and bruised bulk on the couch with pillows and blankets.

"I'll fire your ass if you even stick a toe out that front door," Warren told Joey in no uncertain terms. "Your only job tonight is to watch out the front window."

To manage my own nervousness, I canned a batch of green tomato mincemeat and tested Deputy Delilah to make sure she still worked. Praise be, she lived. As I added raisins and apple pieces to chopped green tomatoes, I wondered if all this effort would get us any closer to capturing my harasser. Even if it did, was it worth putting my friends in danger?

We had dinner early, a barbecue in the backyard to masquerade our entrapment setup and make everything look as normal as possible. In muted voices, Warren, Roger, and Philly rehearsed their capture strategy several times during dinner, which consisted of running through what they called code scenes one, two, three and four. Joey and I would station ourselves inside my darkened house after we'd driven our cars away and covertly walked back, post dusk, to make it look as though no one was home.

We cleaned up dinner right as the sun set. I left the bait - the package - on the porch before I took off in my car. This time the package was a large Dick Blick art supply catalog wrapped in brown paper, along with my letter to the abusive predator who demanded Joon's almanac.

Dressed in camouflaged hunting pants and jacket, her face smudged with black face paint, Philly installed herself between branches of the big apple tree in the front yard. She oversaw the switchboard, as the crew called it. Roger and Warren, also dressed in camouflage hunting gear, stationed themselves strategically behind two thorny quince bushes and waited. No one carried weapons, just flashlights.

Joey slipped in the back door, and we waited almost two hours before we saw any movement. In the meantime, Joey consumed a whole package of chocolate dipped biscotti.

As Joey scanned my cupboards for more carbohydrates, a figure vaulted over the side fence from Mr. Curly's backyard. My phone vibrated so I took it out of my pocket and shielded the screen to check the message, as did Roger and Warren. Philly sent us a text: *Code one*.

Code One meant the subject was on the porch and had lifted the package. As soon as the subject crossed back over the grass, or headed for the front gate, Code One became Code Two. When this happened, Philly turned on the electric fence line the crew installed around my property. When the subject touched the fence, he would absorb an unhealthy jolt of electricity, enough to discourage a one-ton Brangus bull. Code Two would then advance to Code Three.

Out there in the shadows, the subject's dog-like yelp told us that Code Three was in effect. The marauder abandoned the fence line and bolted toward the front gate, which was short enough to jump over. Code Three meant that Roger and Warren were in motion, closing in on the subject. The subject didn't go down easily. All I could make out from the window were two dark forms, Warren, and the trespasser, rolling around in the front yard. Even inside the house, I could hear the distressing sounds of grunts, growls, and groans. I had to gulp down my own yell, which felt like swallowing a chunk of un-chewed celery. Roger relieved my sense of urgency by grabbing the back of the subject's jacket and pulling him away from Warren.

My right hand was on the front door handle, my left hand raised above my head clutching a wooden spoon. I was ready to jump into the fray and whop some sense into all of them. Roger and Warren both worked to pin down the trespasser's arms and legs and that was when Code Four came into effect. Philly pushed the button to turn on an array of outside lights.

When the lights came on, Warren and Roger pulled the knitted face mask off our prisoner.

I don't know who I expected, maybe Mrs. Hester's husband, or even Lester Stoats, but I felt myself rear back in surprise when I saw who it was. Our prisoner's face mirrored our own shocked expressions. I threw down the wooden spoon in exasperation. Philly howled at the sky, and I didn't blame her. After all, she'd been sitting for two hours in a tree - on a branch that made a crease in her derriere - and it was all for not.

Roger gave the prisoner a rough push till he fell on his side, and as Joey's younger brother Maynard worked to sit back up, he bleated, "Okay, I give up. You win! I've been owned."

I'd never met Maynard in person, but during lunch, Joey showed me pictures of himself and his brother receiving their purple belts in jiu jitsu. For brothers, they didn't look much alike. While Joey was all compact muscles, dark hair, and brown skin, Maynard was tall and wiry, with a blond mop cut and thick white eyebrows over brown eyes.

"Sh't," said Joey from his position at the front window.

"Maynard?" blared Roger. "This is one mell of a hess. What in Sam Hill are you doing stealing from Betts' porch?"

"Got hired," Maynard said, breathing hard and looking chagrined. "Someone gave me a job to get this package. I needed a few bucks for cannons." Warren and Roger gaped at him. "You know, paint cans," he said. "I'm an all-city graffiti artist. You've seen my gallery on the bridges and the parking lot wall of the old hotel. Anyway, those cannons cost bucks. This guy rented me to snatch a package from Ms. Harvey's porch. He said I had to be very secretive because it was a kind of game. To win the game I had to get the package without you seeing me."

"And just where are you supposed to take this package?" Warren's voice came out low and dangerous, his arms folded like menacing crab claws over his torn, grass-stained camo shirt.

"I was supposed to leave it in the newspaper box on the corner of Byron and Seventh Street where I would pick up an envelope with my payment."

"Maynard," said Warren, "this is serious business. The person who wants this parcel is probably the one who broke my truck windshield and is bullying Betts with poisonous spiders. This guy is sure to be responsible for your brother's trip to the hospital last night. The person who hired you extorted Betts into putting this package on her porch, and now we've caught you with it."

Maynard took hold of his stocking hat, wiped his brow with it, and said, "I thought the whole thing seemed dodgy, but it was easy money, and I've worked for this guy before. He's never done anything to cause me stew."

Warren lowered himself to the ground next to Maynard. "Tell us who hired you."

"I can't," Maynard whined. "One, I don't know who he is for sure. He always wears a Mexican wrestler mask when we meet. Second, I wouldn't get paid. Third, he said that if I told anyone, he would turn me into the police for being a wall writer." Maynard paused. "Yeah. It was when he threatened me that I began to wonder about his jive. I just thought you folks were playing some crazy game, and I thought it would be fun to mess with you."

Philly leaned against the apple tree. She looked skeptical and said to Maynard, "There's something big you're not telling us, isn't there."

"What?" asked Maynard, on the defensive.

Joey and I came out of the house then, Joey limping after me. I walked up to Maynard and indicated Joey. "Someone came here last night and assaulted Joey. Was that you?"

"No, Ma'am." Maynard looked shocked at the idea.

Joey scowled at his younger brother. "The wheel is turning but the hamster is dead. Hey, we never do things for the wrong side," he said. "Tell Ms. Betts what's up."

"Hey, can't Joey," Maynard said. "I'm hat. It's about honor. I made a promise to a client, and I can't break it."

Joey looked like he was going to belt Maynard, and

Maynard flinched at his brother's accusatory glare. "You're a better hot air artist than a painter," Joey said, spitting on the grass. "I'm not getting you. This guy who hired you might have had something to do with putting me in the hospital. Where are your loyalties? Mom and Dad never got us this training so we'd be thugs. We're supposed to protect and help people."

"Joey, I don't know. I'll talk with this guy. It's not a game anymore, and I don't want to be on the wrong side of it, but in the odd jobs business, I gotta be fair to whoever hires me."

"So, you know how to contact him." Joey's mouth was a bitter furrow.

"Just be careful." Roger said. "If the fellow who put you up to this is involved in the nastier aspects of this business, and by that, I mean murder, then you might be in danger too."

"I can't believe it." Maynard thumped both fists on the grass. "This dude so isn't like that. I've worked for him before, like I said. He's not out to hurt anyone." Maynard lifted the brown paper package. "What's in here anyway, and why does he want it?"

"We're not sure why he wants it." I could see a corner of the brown paper wrapping had torn open during the scuffle. "Maybe it's not even the man who hired you who wants it, but someone wants it very badly - maybe enough to murder for it. We haven't got all the pieces put together yet. We hoped catching the porch thief would bring us some answers. Our goal was to identify the one who's threatening me. With what happened to Joey, can you relate to that?"

Maynard's face was a study in anguish, but he

refused to reveal anything more about his masked employer. "Hey, I'm sorry. I'll ask questions. I'll find out why he sent me here. Can I have the package? Can I give it to him?"

I nodded my head. "Please take it. There's a letter in it I want him to see."

Maynard looked relieved. He could still collect his fee and finish his mission.

Joey surveyed his brother. "Just don't tell anyone about what happened in the yard. We're trying to make Ms. Harvey's house safe from creeps like you."

Maynard winced and nodded. "Your secret is safe with me."

Joey's brother took off. There was nothing left to do but gather up the monitoring equipment and go inside for dessert. I assured everyone the thawed key lime pie was well packaged and purchased that afternoon and so was the coffee I served with it. No one had time to poison it.

"The only thing we really learned," said Philly, a dob of creamy key lime stuck to her pointed chin, "is that whoever put Maynard up to stealing the package is probably local, and Maynard trusts him."

"I'll get the name out of him," Joey said. "I've got ways."

"Joey, you're in no condition to be 'getting' anything from your brother." Philly laughed. "Don't tempt fate. You might lose all your older brother edge if you tried something now."

"Our day wasn't a waste though," said Roger. "We've made your house a little safer, and we might be able to prevent more people from breaking in when you're not here. We can keep the electric fence going."

"There's just one more thing." I sighed and lowered my voice to a whisper, reluctant to share. "I'm scared whoever tore apart my house left a listening device or spy camera." The others didn't think my worry was as far-fetched as I hoped they would. Once the pie was gone, everyone took time to look in every nook and cranny they could think of to find covert listening devices. We discovered nothing, but I remained guarded.

Warren decided to stay at my house that night. The next day I had off, so I would reward Warren for the night's heroism with breakfast in bed or brunch beside the stone fountain. In the morning there would be eggs, pancakes, and time to simply enjoy each other's company.

Before I could get to sleep, though, I had one last job to do. I needed to return to the bakery without delay. Warren was incredulous but I was insistent. I was prepared to go alone, but Warren insisted on coming along, growling under his breath in the passenger seat.

Once in front of Dirty Dozen, I let myself in and tiptoed through the dining and kitchen area without turning on a light switch. Through the bakery kitchen window, the outdoor streetlight afforded me enough luminosity to push the kitchen ladder to the cupboard where I'd stored my package containing the heirloom recipe book. My hands pulled out the mailing box, and I lifted it down with care. I replaced the ladder, locked the front door of the bakery, and got back into the car.

A large box of clothes, ready for recycling at Good Will, took up the middle of my backseat, and that's where I hid the box, under sheets, old T-shirts, and jeans that fit last year, but this year were a size too small. I almost hated to let those jeans go. The upper right leg of each one, just above the knee, had little patches of pulled threads where Dr. Dillinger used to settle his front claws and hold on while I stroked his back every night.

"Joon told me in the dream to use the book to save the book," I said. "I'm going to see if there's anything to that idea. Tomorrow I'll take my large spiral bound Betty Crocker Cookbook and empty it. Then I'll make a reduced sized photocopy of Joon's book and slip the copied pages into the cookbook cover. I'll repack her original book, put it back in the mailing box and re-hide it at the bakery. In the meantime, I can study the pages. There's a key of symbols that goes with the recipes. I'll have that too. Maybe I can figure out what Joon meant in my dream."

Warren looked at me as though I was a confused squirrel changing direction in the middle of a crowded freeway. "It's a good thing I love you and know better, or I might think you're falling out of your tree. It was just a dream after all."

"You love me?" I said, pleased.

"I wouldn't be following you to snitch things out of bakeries at midnight if I didn't love you." He gave me a quick peck on my forehead.

I decided to risk leaving Joon's book in the laundry basket in my car. The car seemed safer, at this point, than taking it into the house. As it turned out, it was a good thing I retrieved it from the bakery that night because by the time Maggie opened the doors at 4 a.m., someone had turned her kitchen into a war zone. The mess forced her to close the shop for the day, and Maggie called to ask for help.

Of course I came. I felt responsible. I told her about the book, the invasion of my home, and the demands that

I turn Joon's compendium over to an anonymous caller.

"So, you think the same bozo who tossed your house made hash out of my kitchen?" Maggie wasn't convinced.

"Whoever wants Joon's book must know I work here, Maggie. They didn't find The Towne Family Almanac in my house, so they decided to look here." I shook my head in remorse. "I'm so sorry."

As I surveyed the piles of cooking utensils, wooden spoons, mixing blades, and measuring spoons, I wondered at the mayhem. Tossing a place to look for something never made sense to me. How could anyone find anything by creating chaos? Kitchen bedlam is the worst. A dusting of flour, like volcanic ash, dulled the shine of Maggie's stainless-steel appliances and workspaces. Contents of egg and milk cartons mingled with corn syrup, potato starch, sugar and cocoa powder, all part of an amalgamation that had the power to cling like hot asphalt to the bottom of shoes. Our shoes re-distributed the glue-like mixture wherever they stepped.

"Honey, even if the prowler was after Joon's book, you can't shoulder the blame." Maggie wiped the back of her hand across a sticky cheek. Her mass of black curls was marbled with flour dust, and the front of her bright red apron sagged from wiping her hands after scooping up thick, wet ingredients. Maggie lost a day of business and several pounds of quality provisions because of the break-in. At least Maggie's apron display was unmolested.

"It wasn't here, was it?" Maggie asked about the book, looking concerned that the kitchen wrecker stole it.

"No, it wasn't." I didn't tell her it had been at Dirty Dozen until midnight. I still planned to return it to the bakery cupboard in the next few days. The fewer people who knew I used The Dirty Dozen as a hiding place, the safer the book would be. If the burglar already looked and failed to find the book at the bakery, the less likely they'd revisit and tear it apart again, at least that's what I hoped.

Three hours later, we had the pots and pans washed and put in order, the spoons and knives back in their proper drawers, and the spilled flour and sugar swept, dusted, and wiped off the floor and counter spaces. After locking up, Maggie took off for home to fill apron orders, while I set out for the copy shop. With reverent care, I took Joon's book out of the box and shook my head at it.

"You, my dear, are certainly causing a lot of trouble," I said to its worn leather cover. I ran my fingers over its border, framed in intricately hand-tooled leaves and flowers. The book had no title, just a family name, *Towne*, and a crest that featured an intelligent looking raven at its center.

As before, I copied each large, thick page, reducing its size to fit inside my spiral cookbook cover and resecuring each envelope of seeds in the page pockets. I had hoped to replenish more seeds by the end of the month, and I wondered, not for the last time, where all those lovely potted plants were, the ones that had gone missing from my greenhouse. On most of them the seeds were still ripening. Was someone else harvesting the seeds? Did they know the significance of each one? Could they use them effectively without the recipe book?

When I finished the laborious job of copying the almanac, I double checked the key to the book symbols. Whoever designed the book cover hid the ingredient list of codes in an almost invisible leather pocket. Without the key, much of the information in the recipes was useless and impossible to decipher. I decided to memorize some of the symbols listed in the key and keep my copy tucked inside one of the plastic recipe holders of one of my other cookbooks.

At last, I rewrapped the original book in the mailing box, put it in the basket of laundry in my car's back seat and headed home, hoping that the book's pages would spotlight a means of ending the insane events that had marred this stress-filled week. Just as I said I would, I emptied out my large, three-ringed, red-checkered Better Homes and Gardens cookbook and replaced its contents with the copied pages of Joon's almanac. Was it a fail-proof disguise? I hoped so.

Now I was ready to take notice of the beautiful fall afternoon - the kind of midday that is quiet and lazy and invites a sit down beside a body of water amongst wild plants and in view of occasional wildlife. I decided to take myself to the edge of the Pacific Ocean and let the wind blow through my hair on the sandy beach. A little convenience store on the way provided me with a snack and a bottled iced tea that I put in my backpack, along with my disguised copy of the heirloom recipe book.

Mmmmm, I thought to myself as I felt my shoes sink into soft, moist sand the waves had only recently backed away from as the tide ran out. It occurred to me I got so involved in work and my backyard that I forgot just how close I lived to one of the most beautiful places on Earth.

A few logs jutted out of the bank near a clear, bubbly stream pouring itself into the ocean. The deep sea was right in front of me, and if I chose this spot between logs to rest, the natural barricade would protect me from the wind. I could rest my back against one log and prop my backpack against the other.

My spot turned out to be perfect for a much-needed respite as I delved into the little wisdoms, vignettes, recipes, and snippets of old lore collected by generations of women and saved in the heirloom recipe book. In spring, when I planted the seeds from the book, I only glanced at the handwritten pages, taking minimal interest in them. For one thing, many of the ingredients and even some of the words in the prose were in code, so to really understand what was being shared, one had to take the time to look at the book's key.

Even as photocopies, the pages were beautiful, each one a piece of art in and of itself with careful handwriting and little drawings of plant stems, leaves, and fruits. Much of the information, and even the language, was hundreds of years old. Joon told me that occasionally the book's guardian re-copied by hand some of the older, worn pages of the book to protect the information before passing the book down to the next guardian. Now, in the days of photocopying, I wondered what methods the more modern guardians would use to preserve their book. Who would be the next guardian of the book? Would Philly accept the title? If so, what would she do with it? Joon said she hadn't recopied or changed anything, nor had her mother, but they both added pages at the end of the book as they gained new knowledge from the plants and the seeds they grew and used.

As I sat, comfortable in the warm sand, I learned comfrey was a favorite herb of Joon's great great grandmother, who put the cool fresh leaves on aching joints to ease pain. She wrote about its early Greek and Roman name, *symphytum*, from the Greek *symphyo*, which means to "make grow together," and she delighted that the name was a recognition of comfrey's healing properties.

On every page, there was a story. Joon's great great grandmother provided a picture of a flowering comfrey and then explained the seeds she included came from a very special plant, one that resulted from a lifetime of saving and cultivating seeds from specimens that exhibited the most potent properties. She depended on comfrey to make high quality oils and dried herbs that she used for cures and medicines.

Every page had, at the bottom, a short line that indicated a more spiritual or magical property of the featured plant and recipe. For her comfrey recipe, Joon's great great grandmother used codes from the key. Translated, her words meant, "Comfrey placed in a soft, cloth bag and carried in the pocket is an enchantment against broken bones or sprained joints."

With the help of the key, pages of the book began to reveal their secrets: ancient ecological knowledge; an account of cultivation and harvest years; uses and recipes; stories; and a smidgen of magical references.

I came across a page from a 16th century grandma Helena. Her script reflected her love of blue violets, and I thought I could almost smell their spicy sweetness as I read the almanac's translation of Old English. As a learned elder, this grandma used the flowers to help her ailing husband with his dry coughs and asthma. She explained that steaming violets calmed their home during storms and helped them sleep at night when they worried about soldiers confiscating their winter food supplies.

Recounting adventures that took place long ago in

the Old World, Helena told how she collected seeds, first from the deepest-colored and strongest-smelling violets on the hillside meadow of a mountain several miles from their home. She tended violets in her home garden, so that the seeds Helena shared in the recipe book resulted from a lifetime of expertise and careful selection of cultivars. She shared a recipe for asthma relief, and at the bottom of the page she wrote in code, "Blue violets hung from a string around your neck and tucked into your shirt will bring you calm when you must confront someone with dangerous information."

I wondered how these women so many centuries ago could write when most people living in their time could not read, let alone use letters. Joon said that family lore decreed that each generation of women teach reading and writing to the next, even if they had to instruct their daughters in secret.

As I skimmed the pages, a recipe for prevention of theft caught my eye and another one for mental powers. Hope stirred as I zeroed in on these two remedies. Problem solving skills and protection were things I needed in my own life. I didn't really believe plants could be magical, but I knew something about ritual, and I knew when people take steps to honor or emphasize something important, they influence their own strength of purpose.

Joon's insistence in the dream that I use the book gave me something to do. As a start, I bookmarked the pages for theft prevention and mental powers. I would work on the recipes when I got home and after I re-hid the original heirloom book in the bakery.

Satisfied with my studies, I closed my eyes and enjoyed the warm sun on my face, the sound of waves carrying a retreating tide, and the occasional cry of a lazy seagull. I suppose I must have looked funny to passersby, a woman with both legs stretched out in front of her, napping with a slight smile on her lips and a large, checkered cookbook on her lap. It was a reprieve I would remember nostalgically as I worked to survive the next several incomprehensible days.

Chapter 12

"Some of my sisters in herbal lore are accused of using magic. But just as the source of power in the universe breathes perseverance into each of us, plants receive their competencies and purposes too. If we help direct those purposes to good ends, I suppose it is a kind of magic, but if so, then so is everything we do." From The Towne Family Almanac, 1487. Rose Green, daughter of Cecily Gardyner.

Light faded outside. I stood in my warm kitchen where strings of vintage Edison bulbs brightened my counter space. Bunches of leaves on butcher paper shared space with flour and coffee canisters, and I'd stuck into vases and water pitchers several thick foliage-heavy branches and long-stemmed flowers. I might have been building wreaths or constructing fall flower arrangements; instead, I was concocting secrets. I caught myself taking deep breaths of the spicy and pungent fragrance of the herbs and flowers.

After my rejuvenating nap on the beach, I got to work, first re-installing Joon's heirloom book to its previous hiding place in the bakery. Step two entailed hunting for herbs listed for the recipes I was about to prepare. Many of the cuttings I gathered came from garden plants; some had sprouted from Joon's family's heirloom seeds. I wished I still had Joon's potted greenhouse plants, as there were a few leaf and flower energies I needed from them. Joon's book indicated that the strength of each recipe increased by incorporating plants sprouted from the seeds of almanac pages, but since some seed plants had been stolen, I did not have that luxury.

Hoping no one was looking out their windows, I took a few cuttings from neighbors' plants on the other side of short fences or near the sidewalk. I tried to wipe the wily grin from my face as I collected aspen twigs and leaves from the edge of Mrs. Hester's yard, but my lips were uncooperative. I'm afraid my grin bordered on devious.

For the first recipe, the one to prevent theft, I gathered caraway, cumin, garlic, juniper, vetiver from a plant of Joon's in my garden, and Mrs. Hester's aspen. For the recipe to strengthen mental powers, I collected rosemary, rue, summer savory, spearmint, grape leaf, and eyebright.

My fear of spyware had grown to a worry that there might be hidden cameras. I acted out a decoy, using many of the herbs in a chili sauce simmering in two big pots on the stove, which I intended to preserve in pint jars. I wanted anyone who might be watching to think I was canning, not conjuring. I hated the idea of an electronic spy camera or listening device. As much as I wanted to, I couldn't even scratch my behind. It was like being on a reality TV show. The worst part was that it was a hundred-to-one odds that no one was watching anyway, that there were no cameras.

The recipe to prevent theft came from a great aunt, according to the genealogy Joon and I constructed. She passed the book to her niece, Joon's grandmother, because she had no daughters. Joon's grandmother gave the book to her daughter, who was Joon's mother. Joon's mother passed the book to Joon soon after Joon's father cast April from the family. Not long after that, Joon's mother died, broken-hearted about her youngest daughter and frantic to keep her oldest daughter, Joon, from making mistakes that might result in banishment. Family turmoil notwithstanding, the almanac and its seeds survived.

Both recipes I chose called for shredding and then mixing the herbs. Joon's ancestors recommended putting portions of the mixtures into miniature, cotton, drawstring bags so the leaves could breathe and dry within the light-weight material. Herbalists could distribute theft-prevention cotton pouches wherever valuables were kept. The bags with mixtures for inspiring mental and critical thinking powers were meant to slip into pockets or hang around necks.

Keeping a close eye on quantities and measurements, I worked hard to avoid misreading the code key. I strung a small blue bead on each bag for mental clarity and small green beads on bags to prevent theft. When I finished the bags, I set them on my kitchen table and focused on my two pots of chili sauce, bubbling and as thick as hot, Korean military stew. I decided to experiment by making one batch of sauce using only the herbs for mental clarity. For the other batch I followed my regular chili recipe, but for both batches I used fresh tomatoes, garden onions, and crisp, green peppers.

As I diced shallots, I wondered if Joey had any luck

coaxing Maynard to reveal more about his employer. Would it help to get the police involved? Maynard himself might be in danger. I didn't know if Maynard's employer was the same person who murdered Liam and Joon, but if so, wasn't Maynard a possible whistle blower?

By now, his employer was no doubt enraged. The package from my porch did not contain the heirloom recipe book and my letter explained, in clear and direct language, that this - I tried out an innovative word - this freekflushingbeetmasher, this bully, would never get the book, no matter how dark his threats. His next scourge was spiders. Of course I had no idea how they would arrive, but I imagined that at any time glass jars might crash through one of my picture windows, breaking open on my living room floor, and releasing brown, eight legged creatures that bit people with horrible results.

Working to smother images of spiders from my thoughts, I called Joey to explain my worry that Maynard might be in danger.

"I don't know, Joey, I just got an anxious feeling sitting here. Look at what happened to you, and you were just guarding the house. It might be worse for Maynard."

Joey was his cocky self. "Maynard and me, we're handlers. Stop the worry. We got it covered. But yeah. I'll keep an eye on Maynard."

When I hung up, I remembered another recipe in Joon's book, one for extra protection. Why didn't I prioritize safety over theft prevention? I began making a list of what I would need to complete the mixture. There were two versions, one for drinking and one for little pocket protection bags.

By the time I sealed and labeled my jars of chili

sauce, it was time for bed. Warren had a League of Nations competition online with his regular teammates. He needed to be in his own game room with his rig (otherwise known as his gaming machine), but he had a key to my house.

"I'll just climb into bed next to you when the war's over," he told me over the phone, distracted. I cut the call short. His game had already started, so I wasn't going to get much more out of him.

When I woke in the morning it would be a real day off, but before I went to sleep, I installed my new anti-theft bags around my house, in my car, and in my greenhouse. Did I believe they radiated power to protect me? No, but I felt better for having done something, however nonsensical. I planned to distribute enhanced thinking and protection bags to my friends tomorrow, and I was trying to foresee the best way to execute my plan. Philly would go along with carrying them in her purse or around her neck simply because she was open to trying just about anything and because she was a supportive friend. Warren and Roger were going to scoff. Warren would say, "I don't need protection, thank you, and I don't need to walk around smelling like an Italian meatball."

Tucked under my quilt, warm and satisfied with the day, I said to the ceiling, "Okay, Joon. I took your advice. Let's hope it helps."

I woke surprised and pleased to find Warren next to me. Without rousing him, I slipped out of bed and into jeans and a sweatshirt. In the dew of early morning, I collected more rosemary, rue, violet, and wisteria. On people's porches, laying at odd angles, were the Sunday papers, the comics section up front, prizes for those with a day off before the new work week.

Vine maple leaves were beginning to turn colors, as well as the leaves at the tops of trees and in the huckleberry bushes that served as underbrush in the little wooded areas between lawns and houses. I loved the time of year when summer was giving in to fall and people's minds anticipated fires in fireplaces or outdoor fire pits.

By the time I returned home, Warren had the waffle iron out. He'd beat me to the kitchen. So much for making him breakfast in bed. I caught him holding some of my new jars of chili sauce up to the light to admire their color and clarity.

"How was your walk," he said, eyeing the leaves in my gathering basket.

"Beautiful." I breathed out a happy sigh. "Everything was cool and moist and smelled so fresh. I gathered ingredients for one of the recipes in Joon's heirloom recipe book."

"Oh yeah?" The crackle of melting butter on the stove distracted Warren, and he got busy with breakfast. By the time he arranged our waffle and bacon brunch on the table, I finished filling tiny cotton bags with protection herbs and stringing them with yellow beads for identification. I loved the tangy aromas of crushed leaves escaping from the bags when I rubbed the cotton sides together.

"And the game last night?" I sat down and reached for the plate of over-easy fried eggs.

"We killed it 30 minutes into the first round." Warren lifted his chin, filled his lungs, and exhaled an *I've still got it* whoosh of air. "Our standing just keeps rocketing. At this rate, organizers might invite us to one of those national League of Nations conferences."

I don't think Warren ever met any of his teammates in person, but he talked about them as though they were long-standing, personal friends and gaming visionaries. Though I didn't understand half of what Warren was talking about, I enjoyed watching him wave pieces of waffle on his fork as he explained some of the moves and strategies of the evening.

After we cleared the dishes, Warren grabbed my hand and pulled me in for a glorious kiss before getting down to business. "The electric fence is good for today, but anyone who wants in will figure it out in short order. All he has to do is insulate his shoes with rubber and bring an insulted cutting tool, and he's in. So, we need to figure out some other ways to guard you. Roger and I will work on some ideas today." He whistled a few bars of *Poison Whiskey*.

"If you can protect me from jars of spiders, I'll keep you stocked with apple pies for the rest of your long life," I called out as Warren headed through the front door. He laughed, but I meant it.

Time to catch up on genealogy assignments, I told myself.

While backing up client charts and histories from Deputy Delilah to an external hard drive whose name was Joseph, I took time to examine the lists of Philly's DNA relatives. I hoped to bring her some interesting news, maybe something about her father's African American ancestors. We'd agreed to take a long walk in the nature conservancy that afternoon to talk more about Joon and the upcoming funeral.

By 3 o'clock, the loosely-woven, emerald

backpacks we bought together at the county Renaissance faire leaned together on the hood of my car as we sat on the grass, lacing up sturdy walking shoes. We tried to walk together at least once a week, and the conservancy was one of our favorite spots. The trails led through tall dense trees, past little ponds, and over open grassy meadows. Ours were the only cars in the trail-head parking lot. Before we started, I handed Philly two miniature cotton bags, one to enhance clear thinking and the other a protection bag.

"In a way, these are gifts from Joon," I said, describing my dream and explaining that the recipes came from Joon's family almanac.

Philly giggled, adding merriment to my somewhat solemn presentation. "Well, they can't hurt," she said, slipping one bag in her pocket and the long string of the other bag around her neck.

We started our walk, Philly re-describing the capture-caper fiasco in my yard, her arms waving, animating her enthusiasm.

"God, I wish I'd filmed that," Philly said.

The big news, though, was Philly's new knowledge about her family. She hadn't had a chance to go through Joon's interview pages or look in the manila envelope.

"Are you okay with all of this?" I stopped in the middle of the trail and turned to face her. "I mean, how do you feel about being Joon's niece and knowing what your mother went through most of her life?"

"I feel good about the way I grew up." Philly hugged herself, her tone somber. "I love my adoptive family. They didn't know very much at all about my biological parents. When I told them about the DNA search, they warned me that when adopted kids find their biological parents, it can be strange. It can mess with your head sometimes because you've built up an identity and a story of who you are. My adoptive parents did a decent job of warning me. But it's still a shock to find out my mother was a drug addict and made such bad life choices."

"And you know at the same time that who April became has nothing to do with who you are." I put my hands in my pockets and nudged Philly's arm and shoulder with mine.

"Yes, but it's mind bending just the same. And I wonder about my half-brother who was a foster kid when he wasn't living with our mother out on the streets. I even feel a little guilty I've had such a good life when he might have had some terrible, dark experiences."

"Your aunt Joon wanted to change that. And, heaven knows, you had no control of the situation. You were an infant. You didn't even know you had a brother until this week."

"Oh, yeah. I appreciate all of that. It's just these are the thoughts that go through your head."

"Yeah, I get it. How odd that some people are born in such tricky situations and others are born with everything they need." I reached over to squeeze Philly's arm.

We walked for a time in companionable silence. The woods and meadows were quiet, not even a breeze to rustle the leaves or grass. Our footsteps, disturbing a stone here or a stick there, were the only sounds my human ears noticed until I identified another set of footfalls. They were just minutes behind us. When we stopped, I could swear I heard someone else's footsteps stop. When we started walking again, the other set of footsteps joined ours. Philly looked at me, her head cocked sideways and her eyes narrowed. She pointed at the trail behind us. She'd noticed it too.

We were halfway around the circuit back to our cars.

"What do you think," Philly whispered. "Should we just wait and let this person catch up and pass us by?"

"We could if they keep walking when we stop. But they seem to be pausing with us."

"Maybe they're shy." Philly's crooked half smile indicated she knew it was a feeble suggestion.

Even our whispers seemed to broadcast through the woods on this quiet day. Whoever followed us might have caught at least snatches of our conversation, although what they could possibly gain from listening to us talk about Philly's family was a mystery to me. I found myself curling my fingers around the little protection bag in my sweater pocket; having it there really did make me feel better.

"Let's just keep walking," I said, "and see what happens."

While our comfortable sharing and chatting was at an end, we got our portion of exercise. We began to walk a little faster and then faster still, wanting to get to the safety of our cars and trying to figure out if someone really was stalking us. I could see Philly's famous temper begin to simmer.

"I'm done with this," she said over her shoulder. "I'm gonna turn right around and go after the sneak. I'm going to see who it is and turn the tables on them."

"Well. Okay?" I was unsure about giving Philly my blessing, but I relented. "I am tired of feeling hunted.

Let's become the stalkers."

With a turn of our heels, we changed our direction, hustling until we were speed walking toward the source of those shadow steps. Faster meant louder, so we weren't aware for several minutes that the owner of the interloping footsteps started running back toward the cars. By the time we realized it, our gatecrasher had a good head start on us. Philly looked at me as though in apology. "I'm going to start running, Betts, to see if I can catch up. I want to see who it is. I'll wait for you before I get too close."

"Be careful, Philly. It's not important enough to get hurt over."

She sped off, and I worked hard to keep myself moving at a moderate pace, following in her wake. When I finally came up behind her at the trail head, she was gulping air, working hard to catch her breath.

"Couldn't ... catch ... him," she gasped, pointing to the back fender and brake lights of a grayish sedan, turning right at the stop sign onto the main highway. "Couldn't ... even ... see ... him ... through … his ... car window. No ... license plate. Just ... a Santorum ... election ... sticker."

We both just looked at each other, barely able to talk as we struggled for breath, hair askew and leaves stuck to our windbreakers. An upwelling of mirth took control. Holding our sides, giggles turned into wheezing laughter.

When I could finally speak, I said, "Whoever it was, is up to no good if they felt they had to run and speed away before we got a chance to talk with them." Philly nodded her head, still bent over, arms folded around her middle as though protecting herself.

In another minute, Philly straightened and started stretching. "I'm beginning to understand what you've been going through. Frankly, I feel violated."

"Can you imagine what investigator Crumley would say if we told him about this?" I snorted.

Philly lowered her voice and imitated Crumley's clipped, nasal staccato. "Ms. Harvey, not everyone in this world wants that out-of-date cookbook you're so obsessed with. Other people are going to be walking in the park. Not all of them, I doubt any of them, are after you."

We laughed, but there was a bitter tininess to my chuckles. "I'm sorry our little trap last night didn't help much. I'd love to confront Crumley with real proof," I said.

To my surprise Philly jumped into the air as high as she could, pumping her right fist into the air. "Oooooh," she belted out. "Oooooooh. I've just got a fantisimo idea. I think we should set up a new trap. I think Joon's funeral is the perfect place to catch this guy." She spun herself through a full dance circle in the parking lot, her arms extended upwards.

I inwardly sighed and put my hands over my ears. I did not want to hear this.

Chapter 13

"When life experiences repeat themselves, when you re-live something you have already done and never wanted to do again, then it's time to plow the soil and plant new seeds, but make sure some seeds belong to plants you've never grown before." Towne Family Almanac, 1889, Amelia Delano, daughter of Cora James Penny.

Joon loathed the idea of cremation. She once told us that furnace-incineration reminded her too much of the witch executions in the sixteen hundreds in Europe, when they often burned victims at the stake. "Besides, when were ashes ever interesting or mysterious?" Joon had asked. A few of the great grandma authors of Towne family heirloom recipes were burned as witches. Some were hung. "Of course they were just healers," Joon said.

It was with this knowledge in mind, Philly called the funeral home the day after she learned she was Joon's niece. She introduced herself and promised to pay for her aunt's casket.

"We don't want her cremated," Philly stressed over the phone.

"There are worse things than cremation," said Mr. Bodley, the undertaker. "But hey, who's complaining. The cost of a casket and cemetery plot puts more jingle in my pockets."

Now it was the morning after our park chase and Joon's funeral had been scheduled for the next day. Maggie volunteered to cater the funeral reception, so between coffee and pastry orders, I scanned the memorial service menu and located recipes in Maggie's olive green, tin recipe box, the one her great uncle gave her. It had so many dents and scrapes, I figured it served as an army box in the bloody trenches of World War II. As I looked for finger food, cookie, and punch recipes, I thought about the more toxic formula that was stewing at home in my crock pot. My bubbling crock-pot brew was an essential ingredient of Philly's funeral scheme. But we needed one other item if we had a prayer of making the plan work. That item had to come from Warren.

I pursed my lips and concentrated on the high, latte-colored bakery ceiling. Focusing on the maize of copper plumbing pipes, I rehearsed in silence the persuasive speech Warren was in for as soon as he dropped by for his a.m. coffee.

I almost felt sorry for Warren as he slid into his favorite French bistro armchair chair and sent me a warm and lingering smile. He had no idea what was coming. I let him enjoy a cherry and rhubarb-filled star tart and a few gulps of deep, dark Americano before I launched in. Lowering my voice, I outlined Philly's strategy. Warren had taken his first bite of a second star tart, but the pastry balanced on his tongue, un-chewed between his teeth. When I mentioned the item we needed from him, Warren sucked in air, and that's when he drew part of the tart into a lung. Warren leaped up, bent at the waist, coughed for air after every inhale, and stumbled into the men's bathroom. Other customers looked after him, calling out in concern, asking if he needed help. Benjamin Finch, a local potter, dashed after him.

All I could think to do was replace his partially eaten tart with a fresh, ginger-lemon custard, which, when Warren returned, would go down his throat more smoothly and bypass his lungs. I also brought a large glass of water to the table.

When Warren emerged from the men's room, the hair around his temples and over his eyes was damp. Nobody I know feels self-possessed or dignified after choking on breakfast, so I rubbed the thick, dark hair on his muscled forearm in reassurance and apologized for surprising him. Warren pushed the custard away and said with direct firmness, "No. The answer is no. There's no way I'm going to do anything to support a plan like that."

I stopped myself from arguing with him. I'd blown my chance at persuasion. At this stage of the game, Philly and I would have to get what we needed elsewhere. Standing up, I patted Warren on the back, which only stirred up another bout of coughing. I left him to enjoy his coffee and custard the best he could.

Pinky was out back at the usual time. I let him know about Joon's funeral arrangements, explaining Maggie's instructions for delivering refreshments to the reception. I heard him mumble, "Why so much fuss for a homeless nobody?" He picked up a crate of bread and called over his shoulder, "Hey, how about bear claws this morning?" He cocked his head. "And a mocha. I'm on the foodie track, Sweets." He almost giggled, which was as charming as a grin on a hyena. "I'm going gourmet," he said in that bombastic tone he sometimes used to signal superiority. Pinky nodded toward the cup I keep in the kitchen for my own morning coffee. "Get out of your rut, Sweets. Try something new for a change." I kept my face as straight as I could, wondering if bear claws qualified as gourmet foodie fare and mocha as a magic formula for getting out of one's rut.

"Well, what are you waiting for?" He shot his words at me. "I got deliveries to make."

"You've also got several more crates to load." He was the delivery man, not my boss. "Cool your jets or all you'll get from me is day-old bread and butter."

Was there a recipe in Joon's family almanac to improve goodwill? If so, I could sprinkle herbs in Pinky's coffee in the mornings and we'd all benefit. I also began to wonder about myself. Almanac recipes came to mind more often as remedies to everyday problems and circumstances, yet I'd seen no indication these recipes influenced outcomes or brought solutions. My homemade mind-power and protection bags had yet to prove themselves.

The next ten hours were busy for all of us, baking extra pastries and cookies for Joon's reception, planning the funeral service program, and printing the bulletins. In furtive, whispered conversations, Philly and I sketched out the details of Philly's ambuscade.

"Ambuscade, ambuscade, ambuscade," Philly recited, punching her right fist in the air each time she said ambuscade. "I love my new word. It means suddenly popping out of a forest to deliver an ambush, and that's how I see us once we spring the trap. We're ambuscadors."

Lacking any kind of ambush experience, my visions

of the possible outcomes were less romantic. I pictured myself tripping over a tree root, or falling in a hole, or the whole thing backfiring into some kind of reverse entrapment.

"Have you talked to Roger about the funeral and your plan?" As Philly and I worked to put the finishing touches on our conspiracy, I hoped Roger might be a safety backup.

"Naw. I figure he's already heard from Warren, and if he wanted to help, he'd have come around. Besides, we can do this. We don't need either one of them." She sounded annoyed, and I looked at her, my nose wrinkling with curiosity.

"He's halfway smitten with you," I said, giving her a playful push. Why was she vexed with Roger? "I think you have more sway with him than I do with Warren."

"Warren's smitten with you too, more than you'll admit," Philly snapped. "And stop calling it my plan. You're in as deep as I am, sister. Where *is* Warren, by the way?"

Where was Warren, indeed? It was after dinner and no word. Together Philly and I hobbled together the centerpiece of our scheme, using wood, nails, and cardboard, but it had none of the workmanship and convincing authenticity that Warren's handiwork would have given it.

"I'm ninety nine percent sure whoever killed Joon will be at the funeral." Philly looked with brooding intensity at our lopsided contraption. "But will our target believe this thing is what we say it is?"

I sighed. "It's late. I figure with a good night's sleep it'll look better in the morning."

It didn't.

I started the day earlier than necessary. Sleeping in is a challenge when you work at a bakery. Checking my crock-pot, I determined my recipe for our trap was done. Glory be. It was about time. My house reeked as though scrubbed with concentrated cleaning fluid, and my eyes watered every time I lifted the pot lid. Being careful not to touch the concoction, I ladled the yellowish goo into an old ketchup squeeze bottle and slipped the bottle into a zip-lock plastic bag for safety.

Back at the bakery, the cookies, meat pies and miniature cakes were ready for transport. At home I laid out an A-line, green and white, damask jumper; I ironed my fancy white apron for serving. Today I would be both a mourner and host, and that required creative costuming.

Funeral directors scheduled the service for 3 p.m., hours away, and though I tried to concentrate on genealogy work, my feet kept leading me to the entrance of my kitchen. I felt compelled to mix the ingredients of another Towne Family Almanac heirloom recipe, one that claimed to improve chances of success. Before dressing for the funeral service, I sat Philly down at the table and poured tea-for-success, a pungent brew made mostly of clover, cinnamon and ginger.

"Success," I said, clicking my cup against hers.

"Success?" she answered, inspecting her tea with suspicious little sniffs.

Philly requested an open viewing as part of our strategy. At the Harmon's Funeral viewing room, people who knew Joon, and some who did not, filed past to see the work of art our stately funeral director, Sydney Bonneville, had made of Joon in death. He dressed Joon in a cream, jacquard, two-piece suit, nothing she would have worn in all the days I knew her. Her jewelry included a string of imitation pearls resting on top of a lilac shell. With some kind of modern funeral technology, Sydney smoothed Joon's facial features into a picture of calm serenity, the lines around her eyes softened with makeup, her long hair gone, replaced by a blunt, above the shoulders cut. I recalled, in life, Joon's simple ponytail and the intensity of fierce passion that so often flared in that face when she talked about the trials, tribulations, and needs of the unhoused people she shepherded. Images of Joon's wild, meercat eyes in my dream pushed themselves to the surface of my thoughts, but I drove them back. That was a dream, and this was a time to honor Joon as she was in life. I would remember her as my friend who stayed firmly rooted in a profound sense of justice and who disguised a kind soul underneath her abrupt, truthful words and her gruff demeanor.

Tears rolled down my cheeks. They matched the streaks on Stan's cheeks.

"I would have had Denny be here," he said, putting a hand on the edge of her polished, deep oak casket. "He was one of her closest friends. His grief must be terrible. Denny had a right to say goodbye." All I could do was nod in agreement and put my arm around Stan's thin, shaking shoulders.

Lt. Crumbley lingered by the casket, along with several other city employees, the pastor of the Salvation Army Church, and volunteers for the food outreach services. Lester Stoats was in the room, but he avoided the casket line. Roger was on the far side of the reception area, stiff and straight. He looked over the crowd but kept glancing over at Philly every few minutes with a troubled expression. Philly stood close to the casket, her funeral speech in hand. Why wasn't she standing with Roger? But then, Warren wasn't standing with me either. Was he that peeved about Philly's (and my) plan that he skipped out on Joon's service? Pinky, who helped unpack the reception food, stood against the wall looking on, arms crossed and a bored expression on his face. I wanted to hold a bicycle horn to his ear and squeeze it.

The line was short now, with Mrs. Hester third from the end. I watched her promenade along the casket, head held high. She took a perfunctory look at Joon, strumming her bright pink nails insolently along the casket edge. Her shiny, coral-dyed high heels, embellished with large white bows, pommeled the wooden floor as she walked across the room to take a seat in the back row of the service chapel. I looked for a sense of remorse or some softening under her pinkish blush and foundation, but saw only a thin, straight line between her made-up lips and a cold, assessing stare.

We all followed the strains of notes from Stan's guitar in the worship space. The Salvation Army church choir sang *Be Thou My Vision*, and our short, squat Methodist minister, Arney Smith, with his thin, high voice, read John 14:27 from the Bible. When the time came, several of Joon's friends and acquaintances stood up to talk about her life and her determination to make each day easier for others.

"She was tough, but she was kind," were the words stated most often.

Philly would be the last speaker, and I looked around to find our homemade prop to get ready and bring to her.

Our rather flimsy, wooden box with cardboard layers inside was not on the table where we'd left it. I panicked, running to the kitchen to see if someone commandeered it as a goody container or, more likely, to throw in the trash. As I spun around to get a view of every inch of the counters, someone grabbed my waist and held me still. I knew by the shape of the sturdy, large hands that it was Warren.

"Hey. Stop. I've got your crazy looking box-thing," he said. I turned to look up at him. He was sharing that warm, *you're everything* smile, the one he summoned for special occasions. Warren was also pointing, so I followed the line of his finger to the kitchen's central butcher block. On top of the hefty chunk of scarred and battered hardwood was a glowing, unblemished spruce-wood box, as beautiful as a handmade Boudreau jewelry box. It was much more extravagant than the box I'd asked him to make yesterday, right before he nearly choked to death on his tart.

I hugged his hard, blockish midriff.

"Warren, you're a wonder," I said. "You surprise me every single day. It's beautiful."

"We'd better get it out there and keep Philly from making a fool of herself," he recommended.

"Yes. We better," I breathed, ever so grateful for this man who was becoming such an essential part of my life.

I brought the bottle of crock-pot formula out of my bag, squeezed the yellow goo onto a piece of prepared paper, and slipped the paper into the special compartment Warren created inside the box. Also in the box was a heavy, brown-paper-covered package. "I wrapped up a bunch of old wood-working catalogs," Warren told me, patting the package. An ornate lock, complete with brass key, adorned the outside of this simple, tasteful container. Warren and I returned to the chapel hand in hand, Warren carrying the box under one arm - our bait for the trap.

"Friends and neighbors." Philly worked to capture the attention of Joon's mourners. "Most of you do not know this because I only found out after Joon died, but she was my aunt, my biological mother's sister." At these words, there was complete silence. Philly had her audience. "I learned about it because Betts Harvey is helping me find my birth parents through a DNA search. Joon came up as a relative on my DNA site, my aunt on my mother's side. I just wish I had started the search sooner."

"Sweet sister, I didn't know," blurted pastor Smith in his sing song, scripture-quoting voice. "Can we say a special prayer in honor of you and your aunt?"

Philly lifted her chin, raised her eyebrows, and offered him one of those slow, half nods that usually signals, "I know you're going to do it anyway, so …."

Pastor Smith ambled up to Philly's side and placed his right hand on the top of her head. "Oh Lord," he began. "See fit to bless this young woman. Let her know, really knoooow her aunt, now in the bosom of your loving arms." Pastor Smith's voice rose in volume and pitch. "And may Aunt Joon look down on you, young Philly and, with the help of the Lord, protect you from the fires of malice in this sinful world." He looked out at the crowd and beckoned a response from his audience by waving his hands in a circular motion.

"Amen," the crowd answered him.

"Thank you, pastor," Philly said as he left her side to

take his seat in the front row. She cleared her throat. "I know Joon is looking down on all of us. She left some broken hearts, but she also left an important family heirloom. Betts became the custodian of this heirloom, and Joon instructed her to pass it on to a female relative as soon as she could find the right one. Betts has passed this heirloom to me, and now I want to honor Joon by returning it to her, letting her take it with her to her final resting place. I'm laying this most ancient heirloom, this recipe book, in the coffin with Joon. It's a symbol of her service to so many of us, and it represents her hope for a more compassionate future."

At this point Warren handed Philly the beautiful box with its mitered corners and ornate key. Startled, she gave Warren a questioning look.

"Is this …?" she mouthed. When Warren nodded, Philly took his box with obvious reverence and proffered a half smile and a wink in my direction. "Thank you," she whispered to Warren. She held it up so everyone could see, key and all, and then she took the key and slipped it into her suit jacket pocket. She turned to the casket and positioned the box at Joon's waist, placing each of Joon's hands on top of it. Philly crossed herself then and stepped back. Many in the crowd said another "Amen," but breaking the magic of the moment, I heard a hissed "stupid, stupid, stupid" from the back of the chapel. I turned to see Mrs. Hester stand up, her hands clenched tight at her sides.

Warren and the minister moved forward and closed the casket lid. Pallbearers lifted Joon's coffin and walked it to the hearse, which would take it across the lane to the old town cemetery where workers would lower it into the grave, cut for Joon's final burial. A last grave-side ritual would take place following the reception.

Maggie stood and invited everyone to partake in coffee and snacks. Our serving trays of baked goods, cheese and crackers, and fruit, as well as the coffee urns, tea pots and punch bowl were the center pieces of Joon's reception. The food required little oversight as people talked and ate, standing in small, cozy groups. On purpose, Philly left the wooden box key in plain sight near Joon's photo display, placing it when she knew more than one of our suspects watched her.

Thanks to Warren, our plan was unfolding nicely, but for the first time, I fully realized the enormity of what we were doing. Had we set up a catastrophe? If our suspect took the bait, he or she wasn't going to surrender without a fight. Philly and I had been as naïve as eighth graders who thought they could drive an eighteen-wheeler without instruction or help. We saw ourselves simply running away from the scene with the evidence, leaving our enemy passive and admitting defeat. How likely was that? I looked around for a weapon to defend us. The proverbial frying pan or a rolling pin could do some damage, but neither one would stop bullets if the perpetrator had a gun. I began to panic.

As the reception wound down, Philly and I took our places in the short line of mourners walking toward the grave site. We crossed the road between the funeral chapel and the graveyard, trudged up the grassy hill through the old pioneer churchyard, and strode into the expanded modern graveyard, complete with mausoleum. I breathed easier when Warren joined us. Pastor Smith, Stan, and a few other Tent City residents accompanied us to Joon's graveside. Her coffin was already lowered into a deep, rectangular hole near the edge of the mowed grass. Only a few feet away, a scruffier, wooded area still had control of the landscape. A solitary crow watched us from a broken-topped fir tree. The big, black corvid gurgled a greeting to the newcomer, Roger, who was last to join the group surrounding the edge of the hole.

Standing on the grass, we each threw a symbolic handful of dirt into the grave and onto the casket. The backhoe would come the next morning to push in the waist-high berm of backfill that separated the grave site from the underbrush of the woods. Reverend Smith said a few words and then everyone but Philly, Warren, Roger, and I left the site to return to the reception or go home. We took refuge in bushes in the understory of the nearby grove of trees, which offered cover and a place to conceal ourselves as we watched over our trap.

Before leaving the reception, I covered my green jumper and white apron with a knee-length gray sweater coat. I also tucked a short rolling pin in my deep apron pocket, where it hung as awkward dead weight, banging against my right thigh when I walked and twisting my dress to one side as we sat silent behind the bushes.

Dusk took hold of the skies, and it was dark enough that most Brocklebrook residents would be thinking of going indoors, if they weren't already there. Our suspect should be coming from the direction of the reception, which our hired crew had surely cleaned up by now.

After whispered, last-minute negotiations, the four of us had our parts to play. We'd brought recording equipment under our dark coats and sweaters, which was tested and ready. Philly and I, and now Roger and Warren, were determined to get the proof we wanted to free Denny from prison.

More crows cackled in the trees above us, almost, I thought, to give away our position in merry trickster fashion. But humans usually pay little attention to crows, even when it would be in their best interest to do so. When the crows' raucous clamor increased, I looked with care through the underbrush to see if something was happening. Sure enough, a dark form began to cross over the graveyard. I squinted through the descending darkness, as the figure made slow progress toward Joon's grave, stopping at each classic gravestone on the way. If this man was our subject, he was making his journey look like a simple, curious stroll, with no real objective.

The last rays of sun slipped behind the hills, and nightfall quieted the crows; they flew away to their evening resting place.

We watched the obscure shape shine a pen light on the graves as he passed. I worked hard to ignore my cramped muscles as I struggled to keep myself rigid, all the while focusing an eye on our approaching target. In the glow of his penlight, I could see the man wore a long overcoat over a hoodie, the hood pulled forward to cover his stooped head. Shielded by the shadows of the trees and night sky, he might have been a Benedictine monk, a dementor, or even a ring wraith.

As the figure ambled closer, I wrapped my cold, left hand tight around the rolling pin for comfort. The longer the man took to get to the grave, the more my imagination added to the possible arsenal I presumed he could hide under his overcoat. Pictures of submachine guns, grenades, bayonets, and even poison-tipped spears flashed through my brain. Since I could barely make out Philly under the trees next to me, I assumed and hoped we were invisible to this graveyard invader.

After what seemed an agonizing eternity, the specter in thick-soled black boots approached the burial place. Had I seen those boots before? He stood on the lip of Joon's grave, his penlight-exposed silhouette in full view of our hiding place. The man scanned the obscure graveyard. Was he making sure he was alone?

From his position at the dirt edge of Joon's grave, the shadowy form reach into his coat and pull out something long and black. I breathed in relief when I saw it was only a crowbar. Then I shivered. Could a rolling pin take on a crowbar?

Quick as a black snake, our suspect was over the edge of dirt and into the grave. Time to move. We crawled with as much stealth as four night-blind people could manage.

We slipped behind the berm of excavated soil that would soon fill Joon's casket and peered over it. Inside the hole, with the aid of his penlight tucked behind one ear, the hooded figure pried open the lid of Joon's casket.

"He didn't need to do that," Philly whispered in my ear. "We left it unlocked."
We heard the latch creek and snap. The lid swung open, banging against the far side of the grave. Joon's cream suit absorbed light from the flashlight's beam, and it seemed to glow.

In seconds, the dark figure reached in and lifted Warren's box from under Joon's hands. I feared he would simply take the box and leave, but there he was, inserting the little brass key Philly left on the reception table into the lock. Beside me, Philly turned on our digital recorder, while Warren focused our video camera on my other side. I got ready to animate the battery-powered strobe light.

From my position I couldn't see Warren's box, but I knew there were two parts to its inner workings. The main section held the paper-wrapped, woodworking catalogs. In the latched upper section was our typed list of accusations and the nucleus of our trap, my yellow goo. Not until the grave robber unlatched the top section would we act. I braced myself.

A pain-saturated shriek told me it was time. The four of us stood in unison, working to appear menacing over the lip of the grave. I switched on the strobe and held it up high with my right arm, Warren started filming, and Philly held up the recorder. I squeezed my left-hand fingers tight around my rolling pin and bawled, "You're caught."

"AAAHHH," the man yelled, his voice full of agony. Having dropped the wooden box, and the goo covered paper, he attempted to wipe thick, yellow liquid off his right hand onto his overcoat. When that failed to stop the pain, he held his right hand over his head with his left hand.

"Hurts, doesn't it?" Warren called down into the grave.

The startled man looked straight at us, his hood slipping off his head and revealing his pain-contorted face. With what we saw, someone could have lit a match and set off a whole string of Black Cats fireworks at our feet and I doubt we'd have noticed.

"Freaking, flipping, hellfire," shrieked Philly, who kicked at the berm of dirt so fiercely clods of it rained down on the figure below.

"Damned nation and Deja vu," Warren growled.

"Aren't we the fools," I said.

Looking up at us was the frightened, agonized face of Maynard, Joey's younger brother.

"What the hell, Maynard?" Philly shrieked down at him.

At first Maynard choked on his words, but finally we heard, "What's this stuff on my hand? Get it off me!"

"Climb up here so I can wash it and give you the antidote," I said, disgust and disappointment edging my voice.

"Oh no you don't," Philly said. "He's going to tell us who hired him before you do that, Betts. We want full disclosure."

Maynard breathed hard. I made the goo, so I knew his hand burned with ever greater intensity.

"Someone hired me to do this, and I can't tell you anything. It's like before." His voice, overcome with agony, hissed out the words.

"You need to start talking." Warren used the authoritative voice he employed with difficult fire department volunteers.

"There are blisters on my hand," Maynard wailed up at us in panic.

"There are going to be a lot more if you wait much longer," I said, my impatience growing.

"I'd tell you if I could," he yelled. "But I can't."

"I thought you promised us you wouldn't do more jobs for this guy," Roger said.

"I didn't do it for him," gasped Maynard. "Someone else hired me for this job, a woman."

A woman indeed. "Okay then." I relented. "I think

we can all imagine who hired you to get the book. Come up here, Maynard, and I'll stop the pain."

He sank down to a sitting position, putting his left fist inside the box on the ground, connecting with more smeared, yellow goo. Both hands were burning now, and Maynard was on the verge of sobbing. He sat on the ground gasping and whimpering, hands held out in front of him.

Warren dropped into the grave and helped Maynard climb out with his knees and elbows. I took out my squirt bottle of rich, soothing salve, made of aloe and several other cooling ingredients for burns and skin irritants.

"Here," I said. "Hold out your hands."

I squirted generous amounts of the rich antidote ointment on his skin. The burning stopped in seconds. "You'll be okay," I told him. "The stuff on your hands is a simple mixture of cow parsnip pitch, grapefruit juice and other ingredients. It burns and even blisters the skin, but unless it goes untreated for several hours, there's no lasting damage." I gave him my bottle of antidote to take home with him. "Can you drive?"

Maynard nodded, his eyelids at half mast, his tone accusatory. "You're all wicked mean."

"Don't mess with us again, Maynard," Philly warned him.

"I wasn't trying to," the young man mumbled, looking at his boots.

We watched his pen light bob up and over the rolling mounds and valleys of the graveyard toward the street as we packed our gear, gathering Warren's beautiful box using rubber gloves. My dream and Joon's meerkat eyes haunted me until we closed the lid over her casket. Philly would report the broken latch early in the morning so graveyard staff could repair it before filling the grave.

"Maynard is turning out to be a regular fly in the ointment," Philly sighed when we headed toward the road and our cars. "But hey, let's go get some ice cream. I could use some comforting scoops of Rocky Road with hot fudge sauce on them."

We became a fellowship convoy, with Warren and I following Philly's car to town. Roger had already power walked to his car to follow Maynard and see where the young man ended up.

As Philly slowed to turn into Brocklebrook's fifties-themed ice cream parlor, I noticed a knot of people on the sidewalk under a streetlight. I could swear I saw Roger, Marta Hester, and Maynard deep in conversation. I couldn't for the life of me think why those three would be together talking. When I got into the ice cream parlor, I found Philly staring out the window at them, her arms folded in that "he's making a muck of things" posture.

"What's going on?" I asked Philly, nodding toward the suspicious huddle on the sidewalk. She shrugged.

"I have no idea what those three are up to, but Roger and I had a fight last night, and I'm starting to wonder about him. He's got secrets." Philly's expression turned fierce.

There was more to Philly's story, and I wondered what she meant by *secrets* as we ordered ice cream Sundaes with the works. We found a booth by the window.

"Do you want to talk about Roger?"

Philly took a deep, disapproving breath. "Last night we were at my place. I was so excited to show him the information on the DNA site. We looked at the descriptions of some of my second cousins and the maps that show where family members are located in the world and, you know, DNA connections to different global populations. Roger obviously knew a lot about the site; he showed me how to listen to my DNA music." Philly looked at me and shrugged. "We were having fun, and I appreciated his interest. But then I asked to see his DNA site. I knew he was looking for his birth father. And he just said, 'No. Not now.' It was just so abrupt, and his face got dark and brooding. He does get that way sometimes."

"And what did you say to him?"

"I was kind of shocked and hurt, more than I like to admit," Philly said. "Here we spent a good hour looking at my family connections, and he didn't want to share his with me. I felt like he didn't trust me. He just said, 'Someday soon. Not now.'" Philly turned to Warren. "You're a man. Is there some obvious reason Roger wouldn't share? I'm afraid I couldn't get past his secretiveness last night. I said some rude things, and he left early. Today, he's kept his distance."

We looked out the window at the three still talking on the sidewalk.

"That just looks suspicious to me," Philly said.

"Are you sure you're not just sore at Roger?" In truth I agreed with Philly. Roger talking with Mrs. Hester seemed a bit traitorous. On the other hand, I didn't want to add fuel to Philly's fire if there was an innocent explanation. "He could be trying to do some detective work for our investigation."

Philly sniffed. "Or he might have more secrets than we realize."

"You really like him, though." I kept my tone gentle. "He might have a good explanation for keeping his DNA information secret. Could be he's embarrassed about something."

"Yeah, well, I just don't like feeling untrusted." Philly turned her back on the window. "I trusted him with some pretty sensitive information."

As Warren and I watched, the group ended its exchange and Roger reached over and shook Mrs. Hester's hand. He clapped Maynard on the back and then turned in one swift movement toward the nearby parking lot. He got into his gold SUV and drove off, as though in a hurry.

At that point, Warren got up to get our orders.

"I'm trying not to read too much into their little meeting and Roger's behavior," I said, "but I'm starting to wonder if he still belongs on our suspects list."

"The way I'm feeling, go ahead and include him. I want to believe he's just excited to be helping, but he sure asks a whole lot of questions without revealing much about himself." Philly scowled. "The thing is, he really respects Warren. He asks questions about him, seems to want to know Warren's whole life history. He likes you too. He's intrigued with the idea of Joon's heirloom and wants to learn more about it and why people are so interested in it."

"Don't we all. You've never seen it, have you?" I focused hard on Philly. "I know Joon would have adored giving you a chance to hold it and read it. She would have loved pointing out the parts she liked best and explaining the secret key symbols to you. It really is a beautiful book."

"Is the book safe?" Philly asked.

"As safe as I can manage." I pictured the slot between boxes in the bakery cupboard where I'd slid the mailing box. "I would let you take it home, but we announced at the funeral the book belongs to you. If Maynard spreads the word it wasn't buried with Joon, our burglar might take a chance and try to steal it from you."

"It's just so stupid," Philly said. "Let's find this murderer and this person who's been trying to take the book. I'm tired of you having to be the brunt of so much abuse."

"Amen," said a strong, rumbly voice behind us, making us jump. It was Warren, coming to join us with a foamy root beer float and two ice cream Sundaes piled high with whipped cream.

"What do you make of Roger spending so much time with that Hester woman and Maynard and leaving without joining us?" I asked Warren as he stirred the ice cream into his root beer.

Warren didn't respond until his float was half gone. "He's a good guy to work with," Warren finally volunteered. "I wouldn't want to cast doubt on him just yet."

"Secrets are tough on a relationship," I said. "Once someone discovers their partner has a secret, something usually needs resolving. It's a kind of relationship test. Take Warren and me. Warren, you don't hide any major secrets from me, do you?"

Warren took me by surprise by closing his eyes and whistling off key. Then he looked sideways at me. "A man has always got a secret or two. My most pressing secret right now is in my tool shed. I don't want anyone to see it, especially not you, Betts. Does that mean you and I are going to have to split up because of irreconcilable differences? I don't think so. If Roger has a secret he doesn't want to share about his DNA information, then I think you might just have to accept it, Philly, unless something else comes up that makes it important."

"Something in your tool shed, huh?" I leaned back and studied Warren's ruddy face.

Warren looked uneasy. "It's a matter of trust, and I trust you not to look, Betts. I shouldn't have said anything, but this dispute about secrets came up, and I needed an example." My man was as serious as I'd ever seen him.

Good, Lord, I thought. I rarely went to the back of Warren's house, but now I really wanted to. Warren's tool shed was really a workshop. I only peeked in when I was looking for him and he was out there working. We would both have been better off if he hadn't mentioned anything about a secret.

I looked at Philly. She looked at me, and we both sighed; and then we laughed because it was all so nonsensical, this complicated network of secrets and questions.

Since faith in each other was the topic, I plucked my heirloom herbal bags for Warren out of my pack and passed them across the table.

"Talking about trust, I trust you won't laugh at these gifts I made for you, and I hope you will indulge me by putting this one in your pocket, (I pointed to the bag with the yellow bead), and this one around your neck." I pointed to the bag with the blue bead.

With a long-handled spoon, Warren scooped the last

of the ice cream from his mug before picking up the protection bag and turning it around in his hands.

"What in tarnation are these?" He looked confused.

"You know about the dream I had."

He nodded. "Never saw you so scared about a dream. Never saw you take a dream so seriously."

"Well, I'm following Joon's dream advice, just to make myself feel better. I made these from recipes in the heirloom book. The charm bag you're holding is for protection. The one for your neck is for clarity of mind. I know you don't need either, but I'd feel like I was doing my job if you wore them. Besides, I want to just test some of the recipes and try to figure out why there are so many people who want that book. It's a kind of research experiment."

Then I grinned with a sudden wicked idea. "And I might just make a deal with you. I promise I won't look in your tool shed if you go along with my research."

Warren shook his head, partly in puzzlement and partly in exasperation. He opened each bag and looked inside, shook his head again and then put one in his pants pocket and the other in his front shirt pocket. "I'll carry them for a few days to make you happy," he said, "but I'm not wearing anything around my neck."

I reached over and patted his rough cheek in thanks. Next, I pulled two more talismans out of my bag and gave them to Philly. "If you see Roger tonight, please pass these on to him. If you're the one to ask him, he might be more willing to help me with my experiment."

"I'm not sure I want to see Roger tonight." Philly sniffed, but she took the little bags and put them in her backpack.

When we stepped out of the ice cream shop, the smell of early wood-stove fires and grilled hamburgers seasoned the moist, fall air. As I climbed into my little car and watched Warren and Philly get into their bigger models, I thought of the autumn applesauce cookies I would bake the next morning as a new snack item for Dirty Dozen.

This next week we would solve this case. I was sure of it. We had to.

Chapter 14

"Comparing foes to non-human creatures that we despise indulges human prejudice, but each comparison is also a judgment of Earth's beasts and organisms, who all have reasons for being, of which we are mostly ignorant." Towne Family Almanac, 1897, Hannah Hundman, niece of Amelia Delano.

I learned when I was seven that life doesn't stop just because I sit on a snail. When I was about five years old, I did just that, sit on a big, fat snail who was crossing the cool cement of our front porch. I stood there screaming until my mother brought out a clean pair of pants, but I had to be the one to take the old ones off and put them in the washer.

Now I'm older, I tell myself over and over I've always had to clean up my own squished, terrestrial, pulmonated, gastropod mollusks, shake off my own earwigs, and relocate or dispatch my own spiders. I remind myself I have ultimate responsibility for my own predicaments.

With brutish, even violent individuals forcing their way into my life, I'd reminded myself several times in the last few days about my snail experience and the fact that I had to be accountable for my own affairs. So snails, earwigs, and spiders were on my mind as I talked myself through last week's nightmare. They were so deep in my thoughts I began to compare my fellow human beings with squishy mollusks and long-legged arachnids. Creepy crawly things became metaphors for several humans in my current circumstances.

My daily responsibilities kept me sane, and I was grateful. This particular morning, I would make cookies and serve coffee. In the evening, I would help with an Extension Agency organic gardening workshop, which highlighted fall gardening practices. My part was to demonstrate seed collecting, saving, drying, and storing. I had mounds of heirloom seeds gathered from my garden to share with the workshop participants, but I held back the seeds from Joon's plants. Those were not mine to distribute, as there was no one yet to ask permission. The almanac's new guardianship was still unofficial.

Since our stalker in the woods and the SNAFU in the graveyard, things were quiet, but I was like a captured starling, expecting something to happen at any minute, jumping at little sounds, and worrying about surprises behind every closed door, at home and at work.

After witnessing the suspicious and peculiar sidewalk conference between Maynard, Mrs. Hester, and Roger - so soon after the funeral - I decided to let the police know about Mrs. Hester's threats to get a lawyer and her claim that Joon's book should be hers. I would also mention my discovery of water hemlock on her property, hoping the detectives would be discreet and keep Mrs. Hester's law-enforcement husband out of the loop. At the police station, I asked to talk with the police chief, Clarence McCleary, but to my chagrin, a dispatcher escorted me to

Detective Crumley's office instead.

"This new information could connect to your burglary," Crumley said about Mrs. Hester, his upper torso held stiff and straight, his voice stern. "But I seriously doubt it has anything to do with the murders."

"Well, I thought you'd want to know," I said. "Every little bit helps, doesn't it?" Crumley's logic escaped me. How could water hemlock, found on Mrs. Hester's land, connect to the burglaries and not to the murders? I asked if I could visit Denny and bring him a bag of bakery treats.

"His arraignment is coming up in the next hour, so no." Crumley's glower shifted to a scowl. "He's sure to plead not guilty. We're asking the judge to refuse bail since the man is homeless. He doesn't have anything important to keep him here. He could just take off. We'd have a hell of a time running him down in another state or if he decides to skip off to Mexico."

I rolled my eyes behind Crumley's back. The man was a metaphorical earwig. As with most bugs, I tried to avoid him, but he kept surfacing - much like the earwigs in my garden curled tight around the stems of apples or covertly camped out under flowerpots. I couldn't shake him. Earwig pincers repulsed me and so did Crumley's inane arrogance, but I could forgive the earwigs.

Warren answered his cell phone, and I explained the situation. The least we could do was go to Denny's arraignment to show support.

Warren and I sat near the back of the dim, mostly empty courtroom. The court reporter set up recording devices and a camera, conferring with the court clerk about the upcoming court schedule. My eyes lingered on the palatial judge's bench, finished in dark cherry; it loomed over the floor level below. Beneath the bench, the court staff arranged tables for lawyers and their clients. To the right of the lawyers' tables was the enclosed jury box, looking much like glorified church pews. At the lowest floor level, below the jury box, were the benches for observers such as Warren and me.

A few people trickled in, but it looked to be a light load on the dockets. Court officers brought Denny through a side door. Our friend was dressed in a steel-gray jump suit, complete with ankle chains, his hands cuffed in front. My throat constricted in indignation at his treatment. Displayed like that, the observers and the judge could only see him as dangerous and unstable. I knew him as anything but. Allegorically, Denny was on par with an orb-weaving spider, one who spins webs in gardens and poses no risks to humans. I always leave orb-weaving spiders alone to do their clever work among my vegetables.

A court-appointed defense lawyer stood by our friend's side. Denny's shoulders stayed hunched around his rigid neck, and he kept his eyes on the ground in front of him. When the judge pointed him toward one of the lawyer's tables, Denny turned his head enough to see us. Warren nodded at Denny in a solemn greeting, and I lifted my hand to show support. Denny straightened a barely perceptible inch; I saw a glimmer of relief and hope transform his face, but only for a millisecond. My heart went out to him. Crumley had denied all visits, and without access to friends, he had no way of knowing that many of us still stood behind him and believed in him.

We stayed long enough to watch the judge charge Denny with two counts of premeditated murder and determine that he remain imprisoned with no chance for bail. Denny pleaded not guilty. His assigned legal representative showed little inclination to defend Denny's rights to bail, and the man's face soured when informing the court that Denny was determined to stick with his plea. I detected little to no personal warmth between Denny and his representative, the attorney keeping his distance as though Denny had fleas or contagious foot rot. A snail metaphor came to mind when I thought of this lawyer; he was the kind of slimy invertebrate I might, with glee, threaten with salt. Was I being uncharitable? When the guards escorted Denny from the courtroom, Warren and I took our leave as well.

My sigh was heavy as we stepped out of the courthouse.

"I'm starting to realize they could convict Denny of his old friend's murder if we don't do something." I knew he loved Joon as though she was a sister, and before the hearing, I believed the search for truth would put everything to rights. After the court rulings, I wasn't so sure.

"It comes down to motive." Warren opened the door for me as we left the courthouse. "The police think hot-headedness is all it took for Denny to want to kill. They've stopped looking for other suspects. You and I know there's a whole lot more steam under the cow pie. What perturbs me is the real murderer is still out there, ready and willing to whack people until he gets his prize."

"Joon's book?" I asked.

"Looks like it to me," Warren said, "but figuring out why is beyond my imagination."

"Well, the next thing on my list is to insist on jail visiting hours so we can keep Denny's spirits up. I'm afraid he thinks he's all alone in this." My voice rose. "He needs Stan and us."

"Some homemade cinnamon rolls couldn't do any harm either," Warren laughed.

Cinnamon rolls were missing from my to-do list that night. I had a gardening gig to attend, an expert gardeners' teach-in and workshop.

Returning home, I filled two large baskets with fall produce, and another smaller basket with informational handouts, a rolled-up poster, and a large pile of seed envelopes to share at the workshop. I dressed in loose, multi-pocketed work jeans and a leaf-green gardening vest, zipped closed over my cornflower blue work shirt. I slipped on my purple, waterproof gardening shoes to add color to my presentation. My wide-brimmed, straw sun hat, with its ice-blue ribbon, completed the ensemble. I wanted to model the whimsical freedom of expression that comes with gardening, as well as the serious principles for using and saving heirloom seeds. My free-spirited reflection in the mirror cheered me.

A buzz on my phone told me Philly was outside my gate, ready to attend the workshop with me. She helped carry my seeds and vegetables into the basement meeting room of Brocklebrook Public Library. While I had yet to achieve the status of Master Gardner, many of the other organizers and presenters were masters. Most of them were already moving tables and setting up folding chairs with their mid-grade, tan, upholstered seats. We hung our posters on the vintage, faux-wood, paneled wall, now painted the color of coffee ice cream. Gardener ushers distributed our flyer with the night's itinerary. We hoped for a good crowd.

Below my poster of the progressive stages of seed collecting, I arranged my display of envelopes full of seeds and pictures of the plants that parented them. In one basket I provided empty envelopes and marking pens. My plan was to supply heirloom seeds grown locally as samples that people could take home for next year's gardens. I offered tomatoes, kale, greens from the mustard family, carrots, collards, peppers, cucumbers, salad leaf mixes, tomatillos, ground cherries, and various common herbs. Seeds are part of the magic of gardening because most plants create an abundance of them. One amaranth flower head can sometimes produce half a million seeds.

Within the next half hour, participants occupied four fifths of the chairs, and our workshop began. I was pleased to see Philly paying close attention to each presenter. Knowledge that she might become the guardian for Joon's family almanac inspired her, and I could see she was eager to learn. Marta Hester was also in the audience, though she had her arms crossed in an aggressive manner over her lime green and hot pink Japanese tunic. I heard her whisper to the woman next to her. "There's nothing new to learn here."

"Oh, no?" the other woman whispered back. "It's all new to me. I've just started my garden, and I need all the help I can get."

After my presentation, it was time for a break. I invited attendees to visit my display and take seeds home for spring planting. Chairs creaked and people shuffled toward the coffee and tea table and to view the various posters and displays. Mrs. Hester walked with evident purpose to face me, almost pushing away an older gentleman who wanted to ask me questions about seed gathering.

"I don't appreciate your vindictiveness," she said in a loud, carrying voice. "I don't appreciate what you told the police. You're trying to make it look like I murder people. Well, you're not going to win this war. I *will* get the Towne Family Almanac, and when I do, I'll sue you for damaging my reputation and for giving away seeds that aren't yours." She motioned toward my display table and the people gathered around it sifting seed samples into envelopes. "How many of those seeds came from my family's recipe book?"

There was no help for it. An image of a metaphorical black widow spider intruded upon my consciousness. Black widow bites are painful, and their venom attacks the nervous system causing nausea and death, if untreated. This woman did nasty things to my nervous system, and nausea was inevitable if she kept talking. Still, I was in a situation where I wanted to maintain a sense of professionalism. Time to put on a public mask, even though I really wanted to hit her with a rolled-up newspaper.

"Mrs. Hester." I offered my hand in greeting. "How nice that you could come. We need to sit down over coffee and talk. I think you're misinterpreting things. And I can assure you, none of the seeds I'm giving away have anything to do with Joon's family heirloom seeds or the recipe book. I was careful about that."

Philly was busy gathering seeds at the table. Her head raised up with sudden alarm. She looked in my direction and then back down at an item in her hand. I could tell by her worried expression something had spoiled her enthusiasm. She packed several seed envelopes into her handbag but kept one envelope out and approached Mrs. Hester and me.

"Betts, what is this?" Philly spoke in a low whisper and handed me an envelope.

The envelopes I provided were standard letter mailing envelopes. The envelope in Philly's hand was also a mailing envelope, but it was a different brand than the ones I used. On the front of my seed envelopes, I hand-wrote the name of the vegetable or herb. On the front of this odd envelope were two typed words, *Mystery Seeds*. Inside were seeds that I had neither gathered nor saved. I knew what they were though, and so did Philly, who helped me research what the seeds looked like. They were water hemlock seeds, not yet dried, with a pungent, carroty smell.

Mrs. Hester peered into the envelope as well, a smirk on her pink-painted lips. She announced in a shrill, high voice, "Be careful of those seeds everyone. It looks like Betts Harvey is trying to give us all seeds that can poison us." With that she headed toward the door, but just before leaving, she looked back. "I'm going to tell the police about this." Her voice came out shrill and loud enough for everyone to hear. "Very slippery of you. It's vile. You're a dreadful woman."

I was in shock for a moment, my mouth open in a round, incredulous 'o'. Philly nudged me.

"Do something," she said. "People are asking questions." She put her fingers in her mouth and delivered a piercing whistle. Her whistle did the trick. Everyone quieted, looking in our direction. I cleared my throat and announced there had been a mistake at the seed table.

"We've discovered an envelope at the table full of seeds from a local plant called water hemlock. The seeds and the plant are poisonous. If you got seeds from an envelope titled *Mystery Seeds*, you'll want to throw those away," I said.

"How did the seeds get there?" a man asked. "Are the other seeds safe?"

I assured him that the vegetable and herb seeds were safe. "I don't know where the envelope came from. It's not the same brand of envelope as the others I used, and the label is typed rather than handwritten like mine. I would never want to share seeds from plants that could cause problems in your gardens."

"Was it that woman who just left who put those seeds on your table?" asked one of the master gardeners.

"As to that, I don't know." I didn't know, but I had a strong suspicion Marta Hester planted the seeds in my basket. "I wish it hadn't happened, but it does give me an opportunity to talk a bit about water hemlock and help you all identify it."

After that I explained everything I knew about the water hemlock plant, where it was most likely to grow and how to distinguish it from Queen Anne's Lace. "Most of the time it doesn't cause problems," I explained.

"Isn't it what those two homeless people died of last week?" asked a young woman who had several seed envelopes in her hand.

"Yes. That's what the police think," I said. "That's why it's especially distressing the seeds ended up here at our workshop. I'm glad I had a chance to talk about it and show you what it looks like."

Only two people had taken water hemlock seeds from

the table, as most of our garden workshop participants wanted to know what they were planting and were uninterested in *mystery seeds*. We finished our presentations, and several people thanked me for my seed gathering advice. As we wrapped up the meeting and announced our mid-winter workshop date, two police officers entered the room. It was clear Mrs. Hester went straight to the police department to report the seed envelope, and the police were there to follow up. They took down my explanation, examined the other seed envelopes and confiscated the water hemlock envelope as evidence. I could tell by their stony expressions they were skeptical of my version of events.

When they were gone, I leaned over to Philly and said, "Next thing you know, they'll lock me in a cell and charge me with conspiring with Denny to kill Liam and Joon. It doesn't help I was the one who found Joon's body and that she died at the bakery or that Liam had a bakery wrapper in his pocket."

"They can't possibly think you had anything to do with this foul up." Philly smacked her left hand against the door jam. "It's a sure bet that Marta Hester brought those seeds. I don't know if she did it out of revenge or because she's the murderer and wants to mess with the evidence."

I sighed. "I don't know if she brought the water hemlock seeds, but it's clear that Marta's husband found out I went to the police this morning with questions about her."

I scanned my display table. Workshop attendees helped themselves to the vegetables as well as the seeds, so all I had left to carry to my car were the empty baskets, the markers, and my poster. On our way home, Philly talked about starting a small garden in her backyard next year. She asked to borrow some gardening books she could study over the winter.

"Even if I don't end up being the guardian for the book, my family history with gardening and plant lore has me itching to grow things," she said. "From everything you've told me about Joon's book, I feel as if gardening connects me to my family roots, like I'm closer to those grandmothers and aunties."

I smiled. "Be warned. Once a gardener always a gardener. If you're not careful, you'll end up like the rest of us, at the beck and call of pesky garden spirits who call out in the late winter, compelling us to start our seeds indoors and get the soil ready. Then in spring, their voices get louder until we can't stop ourselves. We put a garden in by May. Next thing we know, we're building a compost pile, and a worm farm, and maybe even enslaving ourselves to a flock of chickens."

I asked about Roger. Philly looked disheartened. "I don't know," she said. "He's left messages on my phone, but I haven't felt up to answering them. I know I'm a hard ass when it comes to relationships with men; maybe our fight the other night is just my excuse to keep him at arm's length. On the other hand, I can't risk sacrificing valuable energy for a guy I can't trust and who doesn't trust me."

"But I think you enjoy his company," I ventured.

"Yes. But it'll be too late to save my heart from a lot of freaking pain if I spend much more time with him and he turns out to be an operator."

How could I judge Philly for being conflicted? So was I. Was Roger a toxic hobo spider or an interesting, but harmless grass spider? His unexplained rendezvous with Maynard and Mrs. Hester on the night of the funeral had me worried. His secretiveness toward Philly was another red flag.

I gave her a hug. We said our goodbyes at the front gate to my house, and Philly drove off while I opened my front door. Inside my compact house, I felt an empty quiet and realized how much I missed Dr. Dillinger, his paws patting my cheeks and his insistent caterwaul. He always ran to the door and greeted me when I got home. I even missed his forays onto my computer keyboard when he wanted attention. He was a good mouser too, even toward the end of his 16 years. An animal shelter was in my immediate future, I realized. Raising two sister kittens to be close companions was a long-standing desire, and this was my opportunity.

Joey would be back to guard the house by 6 a.m. the next morning but for now my place was my own. The evening's events had me reconsidering the direction of our haphazard investigation. I made myself a cup of tea and was just settling down with paper and pen to try and sort through clues when the phone rang. Caller I.D. indicated it was Philly, so I answered.

"Betts?" Philly said.

"What's up?"

"Betts, I got home and found a giant bouquet of flowers on the porch waiting for me."

"Roger wants to make amends," I said.

"They're not from Roger."

"Well then, who?"

"They're from Lester Stoats."

I was speechless; the phone connection was silent for

a few moments as Philly waited for me to recover. "Is he thanking you for your good work?" I knew the suggestion was improbable.

"I don't think so." Philly let loose an involuntary snicker. "The note says he wants to take me out for dinner and dancing this Friday night."

"Bosses and employees aren't supposed to be interested in each other these days, are they?" I asked. "Isn't he taking a significant risk? He'll be in the gossip spotlight if you let on at the office, and he's got to know that."

"Well … yeah …" Philly paused, thinking it over. "But he also knows that if I say something, I'm selling my own job down the river. And if I say 'no' to his invitation, then what?"

"Better to tell him you don't date bosses. That way you're not rejecting him personally. You're just doing the right thing."

"I must have poured it on too thickly when I tried to get information from him yesterday," she said. "What if he thinks I was cupcaking? Jeebus! I'd hit myself in the forehead if I wasn't so opposed to pain."

I laughed. "The suspect I interviewed for our investigation tried to humiliate me in public tonight, and your suspect wants to go dancing. I think your methods produced more favorable results."

"Ugh."

Ugh said it all. Stoats was a brown recluse disguised as a less-lethal wolf spider. A brown recluse bite can fester into what doctors call a volcano lesion. Recovery takes weeks and the sufferer will carry large, permanent scars. I feared that Brocklebrook citizens and businesses under Stoats' self-serving leadership were in for a great deal of long-lasting pain and scarring. Tent City residents could be some of his first obvious victims.

After we hung up, I went straight to bed, praying for dreams sans spiders. *Good grief,* I admonished myself. I'd had enough of comparing everyone with earwigs and web spinners. Time to stop before it became a habit.

Chapter 15

"Some gifts are offered to castigate, and yet they bring un-looked-for blessing. When that happens, the giver can choose to feel thwarted, or glad for another chance at friendship." Towne Family Almanac, 1974, Helen Simmons, daughter of Helen Harvey.

One day I was simply Betts: baker; gardener; and genealogist. The next day I was Ms. Elizabeth Magdeleine Harvey, murder suspect.

As my shift ended late in the morning, Crumley and a young lieutenant, Eva Schwartz, came to the bakery and strong-armed me to the front door, suggesting I accompany them to the station for questioning. I answered Crumley by calling Warren and asking him to locate my lawyer, the same attorney who helped Joon and me draw up our contract protecting Joon's family heirloom book.

By lunchtime, Brocklebrook officers hurried me into the police interrogation chamber. Waiting for something to happen, I focused my tired eyes on two tiny windows, set deep and high in the rough, cold cement walls of the room. These windows seemed like architectural afterthoughts, but they let in bits of cheerful light in a space otherwise lit by harsh, fluorescent, low-hanging light fixtures - the kind that belonged in a welding shop. Crumley and Schwartz left me sitting in a folding metal chair, my elbows resting on a rectangular wooden table, more scratched than the ice surface of a skating rink. Part of me wanted to laugh at the absurdity of law enforcement holding me in a room for questioning, much like a common criminal. Part of me feared the ineptness of officers who had gone this far in mistaking me as a suspected felon.

"Ms. Harvey, you're not under arrest … yet, but you're a suspect. I can only hope you will answer my questions willingly when the time comes." Turning his back on me with an air of patronizing exasperation, Crumley left me sitting more than an hour ago. *When the time comes*, he'd said. The *time* Crumley referred to would only come when the investigator was darned ready.

On the phone, my lawyer, Miles Fox, suggested that I act in "a spirit of cooperation" and that he would meet me at the station. Perhaps that's why the authorities ditched me in this cramped room for so long. Mr. Fox was, so far, missing in action. I had just decided that I was going to open the gray, metal fire door and leave the room on my own, when it opened. Crumley, Schwartz, and Fox filed in. Since there was only one other chair, Schwartz remained standing by the door. Clumps of dark hair framed a rather plain countenance, Schwartz's long nose her most prominent feature. She was short with a waist larger than her hips, but who was I to judge? My own waistline had expanded inch by inch throughout the past 60 years.

Crumley, his right eye twitching every three seconds, positioned himself in the chair opposite me, slapping a brown-kraft file folder on the table between us. Fox moved over to my right side. He leaned over and whispered in my ear.

"We'll allow questions, but as soon as things get out of hand, I'll give you the word. At that point I'll advise you to stop talking." Fox's breath smelled of cheese, mustard, and onions. The discourteous slob had stopped off for a cheeseburger and who knows what else before making it to the police station on my behalf. Was I too critical? Better to have a well-fed lawyer beside me than a distracted hungry one. I sighed.

Fox stood and straightened, puffing himself up to make the most of his six-foot, three-inch height. He looked down at Crumley from my side. "Let's get this started," he said in a tone of condescending impatience, raising one eyebrow as if to imply skepticism of Crumley's methods and motives.

Crumley drew himself up taller in his chair and assumed a sneering half smile.

Posturing, I thought, annoyed. *Male bravado. Just what I need at a time like this.*

"Yes, let's get started," Crumley said. "I have better things to do than wait for dilly dallying lawyers."

Crumley opened the folder with gravity, as though it contained urgent and vital information. He focused his eyes on mine in a long, hostile stare, as though he was an exterminator, and I was an insect. "Ms. Harvey, a witness brought to our attention a public distribution of water hemlock seeds. You were passing them to unsuspecting new gardeners, no less. This took place yesterday in the library. We believe this brings a whole new light to our investigation of the Tent City murders."

"Mr. Crumley." I kept my tone as cool and even as I could muster. "I certainly never brought water hemlock seeds to my talk yesterday. Someone planted them there, most likely the same person who made a fuss about them and brought them to your attention."

Ignoring me, he continued, "We begin to see how you and Denny might have been in cahoots. You planned and carried out the poisonings together. We are reviewing - in a new light - all your recent complaints. Anonymous phone calls, stolen plants, jars of spiders, and break-ins. Isn't it true, Ms. Harvey, that you created these little diversions and distractions? You've been trying to steer us off our course. Isn't it correct that you, in fact, want Ms. O'Neal's recipe book for yourself for some perverted reason? I'm beginning to think you killed her. Then you tried to make it look as though someone else wanted that book and killed her for it."

Crumley folded his hands over the papers in front of him and squinted at me, hard and accusing, his right eye twitching again. The back of my neck prickled with a new kind of fear. I had been naïve. This twisting of circumstances and evidence was something I never anticipated. When I recovered enough, I shook my head, working to blink back angry tears.

Taking three deep breaths, I steadied my reactions. "Investigator I feel staggered by your accusations. None of your speculations have any truth in them. And now I feel more frightened than ever of the person who is really doing these things because I realize the police won't be helping to make sure I'm safe."

Crumley picked up the folder and slammed it on the table as though killing a beetle or fly. He looked forbidding. "There's the bakery wrapper found in Liam's pocket," he said, his tone curt and biting. "Joon's body was discovered in the alley beside the bakery. And there's the fact that you were the one who found her."

My lawyer tapped my shoulder and shook his head as though to warn me against saying any more. I stood then, my chair scrapping behind me and banging against the cement wall. "This is enough." My voice seemed to echo in that cold cell. "You're on the wrong track, like you have been from the start. You have all my police statements, and I stand behind them. Those are my truthful responses to your allegations. I have nothing more to say to you. My lawyer and I are leaving this room, and I will not return to it - ever - because there is no evidence to bring me back here. I never hurt Liam or Joon. I have no desire to keep Joon's book. I have always had her permission to use it, learn from it, and even copy it. I don't need to steal it."

"I have the original written contract to prove that," Fox interrupted.

I turned to face the door, more furious than I could ever remember being. "Move aside Lt. Schwartz," I said to Crumley's partner. Fox raised an aggressive eyebrow at her, and she stepped away from the door. We passed through, and I followed Fox past the front desk, into the lobby, and out of the police station.

I take pride in controlling my emotions, but to my chagrin, I shook with rage.

"Deep breaths," Fox said, taking one himself. "Deep breaths."

"Macaroni and cheese," I said. Fox looked at me, eyebrows raised.

"What?"

"Macaroni and cheese," I repeated. "It's comfort food, and I'm hungry. Cassy's Diner. Now."

"I'll drive you." Fox motioned to a sexy, black Lexus parked in front of City Hall.

I'd expected a much older and decrepit car. Fox struck me as being a kind of Columbo rather than a James Bond. Wrinkled suits were a standard for him, and his bushy, ginger hair was always in need of a cut. He opened the side door, and I saw on the passenger seat the paper wrappings that once secured hamburgers and fries. He tossed them onto the backseat floor, a gesture that seemed more his style. I could see other litter on the floor, and toppled stacks of file folders mingled higgledy-piggledy in the back seat. A basket of recycling dominated the middle. The car smelled new, but in another month, I suspected odors of stale coffee and corn dogs would prevail. The thing was, I respected Fox as a lawyer. Despite his apparent disorganization, Fox struck me as trustworthy, and he had a reputation for being a skilled attorney.

"New car?" I asked.

"Yeah," he grinned. "Always wanted one of these." He proceeded to tell me about all the amenities, the gas millage, and the bargain he'd finagled from the dealer. Fox was in such rapture about the car, the incident at the police station seemed wiped from his memory, but in my mind Crumley's words echoed. *You've been creating these diversions and distractions to steer us off course.*

We sat across from each other in Cassy's 1950's-themed diner, each enjoying a plate of hot macaroni smothered in rich, melted cheese and white sauce. I took a bite and closed my eyes, allowing the aroma and taste of soft, toasty cheese to overwhelm me. We ate in silence until our plates were half empty before Fox started asking questions.

"What's up, Betts? What's been going on, and what does Joon's book have to do with Crumley's allegations? By the way, those accusations are completely out of line. Investigators often do that, you know, to get a reaction. I doubt Crumley believes half of what he said."

"I'm not impressed." I scowled at my plate. "It's been a tough week, ever since the fire at the storage unit and Joon being killed." I proceeded to tell Fox everything, ending with an account of Mrs. Hester and the envelope of water hemlock seeds.

"Well, well." Fox looked thoughtful and drummed his freckled fingers on the table near his empty dinner plate. "I agree the police investigation is off kilter. I appreciate you filling me in. You don't need a lawyer yet as they haven't arrested you. But if Brocklebrook city investigators take firmer action, I've got some background now. I'll be ready to defend you, should the need arise."

I shook hands with Fox as he let me out near my own car near Dirty Dozen.

"Keep in touch," he said and then drove off, deftly speeding his new black toy around the nearest street corner.

I drove home, heavy with pasta, and ready for a nap. I found Joey in the kitchen, stacking meat and cheese on bread, constructing one of the tallest sandwiches I'd ever seen.

"Hey." He topped his sandwich with a piece of rye

bread and patted it down. "Everything's been good here, except you got a present." The word 'except' had me on immediate alert.

"What kind of present?"

"Well, some guy delivered it. Said someone ordered the fellow yesterday, and the man wanted to know where you needed him. You never said anything about it, so I just told the goat delivery guy to let the animal go in your yard. Last I saw, he was in your roses."

"He?"

"Pretty sure it's a him. He's got horns and a beard and everything."

"And everything?

"Well, I didn't check the 'everything' part," Joey said, sheepish.

My bodyguard picked up a wrinkled, official looking, yellow sheet of paper on the counter and handed it over. "Here's the receipt just so you know where he came from."

I looked over the receipt titled UBER Goat Delivery Service, signed by Joey at the bottom to show the transport was accepted. Someone ordered one male goat to be delivered at noon. The receipt indicated that the paying customer wanted to remain anonymous because the goat was a surprise gift for me.

The bearded, beastly surprise awaited me in my yard.

I walked toward my back door, visions of total backyard destruction in my head. It was a good thing fall was here. I'd already harvested the bulk of my garden produce. I had the seeds I needed for next spring. In a way, the goat might just be a welcome donation, though I'm sure the goat's sender meant to cause me pain. If this goat ate all the annuals, he might just make my life easier when I put the garden to bed for the winter. Even the perennials would be okay.

Just the same, I dreaded what I might find.

I couldn't blame Joey. He knew nothing about the ways of goats and the vulnerability of gardens. Likely the UBER goat deliverer would have simply tied the goat to the fence if Joey hadn't been there, and goats are notorious escape artists.

I took a deep breath, turned the knob of my back door, and stepped out to meet my unwelcome guest, formidable horns and all. At first, I didn't see him. I saw trampled rows of fallen tomatillos and bean frames askew, but not the goat. Lord. What if he got over the fence into someone else's yard? I'd feel responsible.

My grape vines wiggled, and not in rhythm with the wind. I squinted my eyes and focused on the squirming vines. There, sticking out from the thick yellowing grape leaves was a white rump with a furry tail. The tail waggled in a cheerful manner, like a truce flag. Grapes were always the last to ripen, and I was waiting for them to sugar and sweeten so I could make them into honeyed grape juice and wine. My yield was taking a beating – well, an 'eating'?

I approached the twitching tail with caution, making enough noise to alert the goat to my presence. One minute the tail was in view, the next minute the back end disappeared into the grape vines to be replaced by a short-haired, white head, complete with a long, thick beard, gyrating mouth, and gray eyes rimmed in pink. Both eyes regarded me with interest. As I watched, the goat aimed its mouth at a bunch of plump, purple globes and with his teeth, stripped off several chubby fruits, juice dripping from his chin and into his beard. If a goat can grin, he was doing it. A large bell hung under his beard from a blue and red collar around his neck. Painted on the bell in big, black letters was the name Mr. Chew B.

I said to him, "Well, Mr. Chew. Haven't you had enough already?" Mr. Chew answered by grabbing another mouthful of grapes. With trepidation I eyed his substantial horns. They extended back from between his ears like dense, curved javelins. What might happen if I grabbed his collar and led him to the fence where I could secure him? I reached out my hand to pet him above his wide, pink nose, and he backed away, tossing his head in warning. I sighed. I knew so little about supervising goats. It might be just as well to call the UBER goat delivery service and have them handle Mr. Chew. After the day I'd had, a goat in my garden seemed almost trivial. I was not going to call the police about my four-legged visitor. Who knew what Crumley would make of this new turn of events and my anonymous gift.

"Okay, Mr. Chew, help yourself," I said, and then reached out and gathered a few grape bunches to bring in the house for Joey and me.

No one answered the phone number listed on the UBER goat delivery receipt, so I left a phone message stating that, as handsome as the goat was, the Uber driver needed to pick up Mr. Chew and take him away as soon as possible.

Joey made quick work of the grapes and let me know he had a date that night and would be back to resume his guard duty in the morning.

After he was gone, I cleaned up his mound of

crumbs on the coffee table, straightened the couch pillows, locked my doors and windows, and settled myself under a soft, cotton quilt for a much-needed nap.

Warren was out of town for a volunteer fire-fighting workshop. My troubles had taken up hours of his energy in the last several days. He didn't need more unwelcome news while he was gone, so I would wait to tell him about the police interrogation when he got back. I wasn't sure what Philly was up to that evening, and I thought I would tell her the news later. I was tired of burdening my friends with the crazy-making details of endless, bizarre predicaments. That night I would go about my life as though nothing had happened. I would pretend there was no goat in my garden.

My make-believe, holiday-from-reality lasted through dinner and a Netflix movie. Not until I sat down at my computer to check my Facebook account did all hell break loose. A powerful thump against the wall outside my kitchen shook the foundations of the house, and someone out there in the dark screamed in terror. I considered putting on my earphones and pretending that I hadn't heard a thing, but the second scream convinced me I had to face facts and turn on the backyard lights.

I grabbed a shovel stored against the wall in my mud room, turned on the yard lights, and poked my head out my back door.

"What's going on out here?" I yelled in my firmest, teacher-on-the-playground voice. I felt so irritated at intruders and trespassers interrupting me once again I swore loud enough for the neighbors to hear.

"Help," said a weak voice around the corner to my left. "It's going to kill me."

Retrieving a flashlight from the mud room shelf, I tromped one determined step after another out the door and around the back of the house. With an aggressive thrust of my arm, I pointed my light toward the sound of the voice. Two shadowy forms turned toward me. The four-legged one looked at me and lowered his horned head, aiming it at the two legged one, who backed up against the outside wall of my house.

"Get it off me," squeaked Lt. Schwartz.

I'm afraid that I grinned. I just couldn't help myself. "I would if I could." I said, trying not to laugh, "but I know next to nothing about goats."

"What do you mean?" Ms. Schwartz wailed, "you've got a goat."

"Not my goat. Mr. Chew was in my yard when I got home. I don't have a clue who sent him." I shrugged my shoulders.

"Mr. Chew?" Shwartz's tone was incredulous. She started to step away from the wall, and Mr. Chew pawed the ground, huffing in what I interpreted as a goat command. Ms. Schwartz was to stay put.

"I have some idea of why the goat is in my yard, but I'm not sure why you're here," I said.

The lieutenant mumbled something I couldn't hear.

"Didn't get that," I said.

"Okay, okay." The lieutenant sounded resentful. "We're keeping an eye on our suspects. I was just looking around."

"I see." My words came out like dry ice. "I think I'll let my lawyer know about this. In the meantime, I'll try to distract Mr. Chew so you can leave. Don't forget to close the front gate on your way out."

Joey must have forgotten to turn on the electric fence when he left. I walked back to my mud room and grabbed a few apples from one of the apple baskets. I reappeared and called over to the goat, holding out the apples. Mr. Chew raised his head and looked over.

He lost interest in the lieutenant and stepped toward my outstretched hands. As he took one of the apples in his mouth, Ms. Schwartz slipped toward the front of my house. As the goat finished his first apple and reached for the second, I heard the delicate creek of front gate hinges. This time when I reached out to rub Mr. Chew's forehead, he closed his eyes into agreeable squints and then gently pushed his nose into my belly.

"Thank you, my new friend," I whispered in his ear.

As I turned on the switch to the electric fence, locked the back door, and prepared for bed, I realized I was going to sleep well. I had a supreme, four-legged bodyguard by night, who could clear my garden debris by day. Someone intended mischief by sending me Mr. Chew, but I looked forward to thanking them in person in the future. Before climbing into bed, I left another message at the UBER goat delivery phone number asking to keep Mr. Chew for a while.

"Charge it to my anonymous benefactor," I said.

Chapter 16

"Jealousy can be that house cat you just finished brushing and snuggling who attacks his sister because she sweeps around your leg for her share of cuddles." Towne Family Almanac, 1798, Mattee Singeton Hireman, daughter of Ellyner Salter.

Mr. Chew met me at the gate at 3:45 a.m. as I left for the bakery. I stroked his ears and let him know I appreciated his morning hello. He bleated a goodbye, and I took off with the surety that my house and garden were well protected. I left a note for Joey explaining that Mr. Chew B. was there to stay for a while in case the UBER service failed to get my message.

Cool dew beaded the leaves and grasses along my route, and a tiny spark of joy brightened the moment as I breathed in the sweet smells of pre-dawn. Fully rested for the first time in days, I refused to think about police, murderers, or burglars. I was determined to enjoy my morning baking routines and the customers. My traveling bag bulged with zip-locked, plastic bags of ground cherries for that day's special. I'd slipped a recipe into my skirt pocket for ground cherry coffee cake. Ground cherries are a nearly forgotten, heirloom fruit related to the tomatillo plant. They are marble-sized, golden globes of caramel-tasting fruit that grow inside papery shells, easy to harvest and easy to freeze.

The coffee cakes I made boasted crusty oatmeal and brown sugar toppings. Below the toppings, jellied layers of hot ground cherries took center stage over buttery, yellow cake. Customers loved their generous helpings with hot coffee or tea and could never quite identify the warm, honey-like, fruit flavors.

I was just taking two ground cherry masterpieces from the oven, when I heard a knock at the bakery door; it was too early for Stan, Denny, or Pinky. I poked my head around the kitchen door to see who it could be and was surprised to see Roger's silhouette on the other side of the large, plate-glass window. Unanswered questions about Roger percolated through my thoughts all week, and my doubts about him caused me to hesitate before showing myself. Who was he, really? I sent myself a text so there would be a record on my phone about Roger's visit, in case something happened. I tucked my phone in a corner of the coffee cup cupboard, put a smile on my face, stepped out where he could see me, and waved.

When I opened the front door, I could see Roger was wearing the hat he bought from Joon. Temperatures were near freezing, so his hands took refuge in his barn-coat pockets while he shuffled his feet. Roger reminded me of so many 12-year-old boys I'd encountered as they worked up the nerve to explain why they were late, or why they crumpled their worksheet into a ball and threw it on the windowsill, or why a locust had just crawled out of their school desk. I beckoned Roger in, and he greeted me with a half-hearted smile and worried eyes.

"Sorry Betts. I know this is selfish." His voice

sounded low and weary. "I won't take much of your time. I just haven't been able to sleep, and I couldn't think of anyone else to talk to." He paused and sighed. "I hope you can help me answer some questions. They've been bothering me."

I re-locked the door and ushered Roger to a seat in the kitchen, where I could hear him out and still finish my baking. I cut him a big piece of warm coffee cake to go with a mug of coffee. Roger kept his eyes on his breakfast cake. It was heavenly, I'll grant you that, but it didn't warrant that much attention. I knew from his stiff back and tensed arms held close to his body that Roger was reluctant, even embarrassed, to tell me why he couldn't sleep. I refilled his mug again before he finally put down his fork and looked at me.

"Does this have something to do with our case or is this about Philly?" I tried to ease the awkwardness and offer him an opening. Roger cleared his throat and wrapped large, brown fingers around his full mug.

"It's about Philly," he said, sounding resigned.

"Have you two spoken recently?"

"Not since the other night. I offended her more deeply than I realized. She was showing me everything she could about her genetic test results. She told me everything she knew about her DNA family members. Then she surprised me because she wanted to see my DNA family, and I told her I would show her later." Roger shook his head. "She took that badly." He looked over at the kitchen island where I was cutting butter into flour for shortbread. The furrows deepened between his eyes, not in anger, but in puzzlement. He re-directed his stare from me to his empty plate.

"I thought we would work out our disagreement the next day, but she's not answering my calls. Then, last night-." Roger stopped talking, looked up at me again and shook his head. "Normally I'm not so concerned when dating doesn't work out, but with Philly-. Like I said, I haven't been sleeping. Anyway, after last night, well, I need to know if Philly's ever going to give me the time of day again."

"What happened last night, Roger?" I asked, mystified.

Roger leaned back in his chair, his right-hand raking through his dark buzz cut. He slapped both hands on his knees as though deciding on the spot to go ahead and get it over with, however uncomfortable this kind of talk made him.

"Okay," he said. "Okay. Last night I went to Rubio's for dinner, by myself. And there, in the next room, was Philly sitting across a candle-lit table from another man. They were drinking wine, and she was so- so focused on everything he said. She laughed at all his jokes, and she even allowed him to taste her halibut."

"Oh?" I tried to hide my own surprise. "Did you recognize the man?" The fact that Roger's observations included a description of what Philly was eating demonstrated how close his surveillance of her dinner date had been.

"Yeah, I did," Roger said. "It was that city guy, that Stoats."

I choked on the bite of snickerdoodle cookie I was sampling.

"Oh Lord." I tried hard not to laugh. The whole situation reminded me of a romantic farce in a comedy.

"Roger I can guarantee Philly is not into Stoats. I don't know how she feels about you right now, but I'm certain she detests Stoats."

"Then why go out with him?" Roger's voice deepened with embarrassment.

"She's still investigating him. As you well know Philly is pretending to be interested in his goals to gentrify the city. She's asking him fact-finding questions."

Roger's face was a picture of doubtful misery.

"He's a self-conceited jerk, Roger, so he decided that Philly's attention in the last few days meant she must be flirting with him. Stoats thinks Philly can't resist him, so he sent her flowers, and he asked her out on a date."

Roger pushed away from the table and threw up his hands. "But she's playing with fire," he said.

"I sure hope not." Like Roger, I was concerned. "I'm a little surprised to hear Philly went out with Stoats, but she assured me she would be upfront with him. She was going to be firm about boss and employee impropriety. I'm thinking she pigeonholed the dinner in her mind as a business meeting."

Roger continued to glower, but he asked for another piece of coffee cake, so I knew he felt at least a pinch better. Rolling out the shortbread cookie dough for cutting, I thought about Philly "playing with fire" and had to agree with Roger. She was taking chances.

"Roger, Philly does like you a great deal. I've never seen her so interested in a man before she met you. I don't want to talk on her behalf, but she's worried about trust. She wants you to trust her, and she wants to be able to trust you."

Roger nodded. "I do plan to tell her everything.

Right now, the timing's just not right." He stood and slipped his barn coat from the back of his chair. I admired its genuine sheepskin lining and wondered how much it cost. "Thanks Betts. I think I'll have better luck sleeping now."

I gave him a reassuring wink and grabbed my keys to let him out the front door. "I really do hope it works out," I told him as he stepped into the street.

By 10 a.m., I, too, was on the street walking home. Business had been brisk, and the everyday greetings and banter of customers brightened my outlook. Life seemed normal again for at least a few hours. At home, the white picket gate to my front walk creaked its familiar disjointed notes. The raspberry vines near to the left of the house shuddered and shook and a bearded white head pushed out from between them. Mr. Chew chewed with ferocity as he regarded me with his almost transparent blue gray eyes. Joey opened the front door before I could get up the front porch steps.

"There's some trouble," he said in his rich, drawling voice. "You know, with the goat. But I put a stop to it."

Sitting on one of the porch rocking chairs, I motioned for Joey to take the other chair and continue his story.

"Yeah," Joey said. "I heard a car engine running outside the house. One look out the window and I knew something was about to go down. I grabbed my gun when a guy in a ski mask got out of the car."

"You grabbed your gun?" That he had one alarmed me. "What time was this?"

"Still kinda dark," Joey said. "Anyway, this guy leaned over the fence and dropped a pile of plants in your yard."

I got up from my chair to take a closer look. "It's not there," Joey said. "I took care of it." He patted himself on the back for his Johnny-on-the-spot handling of the situation and continued his story. "But when the guy did the dumping, I opened the door and was on the porch. Before I could get off the steps, the dude was in his car and gone."

"What kind of car?"

"Couldn't see it much in the dark, but I'm almost swearin' it was gray," Joey said.

"And the plants?"

Joey grinned. "Got em in a plastic garbage bag, in your green-."

"Show me."

Joey leaped off the porch and waited for me before leading the way to my mini conservatory. I could smell carrots as soon as he opened the door. The bag, which leaned against one of my worktables, was full to the brim with freshly cut water hemlock.

"For the goat, I think," Joey said.

"For Mr. Chew," I agreed.

"Someone is tryin' to make you out as an animal killer." Joey's surety startled me. Mr. Chew chose that moment to nibble at the elbow of my left sleeve. He lowered his horned head, sniffed at the bag of water hemlock, startled, and backed away.

Goats are smarter than we give them credit for, I thought. *It's very possible Mr. Chew knew enough to leave poisonous plants alone.* Between Joey and I, we herded Mr. Chew out of the greenhouse, carefully tightened the closure on the bag of hemlock, and locked the green house door.

As I surveyed my garden, Mr. Chew pushed his rough, boney head against my hand. He wanted a scratching and wasn't too shy to ask.

"Impressive," I grinned at Joey, motioning my head toward the garden.

"Whoa," was all he said.

"Whoa" summed it up nicely. Mr. Chew had turned my garden upside down in less than 24 hours. Wire tomato cages were mis-shaped, tipped, and askew. Uprooted tomato plants wilted on their sides, and red, orange, and green tomatoes peeked out from under torn and trodden squash and cucumber plants, looking like partially hidden Easter eggs. Round, yellow zucchinis, and paper-skinned tomatillos had rolled into beet and nasturtium territory. Bean trellises leaned into and supported each other like windfall, and cornstalks lay flattened among the drooping sunflowers.

I threw my arms out as though to embrace the whole chaotic scene. I would retrieve and preserve what I could when Mr. Chew left, but a good night's sleep and the thought of feeling safe made Mr. Chew's cataclysm worthwhile.

Joey chuckled as I knuckle rubbed Mr. Chew's neck and back. When my goat friend pulled hard on my sweater sleeve, Joey's amused burble turned to outright hilarity, and he almost choked he laughed so hard. I realized Joey had been afraid of my reaction to the water hemlock delivery, worried that he was somehow responsible.

"Mr. Chew, I'll leave you to it," I said. "You haven't finished yet. There's still dahlias and cornstalks left standing."

I spent the rest of the afternoon working on genealogy for a paying client. At 4 p.m., I gave Joey leave to go. Warren was coming home from his fire safety workshop, and I was ready to rescue produce from the garden and turn it into something edible and substantial. For green tomato pie, I gathered tomatoes from the toppled cages. I rescued squash to bake with butter and brown sugar, and I picked flowers for the table. Roast chicken and thyme simmered gently in the crockpot, and I had an assortment of yeast rolls from the bakery.

My heart swelled at the sound of the gate closing outside and heavy boots on my front porch. Warren was back. He wrapped me in a bear hug, then grabbed my shoulders and held me an arm-length away to just look at me.

"Got something to tell you," he said.

I could see Warren had serious news, so I held back on relating my own misadventures.

"You know the volunteer firefighters carpooled to and from the workshop," Warren began. "On our way home, one of the cars full of men was in an accident. Ambulances took Stu, Tom, Justin, and Matt to the hospital, all injured. Turned out the brakes locked on a tight corner."

I groaned. How many more terrible happenings were even possible? "What can I do to help?" I said, offering Warren a comforting squeeze.

"They're going to be okay. A few broken bones, contusions, and Tom's got a concussion. They'll live," Warren said. "The strange thing is, I was supposed to be in that car."

"Oh Warren."

"Yeah, but at the last minute I switched with Matt to take a later car. You wanna know why?"

I studied Warren's pensive face and waited.

"See, I'd left your little protection bag in my hotel room, in the drawer by the bed. I didn't want to see your disappointed face when I told you I lost it, so Matt and I switched cars so I could go back to the room and get the bag." Warren looked me in the eyes, as though appealing to me for a response.

He doesn't want to say it, I thought to myself, so I provided the words. "You're thinking the protection bag saved you from the crash." My heart rate jumped faster than normal.

Warren leaned against the kitchen door frame. "I just wanted you to know what happened."

I took a deep breath. It might have been the herbs working or it might have been a coincidence, but it didn't matter. Warren was safe.

"By the way," Warren said, looking out the window, "you've got a goat in your garden."

Chapter 17

"We thought the flames that blackened our forest hillside brought the end of our world. In the spring, when the hillside was green with grass instead of dark with trees, we saw that the fire delivered us deer, and rabbits, and a new kind of life." Towne Family Almanac, 1452, Rose Green, daughter of Cecily Gardyner.

Stan had taken to coming early in the mornings, in Denny's place, to pick up the daily bag of sandwiches and day-old bread and muffins. He looked more tired than usual, and despondent. I realized that he must feel the weight of Tent City on his shoulders even as he mourned the loss of Joon and worried about Denny. It was a lot for one soul to take on. I would check with Warren for the best time to invite Stan to dinner some night. In the meantime, I sat with him when I could, between serving customers and taking baked goods out of the ovens.

Customers crowded into Dirty Dozen; talk focused on the early edition of the Brocklebrook Journal, our weekly paper. Customer voices rose to an indignant buzz, and I soon found out why when Henry Fritch, our postmaster, thrust the front page under my nose.

Above the fold was a story featuring Brocklebrook's city manager. Effy Gordon, our local reporter, described

Stoats' announcement of a potential deal with the King Leopold Hotel Corporation for a conference, retreat, and shopping center. The city manager revealed that hotel developers were vying for the place currently occupied by Tent City. Gordon asked Stoats when the public would have a chance to respond to the proposal and where the city council expected to move Tent City if it approved the hotel project. She quoted Stoats as saying, "With the heinous behavior of our homeless residents, murders and arrests included, we need to consider terminating Tent City. These people are liabilities and don't add to the integrity of our community."

As I moved with my coffee pot between customers, people's opinions echoed from table to table, both in agreement and disagreement with Stoats.

"Why haven't we heard about this before?" asked Shelly Smythe, who owned the Sweet Nothings Card and Gift Shop.

"Do we want a big company to put up stores that'll compete with our own hometown shops and restaurants?" Belinda Hasselblad, our town barber, tapped her fork on her plate in cadence with her words.

Some customers explored the possibilities that a conference center might bring new jobs for young people. Several times I heard mention of Tent City as I served coffee from table to table. Most people said they didn't realize Tent City was a problem until the recent murders.

"The way the city manager talks about it, Tent City is just one crisis after another with dirt bags and drug dealers in charge," said a woman I'd never met, sitting near the apron display.

"I guess Mr. Stoats would know," said her female

companion. "He's the one who sees all the statistics and works with the police."

"I'm going to call that reporter," I whispered in Stan's ear, "and suggest she do a feature story or expose' about Tent City. Someone needs to dig deeper and write a more complete picture of our homeless camp. There's the good things Tent City does as well as the problems."

"Good luck with that." Stan gave a pessimistic shake of his head as he accepted a coffee refill.

I believed a good investigative piece would examine what might happen in Brocklebrook should Tent City disappear. Knowing the work Joon, Denny, and Stan did for unhoused people, I thought Brocklebrook might be worse off without an official place where people could gather and camp.

The two unsolved murders clouded people's view and sent discussions about Tent City in mostly negative directions. That police charged Denny Woodman with killing two unhoused campers, made things one hundred times worse in people's minds.

I was busy filling cups around our biggest table when I heard the bell over the front door. Talk faltered, and I turned to see Lester Stoats stride in, his own copy of the newspaper in hand. He went straight to the counter to order, looking at the other coffee drinkers out of the corners of his eyes, but not stopping to talk, say hello or even acknowledge anyone else's presence. He ordered his five-ingredient usual and two Morning Glory muffins. He unfolded his paper and scanned the front page. I was sure this was just for show, as I imagined he'd read his own quotes in the story several times already.

Edmund Russell, who owned the town hardware

store, stepped up to the counter and directed his truck-motor voice at Stoats, "Lester, a good morning to you."

With slow deliberation, Lester looked up from the paper and surveyed Edmund without changing his expression. Edmond was equal in height to Stoats and met the city manager's condescending gaze with comfortable ease. Tucking his thumbs behind the straps of his Carhartt work overalls and rocking back on his steel-toed work boots, Edmond raised his right eyebrow as though signaling a challenge.

"Lester, I've got a question," Edmond said when Stoats attempted to move past him. "See, we just found out there might be a hotel company bringing a retreat center and stores to our town. But the thing is, I don't remember city officials inviting us town citizens to talk over this kind of thing. In my mind that's a priority, you know, for us people who live here to really hash things out before we start inviting big companies to town. What do the people want for Brocklebrook? Can we expect town meetings, properly advertised and open to the public?"

Lester Stoats drew himself up. "You know, Mr. Russell," he said, loud enough for the whole room to hear, "we don't want to start doing things that discourage investors from building where they want to, and I'm sure we don't want to interfere with the timing of an important deal. Inviting uninformed, naïve citizenry to unnecessary town meetings would send an unfriendly, unhelpful message. City planners and council members have talked about this, as your representatives. Be grateful someone's looking after town business for you, so you don't have to." With that, Stoats tossed bills and coins on the counter, grabbed his coffee to go and his sack of muffins, and strode past Edmund. When he got to the front door, he looked back and spoke to the room at large. "Let's not run the city the way most of the people in this town run their businesses." The door closed hard behind him.

"What the hell did he mean by that?" Edmund growled. "I'm beginning to wonder who our city government is serving, its people or the political and economic aspirations of a despot?"

"Well said, Edmund," Belinda Hasselblad called out. She yelled instructions to bring Edmund another cup of coffee, on her. "We've kept clear of strip malls and corporate fast food boxed buildings so far. Our village has a lot of charm. That's what makes it look so good to those corporate guys in the first place. Are we going to let them turn us into a copy of every other tourist trap?"

Someone called out, "If city government has been talking about a conference center, why didn't our newspaper know about it before now? Was this all hashed out in private? Is that even legal?"

"I think we better hold our own meetings," said Tony Gonzales, who owned a lunch food cart. "Edmond makes sense. We need to decide what we want for this town. It is our community after all." Tony stood and addressed the bakery crowd. "I came here to live the life I'm living right now. Stoats doesn't approve of my business or my methods, but they work for me. I love this place. I don't want a big change."

"Sure, we can make improvements. That's always important." Shelly Smythe walked over and stood by Tony. "We want a healthy economy, but I think it should be us who decide what that means. We need our own plan.

Should Brocklebrook stay small, or do we want it to attract crowds of tourists?"

"Gonzales, Edmund, Hasselblad, Smyth, let's call our own meeting," said Dirty Dozen's owner, Maggie, coming through the kitchen door. "And let's invite a representative from Tent City to join us. Stan?" She nodded with an air of authority at Stan in his corner. "If we need a place to meet, we can do it here. Let's get to work letting everyone in town know."

Maggie put her arm around Edmund's shoulders. "I nominate you chairman of our first meeting," she said. All our bakery customers applauded. "Free cookies and coffee for the first meeting, but after that, we'll need to pass the hat to help fund the refreshments."

My heart sang to witness the take-charge spirit that came over the customers that morning. They were less apathetic than I imagined. This was real democracy in action. People felt motivated when someone like Stoats ignored them and made them mad. Sometimes a crisis starts people thinking. Sometimes they get outraged enough to demand a hearing. My eyes glazed in dreamy optimism. What if this was the start of an upsurge of local empowerment?

"Yeah. I'll do it," said Edmund, energized. "Let's spread the word."

The morning crowd dispersed, and Maggie went over the baking menu for the next morning. She tried my applesauce bar cookies and pronounced them first-rate. "Let's make several batches of these for the community meeting," she said. "Now, fill me in on what's going on with you. I heard a rumor the police escorted you out of Dirty Dozen yesterday morning."

Of course I told her everything.

"I'm more worried now about getting falsely accused of murder than I am about the threats," I said.

"If women were in charge, we'd have identified the real culprits by now. You'd feel safe." Maggie put her hands on her hips and sent a penetrating glance at the ceiling as though questioning 'the big guy.' "If women were in charge," she said, "we'd be leading our city in a more democratic way." With what I knew about testosterone and its hormonal effects on many males of our species, I felt inclined to agree with Maggie.

Nearly ready to call it a morning, I finished scrubbing down the last counter when Philly as much as threw herself through the front door, stumbling on the door mat. I dropped my wash rag to go help steady her.

This woman, who loved competition and thrived on pressure, looked almost panicked. Philly is a careful dresser, but today, puckered wrinkles spoiled her blue green, A-line dress, and there was a large, brown, stain on her left backside as though she had fallen in wet dirt. I spotted bits and pieces of dead leaves in her hair, and mud soiled her crystal back, open-toe, cream pumps. Before I could reach her, she ran over and hugged me close. She was trembling.

"Philly? What happened?" I guided my friend to the nearest table.

"You won't believe this." Her words came out so fast I could barely make them out. "Your little protection bag saved me, at least I'm pretty sure it did."

Maggie joined us with hot tea and water. "Philly, girl, sit down. You look like you've been ambushed." Philly accepted both offerings and asked for scotch, served neat.

"No scotch. The only spirits we keep around are rum for our rum cakes and brandy for our mincemeat," Maggie told her.

Philly waved her off. "Wasn't serious about the scotch." She tried to laugh but couldn't quite manage it.

Worried and impatient, I waited until Philly had a swallow or two of her tea. When I'd delayed as long as I could, I thumped the table. "Okay. What happened? Your dress is a mess, and you look as though you could use a long soak in a hot tub."

She tried a wan smile. "Well, there's nothing I'd like doing more." She crossed her arms in front of her and stretched her fingers over her shoulders, rubbing and wincing as though in pain.

"Philly," I admonished with a sharp bark. "I wanted to know what's going on."

"Pipe down and I'll start from the beginning." Philly hissed at me, so I knew she was recovering. "Look, I went to work this morning, and while I was putting together the minutes for one of our committee meetings, I discovered I took my notes home. The notes were in my Emerson Satchel, which I left on my home office desk. So, during my break I sped home to get them." Philly stopped and took a deep breath. "You know how my driveway is set off from the street and my house is kind of hidden behind those two large oaks and the Hawthorne hedges?"

Maggie and I both nodded.

"Well, a limb fell from one of the trees sometime this morning. I had a cat's chance in hell driving around it without a brush up with the car, so I decided to walk in on the path and leave my car parked on the road. Well, it was all fine until I stepped onto the porch and reached in my bag for my house keys. The keys wiggled their way to bottom of the bag, like keys do, and as I lifted them up through all my stuff, your little protection bag, Betts, fell out onto the ground. I bent down to pick it up, which turned out to be a good thing because a face in a dark ski mask looked out the front door window just at that moment. Whoever it was didn't see me because I was low to the ground with the little bag in my hand, but I got an eyeful."

Philly reached for a tiny packet of non-sugar sweetener, tore off the top, and sprinkled the stuff into her tea before continuing her story. "I didn't really think. I just rolled myself off the porch, and scootched myself around the other side of that Nannyberry bush that grows right up to the porch railing. The man might have heard something because he opened the front door to look around. And Betts, Maggie-." Philly swallowed hard, and tears pooled in her eyes. "He had a big baseball bat in his hand. I honestly don't know what he would have done if he had seen me ... if I hadn't bent down to pick up that little bag."

She'd placed the protection bag of herbs in her lap, and I watched as she gathered it up in her left hand every time she put down her cup.

"I crawled around the hedge, staying out of the view of windows, until I got in my car." Philly shivered. "Heavens above, I locked the doors as soon as I got in, and I drove right here."

"Did you call the police?" I asked.

"My phone is on my desk at work. I just started the car and drove here."

Just as Maggie and I each reached for our phones to

alert the police for Philly, the Brocklebrook fire siren began its long, drawn-out wail to call in the volunteers. Philly shivered again, and I realized she might be in shock. I strode over to the coat rack, grabbed my purple sweater wrap and enfolded Philly's wet shoulders under the soft wool. Warren would already be in his truck, using his phone to bark out instructions to the volunteers who were also on their way to the fire station. I hoped it was a false alarm. My own little cottage flashed to mind as it always does when I hear sirens.

Maggie was quickest with her phone. She'd reached the police and explained who she was and then reported Philly's break in.

"What is your address, chica?" she asked Philly with a wink, and then relayed it back to the dispatcher. Maggie's face darkened. "Oh?" she said. "I see. Yes. Yes, we will be available for questions later. I see. Yes. Thank you." She ended the call.

My sweet, sensitive bakery boss took a very deep breath and looked both of us straight in the eyes. "The address you gave me for the break-in, Philly, is the same address where the dispatcher sent the fire department. It's your house on fire."

At this point Philly put her head on the table, shaking. I rested my hand on her back to comfort her and realized instead of crying, as I'd assumed, she was laughing. Hers was an uncontrollable, hysterical kind of hilarity. I'd never seen anyone react in quite that way to devastating news.

Maggie looked at me. "Go. Just take Philly to her house. I'll take care of the bakery."

"Yeah. We better go," I whispered into Philly's ear.

"I'm positive they're trying to reach you on your phone, and it's ringing away on your desk at work. We better get to the fire and see if there's anything we can do. I know the fire crew will have questions and hopefully some answers."

Philly laugh-sighed, sat up straight, stuffed the protection bag into the front of her dress, put both hands on the table and pushed herself to a standing position. She wiped her eyes on the sleeves of my sweater wrap. "Okay, I think I'm ready." She looked resolute. "You drive."

In a matter of minutes, we pulled behind an ambulance near Philly's driveway entrance. Police and fire vehicles parked at different angles inside the driveway, volunteers having pulled the fallen branch to the side.

I'd been imagining a pile of rubble and was grateful to see at least the front of the house looked whole and undamaged, except for the smoke-tinted front windows. The crews rolled up some of their hoses. Warren saw us coming.

"Philly, I'm so sorry," he said. "There is major damage to your kitchen, but it's not a total loss. Have you got good insurance?"

Between Philly and I, we updated Warren about what happened on Philly's porch that morning.

"The man with the baseball bat must have started the fire," I said.

Warren nodded. "That makes some sense. Lucky you've got a good fire alarm system, Philly. It's obviously arson, and the rest of your house, the part that didn't burn, looks as though someone searched it. Whoever it was, emptied out the drawers in your study. There's stuff everywhere."

Investigator Crumley interrupted Warren, announcing he had questions for Philly. I searched for a hint of sympathy in his ruddy face and detected none.

Scrutinizing Philly with half veiled eyes, he said, "We just got a report that you were here. You were at the property at about the time the fire started. We also checked with your department. Your fellow workers report you left work at break time because you had something to get at home. It looks mighty suspicious, Ms. Rand. Just what were you doing here? It's hard to believe you failed to notice there was a fire before you left."

Philly, shaky voice and all, told Crumley about the intruder.

"I panicked and drove right to the bakery." Philly explained as much as she could about the man with the baseball bat, but she'd never seen his face because of the ski mask. Her description was limited to body type and head shape.

"Why didn't you call the police as soon as you saw this supposed intruder?" Crumley's tone was sardonic.

"I left my phone on my desk at work." Philly sounded exhausted. "I'll never do that again, but I thought I would be gone for just a few minutes."

Crumley continued to take notes, finishing with an aggressive tap of his pen on his writing pad.

"Can we go inside?" I asked, "so Philly can get some things and see what happened?"

"Absolutely not." Crumley examined Philly with an air of shrewdness. "It's not safe, and we're investigating your house for arson. We're investigating you for arson, Ms. Rand."

It was at this point Philly had enough. I could feel Philly's body tense and straighten next to mine, so I removed my arm from her shoulder. Her hands went straight to her hips, as she turned to face Crumley. The forthright, imperturbable Philly I knew and loved was in charge.

"So, Mr. Hot Shot investigator." She saturated her voice with sarcasm. "Your version of police work is to find a victim and further victimize them. Makes your job so much easier, I suppose. But you might want to do your work someday and investigate something. I warn you. If you don't find the guy who was in my house lighting a match to it, then you can be sure that I will. And after I find him, I will investigate you to within an inch of your job. You haven't done anything to help Betts with her harasser, nor have you come close to finding out who really murdered Joon and Mr. Huong. And, you haven't asked me anywhere near the correct questions to find the underlying cause of this fire."

She turned around and started toward my car. I looked at Crumley and shrugged. "She's got valid points."

First, we drove to Philly's office where she picked up her phone and took the rest of the day off. We returned to the bakery so she could retrieve her car, and we drove to my house. I settled Philly on my couch before opening the front window to let in cooler, fall air and went into the kitchen to find something for Philly's headache.

"I should have asked for more of your little protection bags," Philly called from the living room. "I should have hung them around the house like you did." I laughed because I'd over-done it. Cotton draw string protection bags, like insect-spun, bag-worm sacks, dangled from the ceiling, lampshades, window frames and door frames. Twine and ornament hooks secured the bags, and I adorned them with black marker ghost faces to create the illusion they were Halloween decorations.

"I did go overboard," I said, "but my house has been under attack since Joon died, and the little bags help me feel I'm in control."

On my grandmother's silver service tray, I brought two cups of tea, an Excedrin, and some applesauce cookies, baked that morning. We sat side by side, sipping, munching, and thinking.

"Will things ever get back to normal? I mean, we haven't had a break, have we? Not since the fire in the storage unit." I thought about the inconclusive fire investigation. "Whatever is next?"

We heard a car motor rumble to a stop outside the house and a car door open. I was preparing to get up and check when something sailed through the open window, hitting one of my hanging bags. It caught on the hook that secured the bag to the window frame. By the time I got to the window, the car was gone. Caught on the hanging hook, swinging like a surveyor's pendulum, was a miniature lidded jar containing five brown recluse spiders. The edge of the jar lid just barely caught on the hook. I didn't want to touch that jar, but I could see the hook was starting to bend from the weight of the glass. Ever so careful, I extracted the jar from the window frame and set it down with extreme care. I wiped my hands on my pants, even though I knew nothing was on them, not even spider cooties.

Philly's eyes were wide. "What are the chances?" she murmured in awe. "I think we were saved again by one of your protection bags."

We stayed silent, believing and not believing at the same time.

"I wish I'd seen the car," Philly said. "I have a feeling it was gray with a *Santorum for President* bumper sticker."

"Whoever it was has a good arm and good aim." Just looking at the spiders made me want to run out of the house. "It's a fair distance from the sidewalk to the window."

"Whoever threw that rock at Warren's windshield had a good arm, too." Philly got up to close the window.

Neither of us had the energy or the desire to call the police. We simply sat until Philly dropped into an uneasy sleep. With care, I lifted her legs to the couch and covered her with a soft, merino wool Afghan. Feeling numb and a little cold myself, I unfolded another throw blanket to put around my own shoulders.

My phone vibrated in my pocket. It was Roger.

"How is she?" were his first words. "How can I help?"

I wasn't sure how to respond. We could use his help, but I didn't know how Philly was feeling about him, and I didn't want to force an encounter.

"Thanks for calling Roger. Let's all meet for dinner." The invitation was the best I could do. "We're waiting to get into Philly's house to find her insurance company documents and rescue some of her other paperwork. Right now, she's resting, but we're racking our brains to understand why someone would want to search her house and torch it. There's no obvious reason."

After deciding on a place and a time for dinner, I

texted Warren to let him know. Philly had a drawer in my house where she kept a few extra clothes just in case she decided to spend the night at the last minute. I was relieved to find jeans, tops, underwear, and tennis shoes. She couldn't go home and get clothes, and she was too slim and muscular to look good in mine, but Philly would want to get out of her soiled dress when she woke up, so these clothes were perfect.

I covered the jar of spiders with a dish towel and picked it up. There were no air holes. Did spiders need air holes? Did I care? I slipped the jar into a large zip lock freezer bag and considered giving it to the police. Might there be fingerprints?

With Philly in a deep sleep on my couch, my office was a temporary refuge, and I sat at my desk trying to work out connections and motives, my mind raced like an off-road vehicle, taking side roads, and veering every which way. If someone was looking for something in Philly's house, there was no telling if they found it.

Could it have been Roger? Was he so angry about the other night that he sought vengeance? Was he the one looking for the heirloom book, and when he didn't find it in my house, did he decide to search Philly's house in case I'd given it to her? Did he call so soon after the jar incident to see if his pitch through the window was successful?

Was it Mrs. Hester? With that ski mask, could Philly have mistaken her for a man? Was she looking for the heirloom book in Philly's house, and did she get so angry when she didn't find it that she set the house on fire?

Was it someone completely different; someone who drove a gray car with a Santorum election sticker?

As I sat mulling over these and other questions, I

found myself drifting off. Try as hard as I might, my eyelids wanted to close. I dozed into stage-two sleep so that when someone tapped on my office window, I startled and nearly fell out of my chair onto my colorful, tied-rag carpet. Joey's face filled the window, hands cupped on either side of his eyes as he peered in to see me. It hurt to swallow the scream that was hurdling up my throat, but I managed it.

I pointed toward the back door and met Joey there. He could tell I was angry with him.

"Sorry, Betts. I looked through the front porch window. Saw Philly was asleep. I just didn't want to knock and wake her."

I relented and stepped outside to talk with this earnest young man, t-shirt inside out and ball cap perched backwards on his thick black hair. As I filled him in on Philly's house fire and the man with the baseball bat, we leaned against the back porch railing and watched Mr. Chew pull up radishes with his teeth.

Philly poked her head out the back door just then. She greeted Joey with a sarcastic, "How is your brother?"

"Uh, he's okay, but when he loses at X-Box, he blames his hands. Says they aren't working right after the night at the cemetery," Joey mumbled. "Says he's having trouble doing his wall art too."

"He'll be okay." I was blunt and less than sympathetic.

We went in, and I presented Joey with his personal pocket protection bags and a mental sharpness bag.

"Just humor me," I said. "I want to see what happens when people carry these around."

Philly, grateful for a change of clothes, said she still

wanted to go shopping for work outfits. We left Joey hunched over his computer in the front room to find dresses for Philly and to see if she could retrieve some things from her house, especially her important papers. The inspector allowed her to go in and take things from her desk such as insurance documents. She also took copies of my interviews with Joon and her aunt's manila envelope, still unopened.

"It's overwhelming," Philly said, verging on tears. "But the guys in there gave me a few phone numbers for companies that help restore homes after a fire. Sometimes they can recondition furniture and clothing." Philly wiped her eyes and blew her nose on one of my old t-shirts, still left in the laundry basket for delivery to the second-hand store. I had run out of Kleenex.

We went to Main Street to visit the local shops for basic clothing, including work ensembles, pajamas, shoes, socks, and the rest. As we put together a new wardrobe for Philly, we also brainstormed after dinner plans for the two of us, plans that involved black clothing, flashlights, and self-protection objects.

It was getting close to 4 o'clock when I remembered Roger and dinner.

"Roger called," I said. "We set up dinner for the four of us at about 6:30, if that's acceptable to you."

"I suppose," Philly said. "I don't know what to think of Roger anymore. I don't know what to think about anything right now."

Chapter 18

"They say we need real heroes in our lives, the ones who keep trudging through thick and thin with dignity and perseverance, and I agree, but sometimes we need a hero who saves us from a single calamity, because once in a while we need a quick, dramatic rescue." Towne Family Almanac, 1966, Helen Harvey, daughter of Corrie Alzesta Towne Douglass.

Dinner was quiet, as though we were strangers thrown together on a bus, painstakingly trying to make conversation. We talked about the fire and what Philly needed to do because of it. Philly and Roger sat stiff and separate, avoiding the big rhubarb as my mother used to call inevitable confrontations. They couldn't tackle their "rhubarb" very well with Warren and I hovering.

As Philly and I kept quiet about our after-dinner plans, my conscience suffered a ferocious tug of war. The feud in my head between feeling guilty for not telling Warren and defiance about being able to make my own decisions kept me so on edge I barely tasted my hot Reuben and sweet potato fries.

"I don't know how to start with the insurance company," Philly was telling Warren. "Crumley seems to think I might have started the fire." Warren shook his head in disgust, a sort of nonverbal grumble.

"Who knows how many clues were destroyed when we put out the fire," he said, "but when things calmed down, I scoped the grounds and discovered heavy boot tracks leading from your yard to a path through the woods. The path leads to a dirt road. There's evidence that a car parked there this morning. You know the path, I'm sure, Philly. Anyway, I showed the tracks to the fire investigator."

"Damnation. I'm sorry I wasn't there," Roger said for the fifth time. "Maybe I need to volunteer for the fire department so I can keep up with all the news around here. Ask me for help getting the house right again, please." Warren favored Roger with a half-smile, but I also saw him take note of Roger's heavy work boots.

As dessert arrived, warm bread puddings topped with melting, vanilla ice cream, I thought of asking Roger about his sidewalk meeting with Mrs. Hester and Maynard but decided against it. I'd let Philly take care of that when she and Roger had their "rhubarb".

A light rain fell on us as we left the restaurant. Cooler clouds bumped against warm air, stirring up sonic shock waves from lightning. Thunder rumbled in the distance, an unusual occurrence in our coastal town. When I got home, I opened my well-lit house to find Joey plugged into the Internet, complete with earphones and a microphone, busy conversing with his Minecraft buddies.

"Oh shiznet. You scared me," he said, jumping off the couch when he noticed Philly's critical eyes peering down at him. "Uh. Sorry. Didn't know you were here."

Wondering if someone could take off with my whole house and get away with it when Joey was on duty, I dismissed him for the night. When his jeep roared toward the intersection, we rushed to find dark clothing suitable for skulking around in an unlit, smoky house. We'd purchased two pen lights and batteries that afternoon, and I'd confiscated investigative foot covers from Warren's truck so we wouldn't leave footprints. We stuffed pairs of rubber gloves into our back pockets. On impulse, as we scooted out the door, I grabbed Joey's telescoping Billy stick from where he left it on the coffee table - not that I knew how to use it or even how to extend it.

"Let's take my car." Philly pulled on an over-sized black sweater with a front pocket and hood, embellishing her ensemble with a smoky gray and black infinity scarf. She couldn't help it. Accessorizing was a compulsive habit, even when Philly was dressing to be invisible. I turned toward the hall so she couldn't see my smile. My own black sweatshirt sported holes in the elbows and a hood beginning to tear away from the neck.

"Won't your neighbors recognize your wheels?" I asked about her car.

"Oh. Right. How about yours then?"

"We'll park a block away, so hopefully they won't recognize or remember mine either."

"We should practice different ways to walk," Philly suggested. "That way anyone who sees us walking won't be able to describe us. I do a good old-guy shuffle."

I lumbered down my front walk like my idea of Frankenstein.

"The way you're shambling around, they're going to call the police before we even get to my house." Philly giggled. I just looked at her, grateful to hear her laugh despite the fire and the prowler with the baseball bat. She was a glass half full kind of woman.

I got the heater going full blast in my car and we took off toward Philly's.

"So, what do we look for once we get there?" Philly whispered.

"Anything out of place," I breathed back. "I know the intruder ransacked everything, but you're the one who knows how things ought to be. You can see something out of place or something that doesn't belong. The police wouldn't necessarily know the difference."

"Yeah, and I need some more of my papers from the desk and some of my jewelry," Philly hissed beside me.

I cleared my throat and said aloud, "Why are we whispering?"

"We are, aren't we."

I parked on Croissant Avenue, one street over from Philly's house, which was on Scone Street. People liked to call this the half-baked neighborhood, especially since Baker Grade School was on Strudel Road. The story goes that a couple of baking grandmothers were on the planning commission, and they helped pick out street names 60 years ago.

The houses sat far apart, as zoning required each lot to be a minimum of one acre. Strips of fir tree woods and evergreen hedges separated properties and walkways. Several houses, including Philly's, were built a good distance from the street with long driveways.

We approached Philly's house on foot, distorting our strides, and looking like partners in a Sponge Bob bebop. Peering around my friend's front hedge, I made out the outline of her driveway leading to the dark shadow of her house. As the fire was still under investigation, we wanted to avoid drawing attention to our entry. Once inside, we could turn on our penlights and start our search. I also had a pocket camera, but I wanted to use it with care because of the flash.

"My very own house gives me the creeps right now," Philly whispered in my year, "and that makes me sad because I usually love being here." She stepped onto her driveway from the sidewalk. "Here goes."

I followed behind in the gloom, counting on Philly to know where the low places and rough spots were. The closer we got to the front door, the stronger the rancid smell of smoke.

"Holy Beelzebub," Philly said in a soft grieving voice. "I feel like a crook, like I'm burglarizing myself."

I heard the jingle of keys as she prepared to open the front door. We slipped on our shoe booties and pulled on rubber gloves before entering the foyer. Inside it was chiller, moister, and darker than outside. Once Philly closed the door behind us, I could see absolutely nothing. The air was thick and concentrated with that stale smell - like burnt logs saturated with water upon the death of a campfire. My ears strained to catch sounds, but the silence was heavy. Nothing broke the stillness, not even the hum of a refrigerator or the whoosh and clunk of a central heating pump turning on and off. Fire department personnel disconnected Philly's electricity for safety's sake.

I reached into my sweatshirt front pocket for my light, but a tap, click, ka-thump interrupted the hush, and my hand found the Billy stick instead. The sound came from the back of the house, and my imagination conjured visions of a magazine clip sliding over a semi-automatic pistol, or a baseball bat scraping and banging against something wooden. Philly gripped my arm, though I had no idea how she knew where to grab. We stood there together for several minutes, frozen, waiting for more. All we heard was our own breathing and the creaking of floorboards beneath our feet as we worked without success to stand still.

"What nonsense." Philly said the words aloud. "Must have been something settling. It was a critter, or the wind outside. I'm tired of standing here. Let's start." She turned on her pen light and headed toward her damaged kitchen. I shone my light around the front room, my left hand on Joey's collapsed baton. I tried to picture myself hitting someone with it. I'd need a sudden and ample surge of adrenalin to do the job. One thing I was sure of, though. There was no wind outside.

My flashlight illuminated Philly's Bella Berry velvet, button-tufted sofa, and matching wing chairs. From what I could see in the dark, a uniform dusting of ash covered the furniture, and I was sure the chairs and sofa absorbed a hefty dose of smoke. Everything smelled of smoke. While the fire department avoided turning a water hose on the living room, the walls were still damp from condensation, and here and there moisture, like sweat, accumulated and dripped in uneven rivulets down the painted sheetrock. The rivulets looked like runs on a pair of nylons. Even in the shadows, I could see the dismal patches on Philly's beige, 100 percent wool carpeting left by wet and muddy firefighting boots. Philly kept her front room spotless most of the time, so except for the soot, moisture, a fallen lamp, and muddy footprints, there wasn't much to see.

I followed Philly into her kitchen, a cooking fortress of stainless steel and oak. Here was the locus point for most of the fire damage.

"Things have been moved," Philly said, her back to me, "but there's no way to tell if the fire fighters changed things or the guy who broke in."

"What's been moved?"

She pointed to the pantry closet where cans, boxes, pasta packages, bottles, and dry goods lay in a massive wet and irredeemable heap on the floor. The shelves themselves were empty.

"Looks like my house a few nights ago," I commented.

Philly gestured to the bookshelf, built as an inset into the wall near the door to the living room. It too was bare, and below was a soggy hill of cookbooks, many of them turning to papier Mache. Most of them were open, their sodden pages barely holding together, separating from water-logged, broken backs. Her herb and spice containers lay scattered higgledy-piggledy on top of her Capital convection range, looking like the aftermath of a 46-car pileup on the Las Angeles section of Interstate Five. I took pictures, my camera light flashing and blinding us both. Since we couldn't seem to identify any clues from just staring in dismay at the clutter and piles, pictures might help us see better in the future.

"I'll ask Warren about the fire investigation report." I tried to orient myself with my pinpoint light. "It should tell us what the firemen saw when they first entered the kitchen."

"Looks to me like the guy who started this fire was in a hurry to find something." Philly wiped a gloved finger over one of the empty bookshelves. "I've got cookbooks in this pile of mush that are very precious to me."

"There's eBay and Amazon," I said, "in case you've got to replace them."

"My fourth-grade soccer team fundraiser cookbook?"

"It's just possible. I've seen everything from church to yachting club fund-raising cookbooks on Amazon."

"It's just so weird." Philly aimed her penlight at a heavy book full of bread recipes. "You get attached to things like recipe books, and if you find a replacement, it doesn't feel the same, even if the recipes are exactly like the ones in your own precious book. I mean, the replacement already belonged to somebody else."

I put my arms around Philly's slumped shoulders.

"I don't see anything that points to who did this." Philly sounded discouraged.

"Let's try your other rooms," I suggested. "We'll take lots of pictures, and something may reveal itself in one of them later."

Philly's home was a reclaimed Craftsman, complete with picture-rail baseboards and crown moldings, substantial door frames, and thick oak doors, including her pantry door. Elegant old-fashioned, crystal doorknobs turned the latches of even her broom closet. Her art-glass kitchen cabinets, framed in blue-painted wood, were ornamented with upmarket but simple sterling silver pulls.

A door on the east side of Philly's kitchen led to her bedroom, and next to it was a door to her bathroom. The door to her office was through the living room, which was where Philly headed. I started taking pictures in the bathroom, untouched by fire or marauder. Philly's bedroom was another matter. Someone pulled clothes out of drawers, dumped them, and then left them for fire fighters to trod on. I took pictures of everything and looked to see if there were any items left in the bureau or nightstand.

While I hated walking on top of Philly's beautiful blouses, skirts, and lingerie, I had no choice as I made my way toward her clothes closet, shut tight. Her plush burgundy robe hung limply from its door hook. It occurred to me that every cupboard, drawer, and door in the house was open, except this one. Yet the area in front of the door was cleared of debris, as though someone pulled the door open after the ransacking. With fire investigators, fire fighters, and police in and out, who knew what got opened and closed by whom and for what reasons.

The dark bedroom felt humid, and the shadow of Philly's velvet bathrobe, cast by my flashlight, loomed over me like the transformation of Professor Gordon Crowley in the film 'Monster Slayer'. I considered waiting for Philly before I opened her closet. Was I afraid of being a snoop? Not really. Was I simply uncomfortable opening closed doors in a spooky house? Something felt more amiss here than in the bathroom or living room.

I wrapped my gloved, right-hand fingers around the doorknob, turned it, and pulled. To my surprise, Philly's suits, coats, and dresses hung untouched, squeezed close enough together that I couldn't see the back wall. Why had this closet escaped the carnage? I leaned back to take pictures. The shelf above the coats supported three-high stacks of shoe boxes. They, too, seemed unmolested. My eyes drifted to the closet floor where Philly had lined up several pairs of her shoes, toes facing front. Among the women's dress boots was a pair of men's fawn-colored work boots, discolored with water stains and soot, incongruous between the many pairs of stylish, leather footwear. I looked more closely and saw that above the boots were the cuffs of a pair of men's pants, also smudged and dirty. And then I realized the boots and pants contained feet and legs and behind the wall of clothes someone stood hiding.

As I waited there, paralyzed with surprise and panic, the wall of clothing began to move. This hiding man was about to make a move, and I really wanted him to be still, to be a figment of my imagination. Even though I was on the verge of peeing my pants with fear, I managed to close the closet door with such force that the slam shook Philly's heavy wall mirror nearby. I leaned against the now quaking door and screamed like a banshee for Philly. She was by my side in a millisecond, having already come to find me. The closet door started to open as the closet's occupant waged a shoulder attack to the wood that was an effective counter force against my own weight. Philly threw her Tri-fitness champion shoulders into the door above the knob, moving me out of the way and pointing with her flashlight to a long, thin metal stick propped against the wall near the main bedroom door.

"Get it," she hissed, and I obeyed. It turned out to be a steel door brace. If Philly installed a brace on our side of the door, it would be almost impossible for the man to open it. As Philly worked to position the brace, she said, "I use this after watching horror movies. It helps me sleep better."

She and I rammed our weight against the door as the man shoved back until the bracing pin of the bar snapped in place and the door held without us. The door had an old-fashioned lock, something I had never seen on a modern closet door. Philly fumbled through the debris of her upended jewelry box and produced a long-handled brass key. She used it to lock the now thumping closet door. I was weak with relief as I sat back on Philly's mahogany sleigh bed. Throughout the whole ordeal, all we heard from the man was an occasional groan or gasp of effort.

"Who is he?" Philly hissed.

"I didn't see his face. He didn't say a thing."

"That's really creepy." Philly turned toward the bedroom door. "Let's get out of here. That door will not hold forever."

Her beautiful, hardwood door was taking a walloping as the man pounded his shoulder against it, one blow after another.

"What about calling the police?"

"Not if we don't want a piss pot of trouble on our own heads," Philly called back over her shoulder as we sprinted toward the kitchen and the back door. "Does that man know it was you who saw him in the closet?"

"I don't know what he knows."

"Let's go down the trail in the back of my house." Philly pushed the screen door open onto her back porch. "Let's see if his car is there on that dirt road through the trees. We can figure out who he is without having to see him face to face."

"You think it was the guy who set fire to your house?"

"Yeah," she yelled, twisting her head to look back at me as she started to jog down the little trail in the woods. "Maybe Mr. Fire Bug didn't find what he wanted the first time. Someone searched my office since I visited it this afternoon."

Philly led the way with her flashlight down the soft, muddy trail with its obstacle course of zig zagging roots, fallen branches and loose stones. While the wooded grove was murky, it could have been the middle of a floodlit stadium compared with the inside of Philly's home.

I breathed cool night air into my lungs, grateful for every gulp. We ran out onto the dirt road, stopping our flight with hands and arms outstretched to thud against the passenger side of a parked car, gray with no license plates and a Santorum bumper sticker, its curled corners pealing from the back right bumper. To our amazement, the driver left the car doors unlocked.

"You take the back, I'll take the front," I said.

"Sure," said Philly. "As soon as I relieve myself in those bushes. I can't do anything more until I take care of business."

My hands explored every crevice in that front seat. I looked in the glove compartment and found nothing, not even car registration papers, nothing but a Dirty Dozen bakery wrapper. Was the man who burned Philly's kitchen and who maybe murdered Joon and Liam a regular bakery customer? The idea that I might have served coffee to this arsonist turned my stomach. It wasn't until I lifted the floor mat on the passenger side that I found something. It was a key ring holding three keys with no identifying markers. I slipped them under my sweatshirt and between my girls for safe keeping.

Where was Philly? I backed out of the car feet first and butt next, right into the thick frame of a man wearing fawn-colored work boots, sooty pants, and a ski mask. The man pulled me hard against him and pushed something sharp and metallic against my throat.

Blood and sand, I thought to myself. *Just when I need it, I've left Joey's night stick on the passenger seat of this guy's car.*

"Betts? Crap!" I heard Philly screech from the other side of the car. I felt pressed against a loaf of Challah bread. The ski-masked man had padded his large coat to increase his girth. By now I thought of my captor as Mr. Lump. Had he cushioned himself to the hilt to look imposing or as part of a disguise? Mr. Lump's voice came out a strained, unnatural, monotone of a growl. Why was he disguising his voice? Did that mean I knew him?

"Get back," he snarled at Philly. "Get away from the car. Sit or I will hurt your friend." He reached up with his empty hand to turn on a head lamp, banded onto his forehead.

Philly stood glaring in the spotlight.

"Right now!" the man ordered with a sharp bark that had to strain his throat. He pulled me step by step toward the rear of the car. "Left pocket. Get keys," he hissed in my ear, increasing the pressure of the blade. I did as he asked, struggling to remove the keys from pants that strained tightly against the stuffing hiding the man's shape. Once the keys jingled in my hands, he pushed me closer to the car.

"Open the trunk," he rasped, switching the knife to the back of my neck, stroking it along my vertebrae like an instrumentalist running a pick along the strings of a guitar. I got the message. I fumbled with the keys, my hands shaking so I had trouble inserting the right key into the lock. When I finally succeeded, and the trunk lid lifted, I could see only outlines of items in the dark interior. Our assailant aimed his headlamp at the trunk revealing a spare tire, a jack, and an open package of Dirty Dozen pumpkin garlic dinner rolls. I recognized them from a batch three days ago when I experimented with sesame seeds as a topping.

"You and your friend will have a picnic." Mr. Lump's voice was changing from forced huskiness to involuntary hoarseness. "Eat the rolls or I will force feed you. I will use this knife to drive these rolls down your meddling throats."

This overstuffed bully with his cold blade instructed me to put the keys back in his pocket, remove the rolls, and give half of them to Philly. Whiffs of carroty tang waylaid my nostrils as I tore at the wrapping. I stumbled and rolls fell out onto the mudded gravel.

"Pick them up," the man snarled.

When I had the rolls gathered, he grabbed them and then shoved me toward Philly. I landed on my hands and knees, cursing because those old scrapes from falling in the alley only days ago were torn open again, and the aching muscles in my back felt wrenched and strained from our assailant's push and my plummet. Mr. Lump Man grabbed my hair to pull me back to my knees, knife digging into my neck. Philly stood to face our attacker.

"You coward," she said, almost screaming at him. "Who in nuckin futs do you think you are?"

Mr. Lump Man loomed over me toward Philly. "Sit down, you nasty woman," he howled, spit flying out of the mouth opening of his ski mask, and close to my ear. He jerked me into the knife, and I could feel it slice through my skin. Philly's mouth formed a horror-struck 'O', and tears sprang to her eyes. I thought she might charge forward, but she sat down in one quick motion, her blazing eyes never leaving my face. My fingers grabbed to feel the cut and touched the string around my neck attached to my little protection bag, tucked with this man's keys between my girls. Feeling the string reminded me that I could stop being a victim if I chose. I could fight back if I decided to.

The cut seemed shallow, but blood leaked down past my collar, soaked up by the cotton t-shirt under my sweatshirt. Mr. Lump wiped the blood from my cut off his hands and onto my sleeve. He seemed repulsed by my sticky, red body fluids.

"I'm going to enjoy watching you die," he raged, pushing me once again toward Philly.

I fell in an awkward heap, Mr. Lump Man looming over me, shoving a stale, muddy roll to my lips and ordering me to open my mouth. Philly batted his hand away and the roll went flying. He kicked her hand, and I heard her gasp in pain. The man aimed a large butcher knife at the left side of Philly's face, and I kicked out. My foot crunched into this hellish brute's shins, his lower legs unprotected by padding. Then I levelled a second blow towards his unmentionables, but he wore so much padding around his hip area, I doubt he felt much. Still, I was able to change the course of his momentum and force him to take a stumbling step back. The knife missed Philly, but Mr. Lump Man swung his arm around to take another stab. The events of the next minute astounded all three of us.

A shadow emerged from the other side of the car and lunged for Mr. Lump Man, hitting him hard along the back of his knees and bowling him over. The knife flew out of his hand, barely missing Philly's right shoulder, and disappeared in the tall, crispy grasses at the edge of the road.

Our rescuer turned out to be a thin, wiry man that Philly and I recognized at once.

Stan from Tent City regrouped and pulled himself up, while Mr. Lump Man crawled out of Stan's reach and managed to right himself, despite his bulky disguise. He rolled over the front hood of the gray car to the other side and dove into the driver's seat, the door having been left open after I backed out. We heard the motor roar to life. Mr. Lump Man put the car into drive and must have slammed his foot on the gas because, with a spray of rocks and mud, the car spun its wheels, lurched ahead and sped away. We could see the battery-powered lamp on the man's forehead inside the car. The three of us watched the light fade away and disappear as the car turned the corner onto the main road.

"Oh my God, oh my God, oh my God." Philly stood and then ran to Stan. She threw her arms around him. "Thank you, thank you, thank you."

I struggled in slow motion to achieve an upright position, moving with a crooked limp, sore knees and all, to join in the celebration and wrap my arms around our scruffy, stalwart guardian angel.

"Oh my God, where did you come from?" Philly hugged Stan one more time. Then we were all one big, relieved, hugging mass.

Only Philly had a light. I dropped my penlight during the ordeal, and Stan's light was a pitiful blinking blivit, low on batteries. With his left hand, Stan shook his flashlight every other minute to encourage battery connection. His silhouetted right arm pointed across the gravely dirt road toward another stand of trees. "Tent City is across the creek, over there. We got a compost pile down in the creek gully and I was puttin' old vegetable scraps on the pile when I heard shoutin' over here. I crossed the creek to see if anyone was needin' help." He pointed down to his boots, and Philly aimed her flashlight to reveal old blue jeans soaked up to the knees. "The rest you saw."

"We can't thank you enough, Stan." I grabbed his right hand to shake it. "I think you saved us from certain death, or at the very least, maiming."

"Who was that man?" Stan shuddered, not so much from the cold, but for the same reason Philly and I trembled. We were all experiencing shock.

"We haven't a clue. My first guess is he's the one responsible for burning Philly's house and maybe even for Joon's murder. Look. You're cold." I reached out to touch Stan's elbow. "You can't cross that creek again, so come on home with us and get dry. I think it's time we got ourselves away from this miserable back road."

Working hard to pick up the rolls with the tips of my fingers, I pulled off my hat and dropped the rolls in it. I didn't want to touch them if I could help it, but I didn't want to leave them behind for an animal to get a hold of either. A dog might not take the time to discern the smell of hemlock seeds that nestled together on top of buttery, brown, round rolls. Would I ever be able to eat pumpkin, garlic dinner rolls again? Probably not, at least not with seeds on top.

We made an odd troupe, Philly leading the way down the trail to her backyard while Stan squeak-sloshed in wet boots and I lagged behind with a limping trudge. I dreaded trying to explain the cut on my neck to Warren.

Chapter 19

"You see, secrets have lives. They are born, and then grow, and then mature in stages. When secrets are fully mature, people have made choices that direct the purpose of the secrets toward goodness or bitterness, love or fear, truth or deceit. A secret in its prime can prevent harm or tear asunder. As in any life cycle, secrets lose energy, and eventually, all that remains is a fading, misrepresented memory." Towne Family Almanac, 1672, Emma Flower, daughter of Anne Barstowe.

Hot blueberry pancakes with warmed strawberry syrup, egg scramble, and sausage-stuffed mushrooms greeted me the next day on my return home from the bakery. We were back to our morning brunches, but Warren cut this one short. He heard my explanation for the large bandage, which showed over the top of my sweater neckline. Madder than Kevin Costner in the film 'Bodyguard', when Whitney Houston refused to cooperate with his safety rules, Warren pushed his half-full plate toward the center of the table. He stood and threw his napkin at his chair seat.

"Elizabeth Magdalene Harvey. If you were one of my firefighters, I would sack you right now, on the spot. Who in Sam Hill do you think you are, Miss Fisher, amateur investigator? You're a baker and a gardener and a genealogist for Pete's sake." Warren grabbed his jacket from the back of his chair and slung it over his shoulder. "I gotta get out of here before I say something I'll regret. But know this, woman, you've gone too far this time."

Warren left me on one side of a slammed door, and he took off on the other side. How long till he cooled off? Did I feel sad for having hurt him? Of course, a little, but he wasn't Keven Costner. He wasn't my bodyguard. I tried to swallow past the expanding lump in my throat, refusing to feel guilty about going to Philly's to look for clues. How were we to know the arsonist would be there too?

By late afternoon, I'd had the police on my doorstep asking leading questions. I referred them to my lawyer, Miles Fox. Philly's insurance company directed her to find a hotel room, so by the time the police came, she'd moved her things from my couch to a bed and breakfast near city offices. Warren was avoiding my calls and texts, so I stopped trying. He would reach out when he was ready.

My job included preparing a few recipes for the community meeting the next night, so I was in my kitchen, browsing through cookbooks. All those dazzling cookbook photographs of deep chocolate torte, wine-tenderized pork roast, and glistening honeyed carrots usually had me mesmerized for hours at a time, but today my eyes kept wandering toward the kitchen table and the checkered cookbook cover hiding the pages of the Towne Family Almanac.

Before I knew it, with a sense of excitement and

trepidation, I was turning the pages in Joon's recipe book.

Did I really believe the mixtures of herbs in my little protection bags had saved me from a recluse spider infestation, Philly from the man who set fire to her house, and Warren from being in a car accident? Did my own protection bag save me the night before by reminding me to fight back? I told myself that each of these examples was an easy coincidence. But, if I didn't believe that the little bags of herbs saved us all from peril, then why was I so nervous and excited about making a new recipe, one I discovered on page 176 of the almanac? Was I fooling myself?

Get a grip, Betts. It's an enigma. You'll never know for sure. For some reason it was Philly's voice I heard in my head, instructing my voracious imagination.

Still, the very thing I wanted most right then was spelled out in front of me, written and embellished with scrolls, leaves, and flowers at the top of the recipe page. My eyes shifted over and over to the one-word recipe title and those five bold, handwritten letters that spelled TRUTH.

As I skimmed the page, I lost myself in a story of a long-ago grandmother, Emma Flower. She and her brother, Samuel, crossed the ocean from England in a crowded pinnace ship. Emma was on her way to marry her fiancé, who had gone ahead to the new world.

Emma was the ancestor who brought The Towne Family Almanac and its seeds to North America.

According to Emma's account, she woke one morning to find a fellow passenger, Harlin Broughton, barely breathing, hanging from the yard arm. When they cut him down, he was able to gasp out one last word before he died, "Samuel." Broughton's last word was why the ship's commanders accused Emma's brother, Samuel Flower, of murdering Harlin. Emma knew her brother was innocent. She also knew there were two other Samuels on board the ship. Was the real murderer Samuel Brink, the ship's captain, or Samuel Howe, a London merchant? Sewn in the linings of Emma's traveling bags were several of the dried herbs her mother taught her to grow and use. Emma was careful to keep the herbs hidden. New world citizens, like those in the old world, were suspicious of healers and herbalists. People both feared and needed them.

Because her brother's life was in the balance, Emma ripped a luggage seam covering the soft, hemp bags of sweet flag and Clary sage. After pocketing the herbs, Emma volunteered to serve afternoon tea for the captain and his cabin-class passengers. Adding her herbs to the existing tea leaves in the captain's large, brown Betty teapot, Emma prepared herself for her investigation. Sweet flag and Clary sage, grown and harvested in the correct time and place, were known to loosen tongues and inspire truth telling.

That afternoon, Captain Samuel's teacups fortified a rousing conversation, stimulated a greater share of candor than usual, and aroused a full measure of competitive boasting and bravado. Almost undetected, Emma slipped a question into the spirited exchange. "Who was the sly and enigmatic soul who really hung Harlin Broughton on the yard arm?" From the lips of a laughing and utterly relaxed Samuel Howe came the confession.

"Harlin knew me. He hailed from a small, pitiful village where I once sold wares for twice their worth and conned a few old people into selling me their land for next to nothing. Harlin knew me well enough to tell all and destroy my reputation in the new world."

"Could you not spare his life?" asked Emma.

"A prosperous man recognizes his enemies and deals accordingly. If he doesn't, he becomes like any other poor bastard who works hard for every little thing he has," said Samuel Howe.

Emma was amazed when the tea guests behaved as though Samuel Howe had said something as innocuous as, "Isn't the sky blue?" His confession had no seeming impact on them, that is, until the effects of the herbs wore off. It was then that people recalled his words and realized their significance. Jailers released Emma's brother. No one fully realized Emma's part in getting to the truth, but every few days she felt the captain's inquisitive eye on her. Emma pretended not to notice his penetrating stare. She could not afford greater scrutiny or questions, especially when people were apt to associate herbalists with witches. So, she kept her head down and the seams in her bags tightly sewn.

After finishing Emma's story, I let go of my held breath in appreciation of her bravery, and I examined the beautiful drawings of birds and fish that framed Emma's recipe page. A garland of tiny blue flowers bordered the truth-incitement recipe at the end of her history. I took out the code sheet and ciphered out a copy of the formula on a handy Post-it note. Would it hurt to try the recipe? I would need to hurry.

I decided to infuse a truth mixture into some of the goodies I was baking the next morning for the community meeting. In addition to applesauce cookies, I would put together savory potato quiche bites. Some ingredients from the truth recipe would be mixed into the cookie dough and some would be added to the quiche bites. If a guest ate both a cookie and a quiche bite within a quarter of an hour, the herbal elements should work together.

With a mounting sense of determination and resolve, I got up from the table to gather ingredients. I hoped the Yellow Moon Tea and Spice Store near the post office was still open. It was 4:07 p.m. and sometimes this tiny, quirky, specialty store, with its bins of common and uncommon whole grains and its jars of herbs and spices, kept its own atypical hours. I sped past the post office, relieved to see an open sign dangling from the crossbar door handle of Yellow Moon. Before anyone had a chance to close the shop, I hurried over the threshold.

Once inside, the fusion of sweet and savory smells overpowered my olfactory senses, but the aromas of licorice and anise always pervaded in these kinds of places, at least for me. Orbiting myself in a circle with my left foot providing the torque and the heal of my right foot the stable force connecting me to the floor, I surveyed the shelves and cases of glass jars, all reflecting light from the big front windows. The store's proprietors displayed the herbs and spices in alphabetical order, so I quickly moved from glass jar to glass jar, scooping out several ounces of Clary sage, licorice, and sweet flag. These were all plants I had been growing for Joon but were stolen from my greenhouse soon after Joon died.

As I plucked bills from my wallet to give to the cashier, my eyes fixed on a tiny vial behind the cash register. Bluebell flowers were the only ingredient I thought I would have to do without, and there it was, just one tiny vial of dried, pressed bluebells. I pulled out another $20 and asked for it.

"What'll you be doing with these?" Rachel, the clerk, cocked her plate-sized head like a bright-eyed owl. "Never seen you buy anything but cloves and allspice."

Tongue tied for several long seconds, I was amazed that she would remember my previous purchases. All I could think to say was, "I've got a new cookbook. I'm trying out some new recipes."

"Mmmmmhmmmm," said the clerk with a knowing expression. "Going to try out some newfangled sugar cookies?" Her mouth twisted into a mocking smile.

"Not sugar," I said. "Applesauce."

"Right," said Rachel, handing me my herbs, packed together in a tiny paper bag. "You know Mrs. Hester, I'm sure. She told me about a cookbook you stole from her family. Your applesauce cookie recipe come from that book by chance?"

"That book isn't stolen," I informed Rachel in my sour pickle voice, the one reserved for complainers and grouches. "But no, there are no cookie recipes in that cookbook."

Dinner was a tuna and tomato sandwich with sliced apple, which I ate alone at my kitchen counter. I was eager to finish mixing the TRUTH recipe and then blending a precise measurement of ingredients in my food processor. That way they would have the consistency of flour when I added them to the cookies and mini quiches in the morning. For the cookies, I mixed rose petals, cinnamon, chamomile, and a pinch of licorice. For the quiches I mixed Clary sage, thyme, sweet flag, and the bluebell flowers.

After funneling each mixture into glass spice bottles, I set the containers on the table. Finding a seat, I stared at them, contemplating the greenish, grayish, dusty-looking substances inside. Questions niggled at my conscience. Was I crossing some kind of ethical boundary? Was I deluding myself into thinking herbs had more power than logic ordained?

Before crawling under my soft quilts that night, I made sure Mr. Chew had enough water and a bed of hay to stretch out on. Joey was busy at his parents' home working on college midterms and keeping a close eye on his brother Maynard. I almost called Warren before climbing the stairs to bed but thought better of it. He was still infuriated with me and Philly for putting ourselves in danger. I pictured him working out his vexation in a series of flash and bang computer games. Despite my apprehension about Warren, I slept like a milk-satiated bobcat much of the night, hypothetical claws at the ready, knowing all the while that my new, bearded, horned friend was keeping an eye on my fence, my porch, and my back door.

About midnight my dreams intensified. I was in a tree-lined meadow, overflowing with bluebells. Rachel, the herb-store clerk, stood talking, her hands on her hips. "Bluebells are as prolific as dandelions, silly. Pick as many as you like, but don't pull out the bulbs. You pull out the bulbs and you'll owe me a good deal more than $20."

All at once Mr. Chew walked out of the trees carrying a large, brown, cloth-covered bundle on his back. He started eating bluebells, mouthful after mouthful, pulling them up with their bulbs and eating those too.

"That your goat?" shrieked Rachel, waving her arms toward Mr. Chew, running toward him, all the while crushing hundreds of flowers beneath her feet. I moved forward, thinking to get between Mr. Chew and the raving store clerk. Just as Rachel raised her arm to strike my goat, I reached him and caught her wrist. We struggled, her arm suddenly around my neck, choking me. It was then that the bundle unfolded itself on Mr. Chew's back, and a pair of bright, meerkat eyes peered from under the brown cloth.

"He's coming for it," Joon's voice cried out from the bundle, and Rachel loosened her hold on me. "He's coming for the book." Joon wailed again, rising to a full sitting position and throwing off the heavy cloth. "Take care," she called. "Take care." At Joon's last "take care," I threw Rachel off me. She fell into the flowers, her snarl the last thing I remember before waking up in my own bed.

I lay shivering, despite cocooning myself in two quilts. There was no Warren this time to wrap his arms around me, but the bright crescent moon sent a beacon of comfort through my bedroom window. I removed the quilts and stood, the light bidding me to the window.

Barefooted, I regarded my moon-lit garden. Mr. Chew's white form reminded me of a revenant as he stood still and alert in the middle of the pumpkins. He lifted his merry face skyward and looked straight at my window. As ludicrous as it seemed, I could swear he winked at me, but no, he was too far away for me to discern a wink. And besides, did goats wink? Just the same, I felt the adrenalin drain away as I watched his peaceful enjoyment of what turned out to be a crisp autumn night.

Waking again at 3:30 a.m. and dressing in a warm calf-length skirt over leggings, I stepped out of my house at 3:45 to trek to the bakery; my feet crunched on ice-dusted leaves and crystal encased sidewalk sand. Of course I was exhausted, but my thoughts drifted to visions of homemade applesauce cookies and bite-sized quiches. I patted the bulky pockets of my navy-blue pea coat where I carried the bottles of truth herbs that would season the goodies we offered at the town meeting that evening. Mostly I thought myself silly to go to these lengths to try out a recipe I didn't believe would work. But part of me was excited to experiment with ancient secrets and the possible influences of dietary mysteries.

Stars revealed the sharpness of a cloudless sky. A family of raccoons ambled across the street under a streetlight a block away. I felt grateful to take part in the early morning ambience of liminality, a time of betwixt and between.

Arriving at the bakery, I went through the ritualistic joining of key with lock, but I drew my hand away from the doorknob as a snap of electricity pricked my fingers. Static electricity added pizazz to our first real freeze, but wild energy seemed to pop inside the bakery as well. Did I bring my own measure of chaotic anticipation to work, with all my scheming and anxious anticipation; or was it one of those moon-controlled days when all hell breaks loose for those of us who are holding things together with the last thread of a frayed shoelace?

Baking is usually a calming, methodical affair, but today, as I measured out butter and sugar, I fumbled with flour sacks, dropped measuring spoons, and misplaced spice bottle lids as my head worked faster than my fingers.

I got the bakery's standard breads and sweets in the ovens before starting in on the refreshments planned for the evening's public meeting. I hoped the mixtures of truth herbs and spices in the cookies and quiches would be edible. With luck, they would even be delicious.

Buttery piecrust dough lined mini muffin pan cups, ready to receive the combination of milk, eggs, cheeses, sage, thyme, sweet flag, and the bluebell blossoms. I'd covered two large, shallow baking pans with parchment paper in preparation for applesauce cookies. Quiches and cookies would bake between customer orders as I served the morning crowd their version of the most important meal of the day.

By 5 a.m., Stan, our guardian angel, was at the front door with the morning edition of the Brocklebrook Journal. This wiry man with his sun-creased face and olive-green billed cap loved Chai tea, but only when no one was round to witness him drinking it. He considered Chai a girly drink. I made him a giant mug of it and put his tea on a tray with warm cinnamon buns.

"It's on me," I told him, setting it on the bar counter where he had the paper spread out. I started to thank him again for his heroic rescue, but he held up a weathered hand to stop me.

"Don't mention it again." He shook his head, forehead wrinkles deepening above his bushy eyebrows. "I was watching yesterday from the trees, and I saw the police find that knife."

"I gave the keys I found in that jerk's car to the police," I said. "One of them fits the lock to the storage unit. Crumley seems to think me having those keys looks even more suspicious. I'm not sure he believes I found them in that man's car."

Stan guffawed, but his amusement faded fast as he read the headline on the front page of the newspaper.

"She did it." He shook out the paper, spread it on the counter and splayed his right-hand fingers across the front page. I peered through his fingers at enough of the headline to see Effy Gordon's byline on top of a story headlined, *Tent City Decreases Expenses and Crime in Brocklebrook.*

I moved around the counter to stand beside Stan so we could read the article together. It was a piece dense with historical research and a wealth of statistics about petty and serious crime levels before and after the establishment of Tent City. Crime had decreased since Brocklebrook organized Tent City because of leaders such as Joon, Denny, and Stan. Gordon gathered the facts and then devoted several paragraphs to quotes from citizens. Some supported the camp while others agreed with City Manager Stoats about Tent City's future.

"Wasting our tax dollars and city land on people who don't work for a living is un-American," said Biff Sherman, a Dirty Dozen regular.

"We need to bring back the old workhouse system," said Arletta Croop, retired home economics teacher.

I snorted at some of the irony. "Sherman lives off his sister's inheritance. I haven't seen him do a lick of work in the six years I've been here. "

"Are they talking about 'work' as work or do they only count paid work?" Stan's utterance was low and quiet.

Stopping short at his words, I nodded my head in his direction. He spoke a truth I often forgot. In our culture, we failed to acknowledge all the work people did that was unpaid, but still valuable and important. Stan was an example of someone who never stopped working, but not for money. Everyday citizens didn't consider his work real because there was no exchange of dollars.

Together we studied Gordon's collected statistics showing petty crime such as shoplifting, loitering, small-scale burglary, and car theft was down twenty seven percent since city leaders established Tent City. Serious crime, such as murder and robbery, never that frequent in Brocklebrook, was down three percent.

Gordon quoted Adrian Childers, governor-appointed secretary of the Washington State Department of Health and Human Services, as saying that the facilities at Tent City give people who are unhoused access to basic needs. "We're familiar with Brocklebrook Tent City here at the state office," she said, "and much of the real credit for Tent City's success goes to the people who have lived there for several years and who work together to enforce rules of conduct. Not only do they make it a community, but they also make it a safer place to sleep and eat."

Gordon's story ended with a recap of the Joon O'Neal and Liam Huong murders and Denny Woodman's arrest. The reporter quoted Crumley as saying the case took a few interesting turns a few days ago, but the investigator refused to elaborate. "Let's just say we gathered new evidence, and we are exploring new angles," Crumley said.

Stan took a deep breath and turned toward me with a grin. "That oughta help tonight at the meeting. Having real facts makes all the difference." His rough fingers were about to fold up the newspaper when I spotted a smaller headline at the very bottom of the page. I stopped his hands and pointed. In a second, Stan spread the newspaper flat again as we both absorbed a godsend of unexpected information.

Homeless Man Dies of Water Hemlock Poisoning Twelve Years Ago.

By Effy Gordon, staff reporter

Water hemlock poison killed a man 12 years ago in Brocklebrook; the circumstances share similarities with two recent Tent City resident murders.

Freddie Pringle, 37, was found poisoned in a wooded area near Hudson Creek, Dec. 7, 2012. While police ruled the death suspicious, the case was never resolved, according to cold case police reports.

Pringle was camping alone, as far as police could determine. An autopsy revealed Pringle died of ingesting water hemlock. Police lieutenant Donald Hester said the poisoning could have been accidental.

"It's possible this Freddie character ate parts of the plant not knowing it was deadly poison," Hester said. "After all, it does smell like carrots."

According to the police report, no water hemlock plants were discovered at Pringle's camp site.

"But there was a Dirty Dozen Bakery wrapper," Hester said. "Pringle had eaten several orange rolls. Forensics found the remnants in the vagrant's stomach during the autopsy."

Police files include a set of fingerprints that were taken from the bakery wrappers, but a match for them in state fingerprint archives was never found.

Harold Roesoto owned Dirty Dozen Bakery at the time. Neither Joon O'Neal, murdered last week with water hemlock, nor Denny Woodman, now charged with her murder, lived in Brocklebrook 12 years ago. Woodman is also charged with murdering Liam Huong, a vagrant who died of water hemlock poisoning last week.

Except for the three Brocklebrook cases, no other incidents of water hemlock poisoning have been reported in Washington State, according to the State Department of Health and Public Welfare.

In an interesting twist, Lt. Hester told our reporter the fingerprints found on the bakery wrappers twelve years ago match the fingerprints on a knife recently discovered at an assault scene this week. The owner of the fingerprints remains a mystery.

"F'n A," said Stan, his crinkly eyes focused on the sidebar story. "They gotta let Denny go now. This - and what happened the other night behind Philly's house - they gotta know they f'kd up."

Throwing a dish towel over my shoulder, I squeezed Stan's shoulder to encourage him. "Let's hope so, Stan, cause I'm on the police suspects list now, especially since

I turned in the keys I found in our attacker's car. Detective Crumley seems to think I used the situation to get rid of the keys and shift suspicion away from myself. The police even suggested Philly, you, and I staged the whole assault the other night."

I left him rereading the newspaper story and returned to the kitchen to check on my quiches and bar cookies. The oven smells blended in a heady, spicy incense. I closed my eyes and breathed them in. Did I feel anything, such as a compelling urge to be truthful? No more than usual, I decided.

As I served up caffeine and breakfast goodies an hour later, I was pleased to hear people talking with enthusiasm about the town meeting. Voices rose and fell in waves of excitement as the talk accelerated to high speed and then dipped to thoughtful silence. Outside, the wind carried flocks of yellow and red leaves across a horizon dark with rain-heavy clouds. I worried about Mr. Chew. If it rained, would he think to take cover under the back porch roof?

When I finally got around to arranging my quiche bites and cookies on serving trays for the coming night, the breakfast customers were mostly gone. Pinky showed up a little later than usual for his bakery wares. He barely spoke, his expression closed and pinched.

"You look like you could use an extra donut," I said, working to coax a smile from him. "Are you still drinking mochas?"

"Yeah. Sure." Pinky barely moved his lips.

"You coming to the meeting tonight?" I kept my voice friendly.

"Got stuff to take care of at home," he answered, not

meeting my eyes. "Kids are sick, and all this murder and mayhem is making my wife nervous. She's scared to go out at night, and she's talking about us moving back to Minnesota to where her parents live."

"That's a big change." I grabbed up a used newspaper and handed it to him. "I honestly think with the help of citizens and investigative journalism, we'll find evidence to clear this up soon. You can show your wife today's paper and reassure her this isn't such a bad place to be."

Pinky expelled a noncommittal huff.

When Maggie arrived, we talked about the newspaper articles and planned out the night's events.

"My parents immigrated here from El Salvadore," Maggie said, her eyes unfocused as she recounted her memories and her family history. "They were homeless for many months trying to make their way as field hands, picking strawberries, beans, and whatever else they could find to do in a new country. Dad discovered a two-room shack they could live in just two months before I was born. They worked hard every day to keep us fed."

And here was Maggie, second generation immigrant, owner and proprietor of a healthy business and a well-respected citizen of Brocklebrook. I hugged her, thanking her for sharing her stories before I took off home. More people than I ever realized had histories that included being unhoused.

As I walked home, I meditated on ways to straighten things out with Warren, but he had to make the first move. I didn't want to intrude when he was in the far reaches of his man-cave mindset.

Feeling as though I had neglected my genealogy

work of late, I spent the early part of the afternoon in my office, powering up Deputy Delila to check on Joon's DNA account. Someone had written back, responding to Joon's latest correspondence. It turned out to be a daughter of Joon's father's brother, Alena Attwater, formerly Alena Stebbins. She knew Joon and April from childhood, and in her email, she described several delightful childhood memories that I would pass on to Philly. Alena also listed her two sons' names, their marriage status, and the names of their children. At the end of her email, Alena included a postscript.

"About April's son. He visited us 13 years back. We were happy to include him in our family summer gatherings. We heard his mother was terribly ill, and Joon was trying to care for her. I'm including his name and address at the bottom, as he might know of someone who would fit the criteria for receiving the family heirloom. I realize the heirloom passes down through the women of the family, or he might qualify to receive it himself."

I looked at the name and address Alena gave for April's son and caught my breath. I marveled Joon never told me the name of her nephew. Now I saw it, I knew who her murderer was. I knew who the burglar was, and I knew the name of the person who set fire to Philly's house and then tried to force us to eat poisoned buns.

I rushed out of my office to find my cell phone. It rang just as I remembered where it was, still in my work bag. Philly's name was on the caller ID.

"Guess what I'm holding," she said, her voice shrill with excitement.

"Guess what I'm reading," I said, my voice low and strained in shock.

"I'm holding the envelope with Joon's autobiography." Philly sounded breathless. "I just now got around to reading it."

"I'm reading a message from one of Joon's relatives," I said.

"I know who the murderer is," we both exclaimed at the same time.

Chapter 20

"They said the founding fathers were flagrant optimists. They said these believers in a more equitable world would never succeed in shaking off the British yoke. The truth is that the founding fathers could never have brought us the hope of democracy without flagrant optimism; now, more than two hundred years later, we still need a flagrant dose of optimism to carry on any hope of democracy." Towne Family Almanac, 2014, Joon O'Neal, daughter of Carol Stebbins.

My feet were almost numb from not moving them. Afflicted with brain freeze, I wondered if my thoughts would ever thaw. Philly and I sat side by side on my couch looking at nothing. We compared notes, hers from Joon's autobiography and mine from the email I received on Joon's DNA account. The town meeting at the bakery was set to start in 45 minutes, and we were ninety nine percent sure we knew who killed Joon and Liam, and who tried to kill us.

"They're all fart blisters," I mumbled.

"Say again?"

"Fart blisters. All of them. The whole dill-headed police department."

That's when Philly started laughing full force,

unable to stop and drawing me into her spectacle of hilarity. I was crying with laughter too, mostly at the strange irony of the situation. We knew the murderer, but we didn't feel we could tell anyone, not the police, not Warren, and not the rest of the world. The police, we were sure, would roll their eyes. Warren, still angry, had shut down his cell phone. The rest of the world? Well, if the rest of the world was Brocklebrook, then the people in it didn't have enough information to make a judgment.

Wiping tears of laughter from my cheeks with my sweater sleeve, I pulled myself to a standing position. "Let's get to the bakery and start things off for the town meeting. We can decide what to do about the murders in the morning."

"From one freak out to another," Philly said about our conundrum. "From the pot into the fire, as they say. I'm not looking forward to telling everyone at the meeting what I found out from spying on Stoats."

Maggie was already busy arranging tables and bringing out more chairs when Philly and I opened the bakery door. Pots burbled with brewing coffee, and Maggie arranged my innocent looking quiche bites and cookie bars, displaying them alongside tiny paper plates and napkins. I'd tasted them that morning. They left an unusual but pleasing zest on my tongue. Since there was no one around, at the time, to hear my confessions, I had no idea if my concoctions compelled truth telling.

As host, Maggie was all business. She welcomed everyone who came through the door, most of them dripping wet from the barrage of rain that had started as soon as the sun set. Coats and hats hung limp over the backs of chairs, and the large front windows fogged with the steam of people's breath. Those walking past on the sidewalk were out-of-focus, misty silhouettes, until they revealed themselves in the open doorway. We brought out more chairs as the room filled.

Out of habit I began to take orders for free coffee and goodies, bringing people cookies and quiche bites on paper plates and handing out paper cups.

Part of me kept saying to myself, *Get a grip, woman. Herbs are not going to compel people to start revealing deep, inner secrets.*

Another part of me worried what would happen if the herbs worked and how much of a *powder keg* I set off. Even Philly knew nothing about what I'd done.

Among the sixty or so people who had come, several were friends, including the hardware store owner, Edmund Russel, gift shop proprietor, Shelly Smythe, Molly Hansen who ran the day-care, George Peterman, manager of the biggest town grocery store, and Ester McMinnon, who owned the plant nursery. When it looked like a standing room only crowd, and just a few stragglers drifted in, Edmund stood to start the meeting.

"Welcome everyone," Edmund called out in his booming, truck-engine voice. The room stilled as soon as everyone had their chairs arranged to best see him. "We discovered, quite by accident, that our city leaders want to invite an outside corporation into our community to build a tourist industry. We want to have a say in what's happening and that's why we're meeting here tonight."

There was a good deal of murmuring until someone in the back shouted, "Let's get started then."

"Look," said George Peterman, "I'll start things out, but I'm only speaking for myself right now. I like this town the way it is. Most of us have been here awhile, so we should be able to decide on our own vision for Brocklebrook. Maybe when all is said and done, we'll want to invite a bunch of multinational corporations to make unprecedented changes. But we want more control over how we live."

The crowd clapped with enthusiasm.

"Down with out-of-town corporations," someone shouted from the picture windows near the front door.

"We can't decide everything tonight." Edmund's voice rose over the clapping. "But we should at least start an exchange of ideas and determine how we can stop the city council from making decisions without our input. We want more time to explore plans. We've raised our families here. We've made the town the charming place it is. We should be the ones to engineer its future."

We were all clapping or pounding on tables. Some of us stomped our feet.

Mrs. McMinnon raised her hand. "I've been reading a lot about what mega corporations do to towns and how people lose agency when that happens. I've been reading about towns that decide to become as self-reliant as they can. People decide their communities come first and their neighborhoods, so they decide on a purposeful goal, to simplify their lives and try to do as much for themselves as possible. Sometimes that means limiting growth. A community can decide to keep their town under their own control."

More cheering and some murmuring and head nodding.

"Sounds like a vow of poverty," said a tall, thin stranger in the corner near Maggie's apron display.

In answer, a robust man with a merry face yelled from the back. "We should be able to vote on these kinds of things rather than just knuckle under to outside money and power. We've seen community after community changed by big pockets until they're all just alike and all run by outsiders."

"When people decide to do things themselves, there's so much more energy and creativity," Mrs. McMinnon answered him in agreement.

"The kids don't have much to look forward to if they are working for hotels, conference centers and business corporations," said the robust fellow in the back, "but if they get to plan and create programs for a self-sufficient community, their lives might just have meaning."

Philly got up then. "You've got a real fight on your hands," she said. "It's worse than you realize. I've been spending time with our city manager. Not only is he arranging a deal with an international corporation and venture capitalists to build a conference center, he and the city council are negotiating a buyout of our main street so they can execute their gentrification project with all the big brand names. They have deals in the works to create a new, exclusive tourist center right next to our ocean shores to bring in wealthy visitors. There isn't much mentioned about protections for us locals. I saw a map that shows projected ideas for new condominiums right on top of many downtown homes and houses. You see, the plan is for Brocklebrook to be a prime tourist location in the future."

The anger was palpable in the room. I heard murmuring about stringing up the council members and the city manager. Some of the cooler heads talked about lawyers and suing for government transparency.

The front door opened then, and the room quieted as figure after figure filed in, including the city council members and the city manager. The six men and one woman stood side by side, unsmiling, in a row along the front window.

Stoats spoke first. "I'm not sure what you all hope to accomplish here, but this meeting is in no way official, nor can any decisions coming out of such an assembly influence city business. For that you need a public meeting, called by city hall."

Edmund stepped forward. "This is a brainstorming and fact-finding meeting, one of the oldest forms of democratic exercises. We're asking each other what we want for our town. Once we know more about what the people want, we are perfectly willing to let you know what it is. In fact, you can be certain we will be at your meetings in droves to bark down your secret deals and counter your backroom, money-making schemes."

George Peterman stood, his chair scooting behind him with a skittering bounce. "We have been here in Brocklebrook long before you even heard of us, and you will not be allowed to take our community from us, Mr. Stoats."

Several people rose up, shouting in agreement.

Shelly Smythe stood on her chair and faced the council members. "We want something that is going to honor the spirit of community and that will be so much different from what you've imagined that your head will spin. I have half a mind to pass around a petition to demand a recall election."

Not knowing what got into me, I brought over a

serving tray of quiche and cookies to the council members and the city manager. They looked unsettled by the oddball interruption as I offered them the last of the goodies. My gifts of food in the midst of an escalating insurrection were poorly timed and out of context, and I think that's why they all took something to eat. They stood munching cookies and quiche while the rest of the room stared and glared at them.

"What in thunderation are these?" Stoats peered hard at the cookie bar in his hand, popped it into his mouth, chewed, and swallowed.

Biff Shoeman, who ran the car repair shop on Seventh Street, got up and looked straight at Stoats. "This here happens to be our meeting. We called it and we're going on with it. If you want, you can stay and listen, but otherwise, keep quiet. Frankly, Stoats, I don't like you. I never have. You're a pompous big city stiff with no idea how to treat people."

Beany Finney, who made custom medieval clothes and sold them online, stood up then. "I'm so ashamed of all of you councilors. We voted for you in good faith, and you've become traitors. What exactly were you promised in exchange for your duplicity, I wonder?"

Honesty was breaking through in a big way. The hidden transcript was becoming public. If people's inhibition had anything to do with the herbs in the cookies, I had no way to tell, but I was getting nervous. How far would this talk go and how much would people say that they would later regret?

I wished Warren had come so we could talk afterward about the meeting and everyone's comments, but he stayed home. My confidence took a bit of a nosedive wondering when and if we would get back together.

A few of our council representatives looked chagrined after Beany's short speech, but Stoats remained haughty and irritated.

"You elected your leaders to do a job," he said, "and that's what they're doing. They brought me here to help improve your economic situation, and that's what I'm doing. Do you have graduate degrees in business and municipal management? I don't think so. You're talking about killing your economic chances with pure stupidity."

"Making it impossible for us to thrive and grow is not helping us economically," Beany shot back. "We're not interested in sacrificing our community so you and your venture capitalist cronies can get rich. We want to keep our unique community intact, not bulldoze it to make room for a cookie cutter copy of other towns."

Stoats' face reddened, and a sneer played on his thin lips. "You and your penny anti businesses are taking up prime real estate for the sake of nostalgia," he snapped.

"You, sir, are taking up too much of my real estate," Maggie said, standing up. She had been quiet up to that point, but as she straightened her shoulders, she reminded me of a fierce, long-haired llama, with strands of curly dark hair in her eyes and a warning trill in her throat. "I'd like you to leave my bakery and not return until you're ready to hear these people out." I'd only seen her mad enough to throw someone out once before. That happened when the health inspector accused her of hiding evidence of a mouse infestation. It wasn't true; the inspector had mixed up bakeries when he insisted customers reported mouse droppings on the floor.

Stoats narrowed his eyes and pointed a long finger

at her. "I can have your bakery shut down." He turned to face the citizens. "I can have any of your shops and stores shut down. I know all the little ways your stores and businesses break city and county rules, and I know who to call to report you." He turned toward the council members and pointed to the front door. "We're done here."

Two of the four men, Timmy Bunch and Harold Crinkfield hunched their shoulders and started to follow Stoats, but Councilman Freddie Schmidt stalled. "I – th-ink - we sh-ould -he-a-r th-em ou-t," he stuttered, his voice barely audible. The two council members behind him heard and stood still. Agatha Cranberry and Wesley Franklin straightened themselves and nodded with encouragement.

"Freddie never says anything at meetings," Agatha whispered in my ear, "so we work hard to support him when he does."

"Mr. Stoats, we're going to hang with Freddie," Wesley said with an amiable half grin. "We'll let you know how it goes."

"You waste your time however you want," Stoats snarled. Under his breath I could hear the words "You'll hang with Freddie alright." Then he, Bunch and Crinkfield let the door slam shut, its greeting bell ringing with bellicosity.

The crowd found seats for the three remaining council members. I poured coffee for those who needed refills, and the meeting continued.

I loved watching this kind of democracy in action and shook my head in admiration. Here were people who worked side by side in this town for years and often decades. They had just endured an attack from a bully, shaken it off, and proceeded with their discussion.

Ester McMinnon went on to outline what she had learned by reading about communities that decided to become more self-sufficient and to take their futures into their own hands.

"It's not easy," she said, "but it allows people to be creative about ideas, and not just wait for someone else to fix things. Community self-empowerment requires thinkers, people dedicated to having enough to live on and being content with that. The tradeoff can be a stronger community, a sense of self-reliance, and a feeling of real accomplishment."

"That's kinda what we've been doing," Beany said. "Nobody's noticed us much, so we could just carry on with our lives. Now, it seems, investors see our beautiful place in the world as a golden goose, but we're not part of their plans."

The group talked about studying what other towns had already done and holding a workshop. Forgetting that the three city council members were still with them, Shirley proposed they get rid of the current city leaders who had failed to bring the citizens into their plans. "They've obviously broken public hearing and transparency laws," she said.

"Ho-o-o-ld on," Freddie stuttered. "How do you kno-o-ow what me and Agatha and Wesley want, . . . or ho-o-o-w we plan to-uh vote on th-i-i-ng-s?"

"Freddie's right," said Agatha in her high-pitched, quavery voice. "I can't speak for Bunch and Crinkfield, but Wesley, Freddie, and I are interested in your ideas."

"No papers have been signed yet between the city

and these big-league corporations," Wesley said. "We've just been told about it."

"Can we rely on you three to bring some of this to a city election?" Edmund asked. "Let's have a town vote to decide between corporate financing and gentrification or empowering us town's people to take economics into our own hands and work to build something of our own."

"Y-es. W-e-e-ll said." Freddie's approval of Edmund's words was almost a whisper, but everybody heard him.

Agatha suggested they pass around pieces of paper to gather ideas about what they want for the town. "Anyone who puts down an idea also agrees to do some research on it."

"Let's meet again next week." Maggie stood. "If you want, it can be right here again, only this time I'm going to need to take up a collection to help pay for goodies."

They all began talking among themselves. Some stood and put on their coats. Their exchanges were lively, full of excitement, and the room echoed with the ring of creative possibility. Several citizens came over to shake Freddie, Agatha, and Wesley's hands.

"It's gonna be a fight, you know," Agatha warned. "Stoats is knee deep into deals and plans for an upscale tourist town."

"I think more tourists might be real nice," said Ester, "but we can give them something unusual and pleasant, not just the same plastic touristy kinds of things the outsider corporations bring in."

The front door swung back and forth as people left for home, the bell above the door tinkling out nonstop. It was only when the bell hung silent that I turned to survey the main bakery room and saw one taciturn figure hidden in the shadows of the farthest corner. Stan was there, wrapped in a dark, heavy coat. He'd been still during the discussion, a sentinel, representing Tent City with a kind of invisibility. As far as unhoused residents were concerned, it was always safer to be unnoticed.

I gave him the very last of the cookies and quiches to take back to Tent City. As I locked the front door behind him, I wondered if sending TRUTH herbs to the unhoused would help or hinder them. Then again, had anyone that night *really* been under the influence of Emma's TRUTH recipe?

Chapter 21

"When the soldiers came to kill us with knives and swords, it was personal. Eye to eye with his slayers, my father fought for his family. Decades later, when the soldiers came to kill us with guns, it was as though we were pieces of kindling. They could kill us from a distance." Towne Family Almanac, 1573, Alis Dinley, daughter of Rachel Ward.

A sense of optimism and self-empowerment pervaded the evening, so completely that I forgot all about the water hemlock murderer. I forgot until the last of the town meeting revelers and Stan waved goodbye, leaving me alone to do the final bakery cleanup. Feeling around in my front pants pocket, I realized I forgot to bring my little protection bag with me. At the very least, it might have brought me comfort.

Trying to be quick, I fumbled with the latch while locking the front door, though I wasn't sure what good a lock would do if the killer really wanted to get at me. I hadn't thought this out very well. Maggie, who knew nothing about Philly's and my discovery, left early, since she was the one who would get up at 3:30 a.m. to do the primary baking. The next day was a home day for me.

Philly left early too, not realizing I would be alone

finishing the cleanup. We planned to meet during her morning coffee break to decide how to approach the police with our new knowledge.

"Maybe we can meet earlier, if I get fired," Philly said in my ear as she adjusted her pearl trimmed, rabbit-wool cap. "When Stoats gets wind of what I said about him, he's bound to cast me out as a Benedict Arnold, especially since this afternoon he still thought I was sweet on him."

Warren's cell phone continued to shuffle my messages into his virtual mailbox, and Joel was up to his neck studying for midterms at his parents' house. My fears about being solo were illogical, however real they felt. After all, on most days I was comfortable with being solitary in the big, familiar kitchen. It was just that I knew who the murderer was, and my situation felt more precarious.

Get a grip, I told myself. *He doesn't know I know. Why would he strike tonight?* I worked with quick efficiency to finish wiping tables, sweeping, and mopping the floors so I could get out to my car. There was no way I'd be taking out the garbage, but I would get the bags tied shut and put them near the side door to the alley. When I determined my cleanup was good enough, I tiptoed over the wet floor to recheck doors and make sure I'd locked them. I reached over to switch off the very last kitchen light and then I heard it, the grating scrapes of a key in a door lock. *Like rats scratching on a metal register inside a basement wall.*

I turned to see the doorknob turn, the one that opened and closed the back loading door.

Oh God, where to hide? I twirled my body in a

pivotal, frantic movement. But it was too late; I was standing dead center along the wall counters. The best I could do was finish flipping the light switch and unplugging the night light. As the overhead lights flashed off, I knew the intruder saw me because our eyes met. My fears were realized.

The man at the door was, indeed, April's son, Joon's nephew, and Philly's half-brother. One of his arms extended toward me from the door frame, his thick fingers wrapped around a gun, some kind of black pistol.

As soon as the lights were out, I ducked down behind the kitchen island, so the bullet fired at me pinged off the steel backsplash behind the countertop. I only heard an intense pop, like the clap of a firecracker; my stalker had equipped the gun with a silencer. I understood about silencers because Warren took me on target practicing dates a few times.

Joon's nephew used his gun to scare me, and he succeeded. No doubt he'd be happy to kill me as soon as he got what he was after. He wouldn't want a witness to his identity, I was sure of that.

I heard his heavy footsteps approach in the dark, and I groped around for a way to defend myself before he found one of the light switches. The man had worked for this bakery for more than 14 years. He came with Dirty Dozen when Maggie bought it, and he knew the building as well as he knew the inside of his delivery truck.

If I could get to the breaker box near the back door, I might be able to stall him, but it would only be a temporary reprieve. I slid open a drawer above my head and reached into it from my kneeling position. My hand closed around the handle of a marble rolling pin. I lifted it with care down to my lap and reached up again. This time I located the size-large dough hook.

As Pinky's footsteps rounded the corner of the work island and drew nearer, I slid around the opposite corner to put the island between us again, carrying the rolling pin and dough hook under one arm. I swore under my breath realizing my eyes had adjusted to the dark, so I knew my stalker could locate me, lights or not.

"Sweeeeeets," he called in a sing-song drawl. "No neeeeeed to play games. You knoooooow what I want." His voice hardened then. "I've got my car outside. We'll drive to where you've got the book hidden, and we can get this finished once and for all."

My back to the baking island, I kneeled on the floor, legs quaking, and listened to his footsteps. He ran into the open drawer and cursed, slamming it shut before he stepped forward, switched on the kitchen lights, and stepped around the island corner. When I looked up, it was eye to eye with Dale Stebbins, the man I called Pinky, and it was eye to muzzle with the gun he pointed directly at my head.

"Drop that rolling pin and whatever that metal thing is." Stebbins, a.k.a Pinky, laughed at my meager weapons, reaching over to grab my hair and yank me up off the ground. I was more revolted than in pain, and I recalled our savage encounter on the road behind Philly's house. Pinky had a thing about yanking women's hair. He pushed me toward the back door.

"Look," I squeaked. "The Towne Family Almanac is here in this kitchen. Taking a drive would be pointless."

"You're lying. I took this kitchen apart, and it's not here." He poked me hard in the back with his gun.

"I hid it here *after* the kitchen was searched." My eyes moved upward toward the top row of cupboards, the ones tall enough to meet the high ceiling. I focused on the cupboard that held some of Maggie's specialty items stored in cardboard boxes. Behind that cupboard door was the box containing the almanac.

"So, it's up there." He pointed, his gesture spasmodic with eager impatience. I nodded.

"Get it. Move that ladder over and get the book," he ordered.

"I'll get it for you, Pinky," I said with as much calm as I could muster. "But why is it so important to you? Why kill Joon because of it?"

"She was my aunt, you know." Pinky's voice was thick with scorn.

"I do know. I also know she loved you and your mother." I manhandled the kitchen a-frame ladder next to the cupboard.

"Pish," spat Pinky. "If she'd loved me, she would have found me and my mother and got us off the streets."

"What makes you think she didn't try?" I put my right foot on the first step of the ladder. "She told me she worked hard to adopt you, only she didn't tell me that you, Pinky, were the nephew she wanted to save. She never mentioned your name. I think she was trying to protect you from your past, especially now you've got a family and a place in the community."

"If she said she cared, she lied." Pinky spat on Maggie's sparkling clean floor. "My mother told me every day until I was sixteen that her whole family wasn't concerned a nickel about us. When I was nine, I started daydreaming about killing every one of them." Pinky kicked at the dough hook so hard it skittered under the ladder and bounced hard against the wall.

Looking down at my booted feet, now side by side on the first ladder step, I took a deep breath. People were often good at taking the gray parts of their lives and blackening them with pestilent emotions, like acidic tar, and locking all the doors to any light that might help them see things with more empathy. The truth was, Joon did love her sister and wanted to help Pinky, but April, in her agony, painted a raw, unfinished picture for her son that was only partly real.

"Move it," Pinky yelled, pointing to the top of the ladder. "Get my book."

I started to climb. Realistic about what was bound to happen before this was all over, I would hand Pinky the recipe and seed book, and he would either shoot me or find another way to end my life. Near the top of the ladder, I reached for the cream-painted cupboard knob and pulled. Once I got the door opened, I grabbed the shelf as leverage to pull myself a little higher. Whoever built the shelf failed to anchor it to the back because it tipped, front side down, and all the cardboard boxes, one of them containing the book, slipped forward, toppling off the shelf past my head and onto the floor with a cacophony of crashes and thuds. One of the boxes hit Pinky's right shoulder. The shelf banged back into position when I let go.

Pinky swore.

I gasped.

"You did that on purpose, stinking broad," he snarled. "You're f*cked, Sweets. Get back down here and get me that book or I will shoot you off that ladder." By the end of his threat he was shrieking, his face the color of a raw pork chop.

I stepped back with caution, my legs shaking just enough to miss a step. I didn't want to land ass backward on top of Pinky, although that might not be such a bad idea. When I made it to the floor, I squatted down to steady myself and moved boxes toward me, opening them one by one. Of course, I knew which box contained Joon's book, but I wanted to open it last to give myself time. There were boxes of napkins, paper plates, spoons, and forks. One box held an old crock pot, and I was sure the fall cracked and broke the ceramic lining inside. Could I use the shards to defend myself? My position on the floor put me behind the central work area so that the island was between me and the back wall. I could only see the top half of the loading door, only partially closed, and I wished that someone, anyone, would come through it. I locked the bakery front door myself. Help would not come from that direction.

Pinky kicked the crock pot box out of my hands, sending its contents crashing against the glass window of Maggie's largest baking oven and bruising my fingers.

"Stop playing around, Sweeeeets." His voice turned fermented and sour. He had gone from flaming rage to decomposing menace. "You'll be rat meat when I'm done with you if you don't find me that book." Pinky reached down and pulled me by my hair to more fallen boxes. For some reason, all the cups of coffee and small white sacks of donuts I'd given Pinky each work-day morning flashed through my mind. All those attempts to cultivate pleasant morning exchanges day after day seemed paradoxical. All those encouraging words I passed along as he talked about his kids, the gossip he shared that he picked up on his deliveries, and his bragging stories about church work - did none of that matter? The spittle from his scowling lips sprayed across my face as he hurled words at me, words like liar, thief, and ding-a-ling.

I sat disheveled near the two last unopened boxes; my throbbing fingers brushed the top of my head to soothe the pulled skin on my scalp and to check if I still had hair.

Pinky bent over me, intensifying his insults and calling me a sniveling rat. He began kicking me, so I reached for the last box that didn't contain Joon's book. I fumbled with the box flaps, opening them to reveal decades-old Lion King party napkins.

I glanced up at Pinky and felt myself flinch in the magnitude of his cold fury, but I also saw something that ignited a tiny spark of hope. Behind Pinky's back the loading door was opening in short jerks. In my most optimistic imaginings, I pictured someone kneeling as they entered, so they could remain unseen. I hoped to God it was a friend, but I also knew stormy gusts of wind often caught and opened that door.

Reaching for the last dented, thick-walled box, I knew before I opened it the recipe book would be inside. I slowed my movements in case someone was slipping through the door. I so hoped it wasn't the wind.

"Get a move on," Pinky yelled, poking my back with the butt of his gun. His booted foot stepped on two of my left-hand fingers and I cried out. His reaction was to kick my bruised hand toward the box. Level 10 pain shot from my wrist to my shoulder. I tried to stifle a terrified whimper. With my right hand, I opened the box flaps.

There it was, Joon's leather-bound almanac recipe

book, full of healing recipes, wonderful stories, and fresh seeds. Tears came to my eyes at the thought of handing it over to Pinky.

"It's the book, alright." I heard his voice, hot on my ear. "My mother told me every day of my life this book was my heritage. Out there in those putrid homeless camps, out where people smelled like dead things and where we slept on dirty mattresses, she told me this book was going to save me. She said it should have been hers and that one day it would me mine."

He reached for it, his fat hand trembling with excitement.

Sighing, I swallowed down a gut-wrenching feeling of loss. Pinky would neither honor nor understand the rules that went with the almanac; nor would he understand the motivation to use it for friendship and healing.

As he leaned in to reach the compendium, I attempted to scootch my hunched and bruised body toward the stove and broken crock pot. Just as I succeeded in distancing myself a few yards, Pinky flew forward. I thought he was tackling me, that this would be his decisive action to get rid of me. But Pinky landed on his face, his arms splayed out on both sides. His gun flew out of his hand toward the refrigerator. Before I could move, he stretched and grabbed it, working himself to his knees.

Wondering what had pushed Pinky, I sat stunned until I looked to my left and spotted Mr. Chew, his head down, his horns aimed, preparing to take another running hit at Pinky. I watched as the gun in Pinky's hand moved through the air until it pointed directly at Mr. Chew. I felt a growl rise in my throat. I was up on my own knees, lunging for Pinky's arm. There was no way he was going to hurt my goat.

My goat?

Mr. Chew and I rose up over Pinky at the same time, confusing him for just a moment. The gun went off and Mr. Chew bleated, an anguished whimper. There was blood on his right flank. I cried out in concern, but Mr. Chew was on top of Pinky, his horns pressing down on the man's chest. I rushed forward, charged with adrenalin, and pulled the gun out of Pinky's hand so fast and with such ferocity that it flew across the kitchen, breaking a window facing the alley. I could hear its thunk and skid on the pavement amid the sounds of falling glass.

Still, I wasn't quick enough. Pinky's left hand reached over and found the marble rolling pin I left on the floor. He raised it over Mr. Chew's head, still pressed hard into Pinky's chest.

"No," I yelled, grabbing around me for something to throw. In one of the boxes were bulk packages of spices. I grabbed the one on top, ripped it open and launched myself at Pinky, package in hand. As he stretched his arm, raising the rolling pin a few inches higher, I poured the contents of the spice bag onto his face. The brown, course granules turned out to be nutmeg.

Pinky made the mistake of opening his mouth to yell and sucked nutmeg into his throat. He coughed and groaned. Shutting his eyes tight, I watched Pinky gurgle and try to breathe as Mr. Chew pressed harder into his chest. Blood streamed down the goat's side onto the floor, and I was more worried about Mr. Chew than Pinky by far. There was no doubt; Pinky was losing his struggle to breathe. Nutmeg grit invaded his lungs, and his chest was unable to expand as Mr. Chew kept his position steady.

When Pinky passed out, I decided enough was enough.

"Mr. Chew," I called, "it's okay. You can stop now."

Upon hearing my voice, Mr. Chew looked up. I could swear he grinned at me, showing off a set of thick, straight, white teeth. He tossed his head and stepped away from Pinky. I approached my would-be killer, the man who caused my life to turn upside down the last few weeks. Pushing him to his side, I began pounding on his back. I had forgotten so much of my first aid skills; I wasn't sure what to do.

And then Warren stepped through the door. His blessed, five-foot-ten-inch, solid-self filled the door frame. This time I could identify who entered the kitchen, and my heart gave a leap of joyous relief. I was so glad to see him. Tears ran down my cheeks.

"I can't get him to breath," I said in loud panic. "Pinky is not breathing."

Warren handed me his phone, told me to call 911, and set to work on Pinky. By the time the police and ambulance arrived, Pinky was sitting up, still rubbing nutmeg out of his eyes, making them sting worse, hacking and spitting brown spicy mush out of his mouth. Keeping my throbbing left hand close to my chest, I brought him a kitchen towel to wipe nutmeg dust off his face and neck and out of his hair. He grabbed it and had enough angry energy left to scratch at my hands.

"I'll sue you for this, witch," he rasped.

As soon as the police entered the kitchen, Pinky accused me of trying to kill him. He coughed nonstop, barely able to talk, but he claimed I attacked him.

"I only came in to ask if she needed help," he said.

My head spun. I stood speechless.

"Check his fingerprints," I finally said with a croak. "I think you'll find they match the ones on the knife you found near Philly's house and the prints connected to that homeless man's murder twelve years ago."

Crumley looked both incensed and exasperated. He handed me an official looking document.

"Write down what happened," he ordered. "Mr. Stebbins is going to the hospital right now. We will interview him as soon as the doctors have had a look at him. In the meantime, what's a goat doing in a bakery? This is certainly a health violation if nothing else."

Crumley's boss, Chief McCleary, was more sympathetic. He sat me down at one of the tables, noticed some of my bruising, and asked if he could get me a cup of water. Warren, in the meantime, took pictures, both for my sake, and for the insurance company's records more than anything else. We had come to distrust members of our police force.

I told the chief everything that happened, explaining Philly and I both uncovered more proof of who the murderer was, and we could bring it to him as soon as possible.

"I knew it was Pinky this afternoon," I said, but I didn't have time to think about what to do with the information. And then, there he was, at the kitchen door demanding I give him his aunt's historic book and waving a gun around. You'll find the gun in the alleyway. I threw it out of the window."

Warren stepped over to the table. "I think if you go to his home, you might find some of the evidence you've been searching for. That gray car you're looking for, the one parked behind Philly's house the night of the assault, well, it's out back. I saw it before I came in."

"We'll call in a team," said the chief.

Crumley shook his head in consternation. "This could all be a setup, Chief. We need to hear more from Mr. Stebbins before we decide who to believe."

"Let's gather the evidence right here and now." The chief stated his order with a snort of impatience.

Maggie arrived to watch the incident-investigation crew work through her kitchen, dusting for fingerprints and then moving outside to work over the gray car. Officers located and bagged Pinky's gun in the alley where it skittered to the very spot I discovered Joon only days ago.

"I think it's finally going to be over," I said to Warren, snuggling close to him as we watched the police document evidence. I put my arm around his waist and said, "Thank you for showing up just in time. I don't know what I would have done without you. Pinky might have died and then Crumley would surely have charged me with murder."

He squeezed me back, looked up at the stars and said in a gravelly voice, "I want to apologize for my behavior the last few days. I left you and Philly without a resource or a friend. I realize I was just plain wrong."

"It's not you," I answered him. "I don't blame you for any of it."

We stood in silence for a long moment.

"What brought you to the bakery tonight?" I asked.

"I came to see you, to apologize, and you weren't home. I remembered the meeting and decided to find you at Dirty Dozen. I walked the few blocks to get here."

"How did Mr. Chew get here?"

Warren looked embarrassed. "I'm almost certain I forgot to close the gate when I went into your yard to the front porch. He must have escaped and traced your steps and your smell to the bakery."

"He helped save me, you know," I said.

"He's an amazing creature. I've a mind to adopt him and take him home with me."

"I wish you would. I can't keep him in my yard, too much garden to worry about, but I've grown very fond of him. I'd love it if he went to live with you and visited my yard once in a while. There's more to him than meets the eye."

We both looked over at Mr. Chew, who Warren tied to one of the garbage dumpsters. He tossed his horns and lifted his bearded goat chin. If I hadn't known better, I could swear he winked. Before leaving for the hospital with Pinky, paramedics looked over the goat's flank, grazed by Pinky's misfired bullet. He shied away when an EMT tried to examine the wound, but it was mere flesh trauma, and he would be okay.

Philly arrived with Joon's autobiography. She offered her proof to the police chief, stepping around Crumley to give it to McCleary. I don't think she did it on purpose, but Philly gave Crumley what we used to call a flat tire when we were kids. Crumley had to bend down and take off his shoe, put it back on, and re-tie it.

I showed Chief McCleary the email from Pinky's cousin I received on Joon's DNA account, the one that identified Pinky as Joon's nephew. We printed a copy on Maggie's office printer so that we could submit it as evidence. Proof of Pinky's identity was important, but I believed fingerprints would be the biggest verification of

Pinky's involvement and of his guilt. There might even be prints in the storage unit. We knew Pinky had a copy of the storage unit key.

Last, Roger arrived, hands in pockets, standing several feet away from us. Walking over to him, I offered him my less-bruised right hand. "I couldn't settle in my hotel room and went out for a drive," he explained. "Those flashing red and blue police strobes light the skies for blocks. I almost expected to find the bakery on fire."

I drew him closer to our little group, and it didn't take long before he and Philly were side by side, sharing sidelong glances and shy smiles. Within a quarter hour they were holding hands. I chuckled. Things might turn out for them after all.

Even after hearing about Pinky's early years, I had little understanding for why the man had done all of this. I could only imagine what his childhood had been like, and I suspected it had been a nightmare at times. His mother gave her son a picture of his relatives and the almanac that would have taken on otherworldly meanings, at least from the perspective of a young boy. His grandparents must have seemed like monsters and the almanac a magical passkey that would make his life all that it should have been, according to April.

It was nearly 3 a.m. before the police allowed us to clean up the kitchen area. Warren and Roger boarded up the broken window. Maggie, Philly, Roger, and Warren did most of the kitchen repair and pick up work. Paramedics wrapped my hand before leaving. I would visit my doctor in several hours to see if it needed medical attention.

Maggie had already shut down the bakery once

because of Pinky's intrusions. She couldn't afford to close it again. Besides, there would be a huge crowd when it opened in a matter of hours. People would be curious about the night's events, and they would want to rehash the community meeting.

Still wired from a surplus of fear hormones, I knew I wouldn't be able to sleep, so I stayed to talk with Philly and watch Maggie bake. When I finally did sleep, I knew my slumber would be tantamount to a coma. There would be no dreams.

Warren and Roger took Mr. Chew in tow. I grinned as I watched the last of Mr. Chew's wagging tale turn the corner toward my house. The goat delivery was meant to be mean-spirited, but Mr. Chew made life easier for me. Indeed, Mr. Chew B saved my life. I was fairly sure sending the goat was Mrs. Hester's doing, but the sender could have been Pinky. One day I would find out and thank them. For now, I had to convince the goat's owner that Mr. Chew was for sale, and we should be his new family.

Dirty Dozen Bakery had a record number of customers for breakfast, brunch, and even for lunch. I stayed until noon to captain Philly, Roger, and Warren as they helped Maggie bake extra cookies and muffins. We almost ran out of coffee grounds, and I called our distributor to ask if he could deliver our new order a day early.

Roger volunteered to drive the bakery truck. Relieved, Maggie gave him a list of customers and a map, and he got behind the wheel, coffee cup and a cheese Danish at his side, to deliver baked goods to restaurants, grocery stores, the fishery cold storage plant, and the woodworkers guild for employee coffee breaks.

When I arrived home, Warren waited for me in my kitchen. On the table was a large, homemade, paper heart and a bottle of Columbia Gorge Merlot. We would wait to drink the wine, but in the meantime, Warren had hot soup on the stove for lunch and an update on Pinky's condition at the hospital.

"And you'll be glad to know the chief took over the investigation. He sent Crumley out with Lt. Hester to check on a series of house burglaries." Warren gave me the news and a peck on the cheek. I was glad for both.

Joon's book came home with me, and I set it out on the table, secure in the knowledge that it was safe now, wherever I chose to keep it.

The more Joey learned about the bakery attack, the more he groaned with disappointment. "What? A goat took my place as your bodyguard?" He moaned. "And I missed the big takedown?"

As soon as lunch was over, I baked Mr. Chew a special recipe for grain-heavy Logan bread, and Warren put together a hefty, tarp-covered lean-to, filled with dry, clean hay for shelter.

When we woke the following morning, Mr. Chew's happy face filled the top half of the Brocklebrook Journal's front page. The headline read, "Goat Rescues Baker From Gunman." On page seven we found more photos, one with my wrapped arm around Mr. Chew's neck and my other arm around Warren's broad waist. I was pleased and amused to notice Warren's right hand in the picture pulling the little protection bag from his front pants pocket.

Chapter 22

"What is the lesson when both the father and the son are prodigal?" Towne Family Almanac, 2024, Philly Delano, niece of Joon O'Neal.

Mr. Chew's pictures in the newspaper were the icing on a glorious rescue. I was in a state of pure joy, glad to be alive on a sparkly autumn morning, and it was Halloween. I realized how much I adored the way Warren's bare head shone through the thinner hair over his bald patch. I loved the water spots on the window above the kitchen sink. I cherished the wrinkles in the throw rug at the back door. I treasured the day as a good time to clear my garden and rake up Mr. Chew's chaotic rearrangement of aging plants and leftover vegetables.

"Look at him out there eating the last of my grapes," I crooned with fondness for my four-hoofed protector.

"Yeah, there goes this year's batch of Cabernet," Warren said with less enthusiasm.

"We'll drink to him with our final bottle of last year's wine around the Thanksgiving table." I chuckled as I gave Warren an exuberant squeeze.

My left hand suffered deep bruises, and my wrist was sprained, but with time it would heal. In the meantime, my right hand would have to pick up the slack.

I refused to take a break from the bakery.

Warren, bless him, gathered neighbors and friends, who came over with rakes and hoes to help me clean plant debris and put my garden to bed for the winter. They even gathered my hanging baskets and emptied them into my compost bins. The sun had melted most of the early fall frost, leaving white crystalline patches in the shady areas of trees and on the north side of the greenhouse.

We heard voices in the front yard and knew they belonged to Philly and Roger. I handed them each a gardening tool and pointed to my bean patch. There was Mr. Chew, masticating the overripe beans that were too tough for me to eat. He didn't seem to mind their stringy, yellowing skins.

With everyone raking, cutting, pulling, and piling, my garden was ready for winter by noon.

While neighbors and friends bedded my perennials and spread the sacks of dried leaves I'd collected last fall over the dark garden earth, I made a large batch of Halloween donuts from a recipe passed down from mothers to daughters and mothers to sons for several generations in my own family. We had always joked that for each donut eaten on Halloween, we saved a soul. I discovered later the tradition was not just ours. It was an ancient All Hallows Eve rite, something connected to soul cakes and the wonderful Celt and Welsh pagan traditions for bringing in winter. I wheeled a cart of hot coffee, cider, and warm donuts to my picnic table and thanked each one of my helpers with a one-armed hug. We consumed piles of donuts and saved many souls by the time we finished our picnic. By 3 o'clock, Philly and Roger were in my kitchen cleaning up for me.

Roger, it turned out, knew a great deal about farmyard animals, including goats.

"Yeah. Every time my mother got a new boyfriend, she'd send me packing to my grandparents in Idaho. They were farmers, and they kept me out of trouble with fence mending and daily chores. They tolerated my obsession with cars, target practice, and demolition derbies."

"Roger, you're full of surprises," I said, my curiosity peaked once again.

"He's full of secrets is what he is," said Philly, giving Roger's booted foot a little kick.

"And I guess I better share some of them if I don't want to get frozen out of your life again." He offered Philly a rueful grin.

"Exactly. You can start by telling us why we saw you on the sidewalk after Joon's funeral talking with Maynard and Mrs. Hester." Philly put her hands on her hips and regarded Roger with a look of no-nonsense expectation.

"Oh." Roger managed a short apologetic laugh. "I was trying to do some sleuthing of my own, you know, get information that I could bring to our next bun fight meeting. Mrs. Hester worked out a deal with Maynard to have you watched, Betts. For some reason she had an idea you might come and steal some of the more valuable plants in her greenhouse."

"As to that," I said, grinning, "I was looking in her greenhouse to see if she was the one who stole plants from me."

At this, Warren expelled a self-conscious cough. I regarded him with suspicion.

"What is it?"

"Later," he said. "I've got something to show you in my tool shed."

Ahhh. The tool shed. Warren was going to reveal his own secret so I wouldn't have to sneak a peek on some dark moonless night.

We decided we needed comfort food. The unanimous vote was for meatloaf, gravy on turkey, or macaroni and cheese at Cassy's Diner. We sat at one of the cozy booths with overstuffed seats and told Roger every detail about the café-kitchen nightmare with Pinky. It was good to have someone with whom to recap our story.

"Pinky with a gun," Roger mused. "I wonder if he even knew how to use it."

"I'm awfully sorry it was Pinky," Warren said. "I've known him since I first got to town, and he was always the bakery delivery man. I know he's a hero with the school kids on his route. He likes to tell them stories and give out treats."

"What he said about his mother-." I trailed off. "There's so much more to what happened that's below the surface. He was without a home or in foster care for so many years as a child, and yet he has nothing kind to say about unhoused people. Joon tried so hard to help him when he was young and yet he killed her. There are some deep psychological themes playing out here."

"You're a baker, gardener, herbalist, forensic genealogist, teacher, and amateur private investigator," Warren said, laughing. "I don't think you have enough time in the day to become a psychologist too."

We all joined in Warren's merriment.

"For your information, survival for middle school

teachers hinges on trying to understand psychology," I informed him.

Done with dinner, we headed out to the parking lot. I heard Roger say to Philly, as he escorted her to her car, that she should come over to his hotel room that night, and he would show her his DNA data. He wanted her to know why he was keeping it a secret. She agreed.

If a heart can smile, mine was doing just that. It was good to see those two together again. Warren followed me to my house that night and we ceremoniously shut down the electric fencing as we came in the gate and did not turn it on again as we went up the porch. The danger of intrusion was over. I was more than ready to feel safe and secure in my little cottage again.

The next day I worked at the bakery the entire day. I was getting good at doing things one-handed, with the help of my left forearm as a ballast. Now that Pinky was in jail, Maggie had to drive the delivery truck until she found a replacement.

"Roger said he'd be interested in job sharing the position," I told her. "He doesn't want to do it every day, though."

By the time I returned home, Warren was already there, in my kitchen, making me dinner. I sighed in relief as I took stock of all the new ingredients he brought from the store. I wouldn't have to worry about poisoned food anymore and could even enjoy leftovers the next day.

"Police found heavy boots with mud on them in Pinky's garage that matched the mud near Philly's house." Warren talked with his back to me as he diced onions on the cutting board. "Right below Pinky's house is a creek, and along that creek there's a clump of water hemlock. There's evidence that some of it was dug out." Warren turned to face me, waving the vegetable peeler toward the kitchen window. "In Pinky's garage they discovered a few jars of brown recluse spiders. Where he got them in this climate I can't guess. They don't live here as a rule. He must have a source for spider eggs. And the police found residue on his work bench to show he had been working with water hemlock roots, sap, and seeds."

"They let Denny go, didn't they?" I asked.

"That's right. He's back at the camp."

Relief for our friend welled up as tears, and I had to wipe my wet cheeks with a dish towel.

"They found a lot more," Warren said, "but right now I'm more excited about something that just popped up on my computer." He seemed restless throughout the meal, and I assumed he was agitated about the murder case. When we finished eating, he got up and helped clear the table, almost in slow motion, as though focused control of his movements would help him contain some strong emotion.

Dishes done, Warren took my hand and led me to my office where Deputy Delilah was already up and running. He opened a link to the DNA data and family tree site. Something big must have happened. Warren sat down and opened a memo on his DNA message board; then he got out of my desk chair and invited me to sit.

"Read," he said.

In the middle of my computer screen was a message from Warren's long-lost son. He didn't identify himself by name, but he said he wanted to arrange a meeting.

"Oh Warren." I smiled up at him.

Warren's son suggested meeting in Brocklebrook

and wrote that he was nearby. He asked Warren to pick the time and the place. We looked at each other. Warren couldn't stop grinning, and yet his eyes misted and blinked as he tried to control unbidden tears.

He typed, "Let's meet tomorrow morning at 8 a.m., if that's not too early, at Dirty Dozen Bakery."

His son answered before we went to bed. "I'll be there."

Neither of us got much sleep, so 3.30 a.m. seemed even earlier than usual.

Back to my old routine, I let myself into the bakery, feeling confident and safer than I had in days. I even sang as I put together the raisin bread dough and the spicy, butter filling for cinnamon rolls. It was autumn, my favorite time of the year. My garden was asleep. The mystery was solved, and the murderer jailed, and Warren was going to meet his son after all these years. Life could be glorious.

Maggie arrived at 7 a.m. to train a new delivery driver, one who was interested in job sharing with Roger. The new driver, Joey, was happy to partake in coffee and half a dozen apple cider donuts before his shift began.

"I'm going to be one bad-ass delivery driver," he said to Maggie. "I've got self-defense skills in case someone decides to steal the goods."

She laughed. "Yeah. Scone thefts are on the rise, and our pre-made pizza rounds get lost and disappear like borrowed Frisbees." The two of them took off in the truck, Joey at the wheel.

As the time closed in on 8 a.m. my heart raced. I was nervous with anticipation, but Warren, keyed up, paced the floor as I ushered my first customers in the front door and turned on the neon sign to let people know we were open. Stan and Denny came in for coffee and our regular contribution of Tent City goodies. Handshakes and pats on the back passed between us for several complete turns. Business owners came in to plan the next community meeting, and Roger and Philly appeared with the rest of the crowd for coffee and breakfast. I didn't see anyone else, so maybe Warren's son was just a bit late. Still, I started to worry for Warren. Philly joined me behind the counter to help make coffee drinks, grinning from ear to ear.

"What's got you so jolly?" I asked, although the week's events would have made anyone giddy with relief, especially because we'd identified Philly's arsonist, now caught and behind bars.

"Look." She pointed.

I looked to see Warren and Roger standing, right hands clasped in a long, solemn shake, tears streaming down both of their faces.

"What?" I asked.

"Don't you get it?" Philly grabbed my arm. "Roger is Warren's son."

I started bawling right on the spot, so of course Philly did too. And then we were there with Warren and Roger, hugging them, yelling, and rejoicing. I jumped up and down, I was so excited.

Roger told Warren he had come to Brocklebrook thinking he might stay if his dad turned out to be the kind of man worth knowing. He kept his identity a secret until he knew more about Warren. His mother said so many negative things about his dad when he was growing up that Roger was hesitant to make contact. He wanted to check things out first.

"Now I know that Mom was jealous. She had a vindictive streak to her, and I knew that too. I loved her, don't get me wrong, but I also knew I had to see for myself if my dad was all the things she said he was and wasn't." Roger tipped his hat to Warren. "I know now I am proud to be my father's son, and I'm just sorry I missed so many years with you."

Philly and I sniffed some more, blowing our noses on bakery napkins. Warren reached over and gave Roger another man hug.

The customer line was growing. I returned to the counter and Philly helped me with orders. "I found out last night when Roger showed me his DNA data. There was Warren's name, clear as could be, as his biological father. That's why he wouldn't show me his DNA site the other night. He was waiting until the right time."

Philly left the bakery to get to her own job by nine. She wasn't sure she'd have it for long, and she was job hunting. I worked through the lunch hours while Maggie trained Joey, so I didn't see Warren and Roger leave to go fall chum fishing and spend the day talking. We would all have a reunion celebration soon.

In the days to come, we became a closer family of friends, making dinners dates together, playing board games, going on walks; Roger even became a member of Warren's League of Nations team. The pair wasted no time in making up for lost years. When they were busy on their computers, Philly and I worked on her family genealogy. We made apple butter, learned to knit, and studied Joon's Towne Family Almanac together. Soon Philly's home would be ready for her to reoccupy, but for the present, she stayed in the same hotel complex as Roger. They were becoming a close couple.

One night, not long after Pinky's arrest, Warren led me to his tool shed.

"It's okay," I told him. "I don't have to know what's inside there."

"Yes, you do," he said. "I've been feeling guilty every day since I stored some things in here, and I think it's time for them to go back where they belong."

He opened the doors to his shed, which was really a large workshop, and there they were: all the plants that someone stole from my greenhouse. Warren had been the thief all along. The day he took them, I'd shared with him my fear that the caller who wanted Joon's book might take the plants.

There they were, safe and warm in his shed, where he hooked up grow lights and did a fair job of keeping the plants alive. Most of them were heavy with seeds, overdue for harvest.

"I got worried," he explained as I rushed over with joy to inspect them all. "I thought someone might be after Joon's plants and would ruin your hard work. I staged a burglary so not even you would know where they were."

I wasn't sure what to think about Warren's heist, but I grinned up at him anyway.

"Thank you, Warren, for contributing to my nightmares." I was only half jesting. "But you've done a wonderful job with them, and now I can finish what Joon wanted me to do." I approached my plants, touching their leaves and breathing in their spicy scents.

A blue, foil-wrapped box caught my eye between the angelica and the yarrow. It fit nicely in my palm as I picked it up and held it. A card splashed thick with gold glitter had my name on it. Warren watched me with a look of apprehension as I removed the ribbon and the wrap and opened the velvet jewelry box. Inside was a stunning ring with an emerald set between two tiny diamonds. Warren had tucked a folded note into the empty space at the top of the box. I unfolded it with some trepidation. Was this an engagement ring I would again have to refuse?

My dear Betts, the note read. *I know we decided marriage is not for us, but I want to give you this ring as a symbol of my love for you. We are two independent people with a commitment to each other. I hope you will wear this ring to show the world that we are loyal companions, even though we aren't married. I love you with all my heart. Warren.*

I turned to him, this steady and much-loved man, looking blurry through the tears in my eyes. Of course I nodded my head, "yes". He came over and slipped the ring on my right-hand ring finger. We held each other close and went into the house to celebrate and tell our friends. Later we would find a ring from me for Warren, also for his right hand.

A few days later, I harvested the seeds from my rescued plants, careful to give them correct labels. By night, the heirloom recipe book was back in my safe under the stair step. By day, I replaced the old seeds with new ones, straightened the pages, and polished the leather cover. It was time to pass the book to its rightful owner. Warren made a new walnut box for the almanac with a beautiful bronze hasp lock and lined it in sapphire blue velvet.

I asked Philly to take a walk with me at the

conservancy one vibrant, crisp afternoon: the box and the book straining the seams of my backpack. There, under the orange and yellow-green leaves of the alders, I gave Philly her heritage. She sat on the path, put her head on the book, and wept.

"I don't think I'm worthy," she said. "I'll need all the help I can get to grow the seeds and use the herbs."

"I love you, and I loved Joon," I reassured her. "I'll help in any way I can." I handed her the two copies I had made of the almanac. She shooed them away.

"Keep them and use them," Philly said. "I trust you to use the recipes only for good. I'm just so grateful Joon found you and made you the temporary guardian."

We both felt as though something ancient and honorable was passing between us. It would be impossible to prove that the recipes helped protect or heal or inspire us, but there was something earthy and magical about the history of the women who created the book and gathered its knowledge.

Philly shared some of the seeds and the recipes with Mrs. Hester to help foster trust and friendship, though Marta was still determined to go to court over the Towne Family Almanac. As for Pinky, he would never see the book again as long as he lived. A few months later, a judge sentenced him to life imprisonment, and I doubted we would visit.

A majority of Brocklebrook citizens insisted that Tent City remain intact. They also demanded more time for creating their own town goals and shared visions. Lester Stoats remained as city manager, even after citizens began to hold independent planning meetings. According to Philly, Stoats figured that Tom, Dick, Harry,

Ester, Jane, Abbey, and all the others would soon get distracted and sidetracked from what he thought of as their temporary political fervor. Apathy would return, he believed, and he could follow through with his original plans.

I hoped he was wrong.

Denny and Stan worked together to keep Tent City as lawful and healthy a community as they could manage, though they both missed the sometimes gentle and often fierce advice of their companion, Joon. She made all our lives richer and sweeter, and I thought of her every time I opened my checkered Betty Crocker cookbook cover to peruse through ancient and magical recipes, words of wisdom, and the stories of healers.

In the middle of a snowy, winter day, I made a new genealogical discovery that drew me closer to the almanac and all its history. I was researching a particularly tough lineage in my own family tree when I saw a name that I'd come across somewhere else. My great (x5) grandmother, Geneva Douglass, had been a Towne and had married my great (x5) grandfather, Reggie Douglass. With a little more research, I realized my family had connections with Joon's family. As a genealogist I should have expected the family link. On North America's east coast, early settlements from England constituted a DNA bottleneck of sorts. A vast number of North Americans trace their ancestry to that bottleneck. Still, however distant, I rejoiced at having a sense of personal affiliation with the Towne Family Almanac.

Picking up my copy of Joon's recipe book, I closed my eyes. I poked my right thumb into the pages and then opened the book to where my thumb held its place. At the top of a page, bordered with little sketches of mountains and waterfalls, was the title *Wellbeing*. Below was a recipe to make a simmering pot of herbs so the steam would drift through a room and promote a sense of contentment and harmony. I smiled. I knew I would most certainly need a recipe like this at some future time, but for now I was at peace with the world and myself.